PRAISE FOR JE...

"For a sexy, fun-filled, warmhearted read, look no further than Jennifer Probst!"

—Jill Shalvis, *New York Times* bestselling author

"Jennifer Probst is an absolute auto-buy author for me."

—J. Kenner, *New York Times* bestselling author

"Jennifer Probst knows how to bring the swoons and the sexy."

—Amy E. Reichert, author of *The Coincidence of Coconut Cake*

"As always, Jennifer Probst never fails to deliver romance that sizzles and has a way of tugging those emotional heartstrings."

—*Four Chicks Flipping Pages*

"Jennifer Probst's books remind me of delicious chocolate cake. Bursting with flavor, decadently rich . . . very satisfying."

—*Love Affair with an e-Reader*

"There's a reason Probst is the gold standard in contemporary romance."

—Lauren Layne, *New York Times* bestselling author

PRAISE FOR *FOREVER IN CAPE MAY*

"Probst's entertaining take on the friends-to-lovers trope hits all the right beats, enhanced by well-shaded characters readers will immediately love. This irresistible finale does not disappoint."

—*Publishers Weekly*

PRAISE FOR
TEMPTATION ON OCEAN DRIVE

"*Temptation on Ocean Drive* was an adorable and sad and sparky and emotional and wedding-y New Jersey Beach Town love story! I loved it! Run to your nearest Amazon for your own Gabe—this one is mine!"

—*BJ's Book Blog*

PRAISE FOR *LOVE ON BEACH AVENUE*

"Probst (*All Roads Lead to You*) opens her Sunshine Sisters series with an effervescent rom-com. The characters leap off the page, the love story is perfectly paced, and an adorable dog named Lucy adds charm. Readers will eagerly await the next in the series."

—*Publishers Weekly*

"The perfect enemies-to-lovers, best-friend's-brother romance! I laughed, smiled, cheered, cried a few tears, and loved Carter and Avery!"

—*Two Book Pushers*

"*Love on Beach Avenue* is a three-layer wedding cake of best-friend's-brother, enemies-to-lovers, and just plain fun. Another yummy confection by Jennifer Probst!"

—Laurelin Paige, *New York Times* bestselling author

"I could feel the ocean breeze on my face as I turned the pages. *Love on Beach Avenue* is chock-full with magic ingredients: a dreamy seaside, a starchy hero with a tiny dog, sparkling wit, and fabulous female friendship—a must-read romance!"

—Evie Dunmore, author of *Bringing Down the Duke*

"JP writes beautiful words, and I just loved this story. There was enough action, adventure, passion, and swoon factor, not to mention romance."

—*The Guide to Romance Novels*

"A read that will not only fill your emotional romance need but will fill your heart with the fulfilling need to care for a goat that needed to be hugged and be besties with a horse to feel safe."

—*The Book Fairy Reviews*

PRAISE FOR *A BRAND NEW ENDING*

"*A Brand New Ending* was a mega-adorable and moving second-chance romance! I just adored everything about it!"

—*BJ's Book Blog*

"Don't miss another winner from Jennifer Probst."

—Mary from *USA TODAY's Happy Ever After*

PRAISE FOR *THE START OF SOMETHING GOOD*

"The must-have summer romance read of 2018!"

—*Gina's Bookshelf*

"Achingly romantic, touching, realistic, and just plain beautiful, *The Start of Something Good* lingers with you long after you turn the last page."

—Katy Evans, *New York Times* bestselling author

So It Goes

The Hot in the Hamptons Series

Summer Sins

Stand-Alone Novels

Dante's Fire
Executive Seduction
The Holiday Hoax
All the Way
The Grinch of Starlight Bend
The Charm of You

So It Goes

JENNIFER PROBST

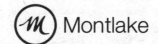

Text copyright © 2022 by Triple J Publishing Inc.
All rights reserved.

Published by Montlake, Seattle

www.apub.com

Amazon, the Amazon logo, and Montlake are trademarks of Amazon.com, Inc., or its affiliates.

ISBN-13: 9781542038324 (paperback)
ISBN-13: 9781542038331 (digital)

Cover design by Caroline Teagle Johnson

Cover image: © Regina Wamba of MaeIDesign.com; © jhayes44 / Getty; © Manuel Breva Colmeiro / Getty; © PeopleImages / Getty

Printed in the United States of America

Ray,
This one's for you.
Happy 50th (book anniversary).
You've been there from the beginning and never doubted
me.
You've cooked endless dinners around deadline and
never asked me to do the dishes.
You're the best publicist I could imagine, hyping my
books to everyone you meet.
Love you, babe.

Know your own happiness.

—Jane Austen, Sense and Sensibility

Chapter One

Malia Evergreen walked into the office of her least favorite client and swore not to lose her temper.

Not today.

It had been a perfect morning. After a solid night's sleep, she'd managed to snatch the last croissant at her favorite bakery and the first cup of a fresh pot of Colombian coffee. She sailed over the Mario Cuomo Bridge on her way to Manhattan without the usual congested traffic. The sun shone bright in a cloudless baby-blue sky with no threat of rain. And she wore her favorite suit—a well-tailored candy-apple-red Vera Wang that screamed BOSS. Even her hair turned out perfectly, the multiple braided strands falling straight down her back.

Mr. Hot Billionaire couldn't even screw this up for her.

Malia nodded at Cassandra, his adept administrative assistant, and was waved immediately in. After a full year of meeting with him every other Thursday at 10:00 a.m. sharp, Malia was aware of each detail of the routine. In the beginning, she'd been confused why the CEO and owner of the multimillion-dollar wedding empire would choose to meet personally with an advertising representative. God knew he had a ton of minions to run the lower-level marketing.

She'd learned the answer quickly and wished she never had.

Because he was a control freak who loved to involve himself in all aspects of his company. He also seemed to enjoy torturing her for his individual amusement, as if it kicked off his early weekend entertainment.

Not for much longer, though.

Satisfaction curled through her. She couldn't wait to make the announcement.

Malia pasted a smile on her lips and breezed through the half-open door. "Morning," she said, moving toward her regular seat at the conference table.

Her gaze swept over Emeril, his assistant, and Andrea, the creative director, flanking the head of the table like knights to a king. The two complemented each other nicely, both sharply dressed, keenly intelligent, and eager to do their king's bidding. Emeril held a tightly bound energy in his body that made Malia wonder if he injected caffeine directly into his veins. Tall and thin, with dark hair and sharp features, he was a multitasking genius who tapped endlessly on his phone while engaging in dialogue and answering questions from his boss. Andrea was calm, with a short blonde bob, cat-eye glasses, and a tendency to dress in classic black pantsuits. For a creative leader, her appearance and personality seemed plain at first, but Malia now respected the hell out of her ideas and laser-like focus to launch dynamic ad creatives for the company.

They exchanged casual talk as Malia flipped open her laptop and got situated. When the clock on her screen switched to 10:00 a.m., Andrea and Emeril looked up expectantly.

Malia refused.

The door clicked shut quietly and footsteps softly echoed. The scrape of the chair and the creak of leather as he settled rose to her ears. The scent of clove and spice wafted in the air. Immediately, her skin prickled and a hot awareness shot through her body—the exact reaction she'd been experiencing steadily since the day they met.

It was a secret she'd never confess. Not even if she were tortured.

"Good morning, Ms. Evergreen."

The deep, rumbly voice shot to all the hidden corners of her body and stroked. Fighting the horrid physical response, she finally looked up and met Palmer Matterson's stare. His sea-green eyes drilled into hers and lingered, as if it were his right to see all of her.

Primal arrogance seethed from his very core. He knew he attracted women like he was a giant chocolate bar and they were gripped by PMS. That thick mane of gray hair was his calling card, falling over his forehead and brushing his collar with just a touch of unruliness. His features were pure aristocracy: the sharp blade of his nose, the curl of his full lips, the defined cut jawline. He wore his fancy Armani suits like they were casual denim, the fabric tailored to emphasize the lean, muscled length of his thighs and ass, the jacket stretching over his broad shoulders. He was a man who ran a female-centered business, surrounded by endless wedding couples and selling the promise of happily ever after. Yet, there didn't seem to be a soft bone in his body or heart. It was a puzzle she'd been trying to solve for a year but was no closer to figuring out.

Malia ignored the punch in her gut like an expert. She refused to allow this man to evoke any type of reaction from her today. Not irritation. Not frustration. And certainly not sexual attraction.

"Good morning, Mr. Matterson." She oozed saccharine sweetness. "It's lovely to see you."

A flare of surprise lit briefly in his eyes and was quickly masked. She usually addressed him in a chilly, polite voice, but he reacted smoothly. "It's lovely to be missed. I assume you've seen the latest figures?"

"While ass-umptions are dangerous for multiple reasons, in this case, yes. I sent Emeril the stats, and I'm sure you'll be pleased."

Satisfaction curled in her belly when his gaze narrowed. She'd always danced along the edge of cheekiness, preferring to cloak her insults with clever folly, but he seemed to volley each of them in perfect retaliation. Malia admitted the man might be a giant jerk, but his banter was legendary. He must exhaust his many female companions.

Maybe in more ways than one.

3

"While many *asses* may disagree, I think there should be some assumptions in business in order to reach a common foundation. Don't you?"

She refused to grin at his obvious jab. "No. Foundations can be reached by an open dialogue where both opinions and expectations are honestly shared until an agreement is reached. It's called democracy, not monarchy. And it avoids making asses out of anyone."

Andrea cocked her head and watched. Emeril tapped rapidly on his phone, but he looked up briefly with interest at the exchange.

"At least you didn't call me a communist," Palmer said mildly.

She widened her eyes in mockery. "I'd never insult you, Mr. Matterson."

"Of course not. It's just a shame you didn't put your motto into action. We could've avoided the disaster of your latest Quench mailing." His voice crisped around the edges, steering Malia right back to the ruthless businessman.

A shred of worry nagged at her current smugness. "What do you mean? The ad is flawless. The sales numbers are solid. The matching web ad clearly shows engagement."

"Along with my competitor." He motioned to Emeril, who slid the latest glossy magazine over the table. "Why would you allow my rival to purchase prime space next to mine?"

Malia blinked and stared at the open photo spread. Endless Vows Bridal Agency held the center ad in the limited quarterly print magazine that had become a staple at Quench, the company she and her best friends founded together. The photo of a bride running from the church easily caught the reader's attention, spotlighting the gorgeous platform sneakers Palmer's company had recently launched with the edgy tagline: DITCH THE GROOM, NOT THE SHOES.

Her red painted nail traced over the full-size ad. "There's nothing else here."

"Turn the page."

She did. Then winced. The Cinderella-type stiletto shoes hit her full force, reminiscent of every royal princess and what many dreamed of wearing at their wedding. Pearls and crystals shimmered with a clear heel that only emphasized the classicism. The groom knelt before the bride, the shoe propped on his knee, and he stared up at her with a look of adoration. The text confirmed Malia was in deep trouble.

Be a Classic.

Kruger Bridal.

She fought the urge to let out a satisfying curse word and mentally calculated how she'd screwed up. Even though Victoria was in charge of the final proofs, as Quench's advertising director, Malia should have made sure Kruger's ad was separated reasonably from Palmer's. Placement wasn't guaranteed in the contract, so they had technically done nothing wrong. But it didn't matter. By allowing Kruger's ad to follow, the pricey ad for Endless Vows' new wedding sneakers had been invalidated.

It'd be easy to blame Victoria but wrong. Malia should've checked, and now she needed to fix it. "I apologize," she said. Her ears burned at the humiliation of admitting to such a rookie mistake. "I should have checked the proofs."

"I'm disappointed, Ms. Evergreen," Palmer continued. His face remained expressionless, contradicting the sharpness in his voice. "I expected more from our business relationship with Quench. Frankly, I'm thinking of pulling back if my company earns such a lack of your attention."

Shit. She may have disliked the billionaire, but he was a huge client. They relied on his massive and consistent ad budget, and that loss could make quite a dent in their bottom line. It couldn't have come at a worse time, either, with her impending announcement.

Andrea looked sympathetic, but her words were direct. "We can certainly pump up our ad spend with the Knot or Bridal Wear, where the product would be better served. Do more television ads."

"You don't need more general name branding," Malia retorted. "You need to sell specific products at this point, and it would be wasted at both of those media outlets, with their sea of wedding ads all trying to sell similar things."

"It was wasted with Quench," Palmer said.

"It won't happen again. I'll guarantee every ad will be double-checked for proper placement away from any similar competition."

"Which should have been done already."

Malia simmered with irritation at his tone and tried not to squirm in her seat. God, it was almost like he was pleased she screwed up so he could gain the upper hand. How did anyone stand working for him? Who cared if he had a voice that sounded like sex and a hard, muscled body created for sin? He was the symbol of everything she couldn't stand: a gorgeous man with a cold heart and a shitty personality.

"Ms. Evergreen?"

"I heard you," she said. Dragging in a breath, she reminded herself this was the last time she'd have to suffer through a meeting with him. She just needed to smooth over this one error and she'd be done. "I'm happy to give you a generous credit toward your next ad package. We're booking our holiday edition, and I can guarantee you prime coverage."

"And if I'd rather not book with Quench any longer?"

Her heart beat and her palms sweat, but she regarded him coolly. "That's certainly your right, Mr. Matterson. I'd hate to see you end a mutually beneficial business arrangement over one honest mistake after a year of great successes. Quench can still give you an audience of millions in a space where Endless Vows has less competition."

"Except for Kruger."

She inclined her head. "Quench is also a business, and Kruger pays a hefty fee accordingly. But we've locked out any other wedding businesses from advertising with us. You'll find most companies won't do that. They concentrate on dollars, not relationships."

Was that a gleam of approval in his eyes?

He remained silent. In a kingly gesture, he rested his hands on the gleaming table, his fingertips touching. She waited patiently, a lesson learned long ago that silence was the best weapon.

"Don't let it happen again."

A shiver crawled down her spine. Bad things exploded between her legs. She hated his condescending tone and at the same time berated herself for responding to it. At least she'd finally be able to have the last word. Sweet victory was so close, giddiness sparkled in her veins. She'd swallow her pride and allow him this one win. "Of course. I suggest we move forward, and I'll send Emeril proof of the credit."

They fell into their usual planning discussion for the next two weeks of marketing and ads—some static, some organic, depending on the news or social media hot spots. Finally, the meeting came to a close and they began packing up.

It was time.

"Before we wrap up here, I wanted to let all of you know I'll be stepping away from my role as advertising director at Quench and moving to a different division."

The room grew eerily quiet. Emeril blinked with a manic swiftness that told of his distress. Andrea pursed her lips with the unasked question of why. Both of them were too professional to probe, and she wasn't on friendly terms with them like she was with some of her other clients who she could relax with while nibbling on sweets during the meetings. But it wasn't their reaction she'd been anticipating.

Slowly, Malia's gaze swung to Palmer.

The breath stuck in her lungs. His usual dismissive expression was wiped away. She'd expected irritation. A bit of surprise with a lot of grumbling. A tad of resentment for forcing him to get into a new routine with a new executive. Instead, she got something much more.

Hot, male temper.

His lower lip curled in a half snarl, and his voice was gravel and sandstone. "Perhaps I misunderstood. Did you just inform me you're leaving as my advertising representative after we spent this past hour planning our future campaign?"

Shock kept her mute for a moment. "Well, yes. I wanted to be sure you felt comfortable moving forward. You'll be in expert hands with our new hire, Hana, and I'm confident in her abilities to serve Endless Vows successfully."

"A new hire?" His emphasis on those words almost caused her to wince. "You're sticking me with a green employee after a year spent building our relationship?"

Once again, Palmer Matterson was hijacking her good news and popping all her balloons. Malia straightened in her chair and regarded him with chilly politeness. "Hana's experience is top rate. She's worked with multiple million-dollar companies, and we were lucky to hire her. As for our business relationship, I'm sure you realize it's not personal. You certainly don't disallow your own staff to move to different positions because you're afraid of offending someone's sensitive nature."

He leaned forward and stared down the sleek mahogany table at her. His gaze trapped her as deftly as his hands would, causing goose bumps to prickle her skin. "Did you just call me *sensitive*?"

Emeril and Andrea glanced back and forth between them. It seemed she was on her own here, because no one wanted to challenge the king.

Malia bared her teeth with a fake smile. "I apologize. I think I meant a different word."

His raised eyebrow invited her to continue.

She purred with satisfaction. "I meant *egotistical*."

Emeril coughed. Andrea grabbed her laptop and looked about to run.

Malia met his stare head-on and refused to flinch. This was her moment. She was done working with him, and there wasn't a thing he could do about it.

Slowly, Palmer rose from his chair. His presence shimmered with command. Malia stuck out her chin and glared back.

"Ms. Evergreen, I'd like to see you in my office."

"I don't think—"

"Now."

Without looking back, he stalked out of the conference room. Eyes wide, Malia looked over at the team left behind.

Emeril pocketed his phone and shook his head. "You better get in there if you don't want Quench to lose this account. Personally, I'm sad to lose you. This year has definitely been . . . interesting." He exited the room with his usual flurry.

Andrea sighed. "Good luck."

"He can't order me around like one of his employees," Malia muttered. "Right?"

"Sure he can. I once saw him give a blistering lecture to Robert Downey Jr. when he played a prank at his own friend's wedding, which Mr. Matterson had personally helped plan. Then he made Iron Man apologize. You pissed him off." Andrea stood up. "I like you, Malia, but that was not the way to inform us you were leaving. Good luck."

She disappeared, leaving Malia alone in the big, fancy conference room.

Ah, crap.

Maybe she'd screwed up. Maybe she should have been more delicate or given him warning. But for an entire year, he'd been slowly driving her mad, and it felt so good to finally give him what he deserved.

Still, her business partners and best friends, Chiara and Tessa, would kill her if she lost this account.

She had no choice.

Malia rose on her red Manolos and headed toward Palmer's private office.

Chapter Two

She was leaving.

Palmer knew he had only a few moments to get his shit together. After endless months of being across the table from Malia Evergreen, he'd finally formulated a plan—a plan he was going to unleash today.

Until her announcement.

God knew the woman was an expert in getting under his skin. Why was he surprised she'd neatly blown up his careful strategy with that fake smile and barely hidden glee? She was consistently two steps ahead of him.

Palmer took his precious minutes alone to pivot hard, a move often required in the manic wedding business of pleasing couples planning their weddings. He switched his brain to action mode and took some deep breaths on the three-point scale to calm the adrenaline coursing through his system. Breathe in for three. Hold. Breathe out for three.

It didn't help.

Perhaps it would be best to let her lead and use his instincts to move in on her weakness. Her defenses would be up, but that legendary temper she loved to hide so well simmered right beneath the surface. Temper was led by emotion. Emotion fueled the soft places between the walls. Palmer would use it to guide him to what he wanted.

Malia.

On cue, she walked into his office. Head up, jaw tight, she vibrated with outrage at his command, but it was the energy hiding underneath that power suit and armor he was interested in.

She was attracted to him.

Oh, she hated it. She'd tried to ignore the heat that flamed the moment they'd met and exchanged handshakes. Palmer was used to the push and pull of sexual tension. He was secure in his world, which was mostly driven by females in various roles. Many times he was the only man in the room, beginning as a wedding planner and working his way up to starting his own business. He adored women, from their soft bodies and multitasking brains to their pioneer spirits that fought back even after years of being stymied by his gender. But his interest in Malia had barely registered a blip on his radar because he rarely engaged in affairs with his work partners. Too messy.

Plus, although she found him attractive, it was obvious she didn't like him. That fact amused him, because he was relatively charming and easy to get along with. But from day one, Malia had challenged him. Her sharp gaze mocked, judged, and found him lacking for no obvious reason. Usually, he initially met with the representative he was investing heavily with, then left it to Andrea. But something about Malia's disregard rankled enough that he'd begun to show up for the meetings in person.

He'd deliberately embraced the role she believed him to play—the ruthless, arrogant, stick-in-the-mud CEO of a business empire. Emeril and Andrea never questioned his sudden shift in behavior, since he usually ran meetings with relaxed ease and casual humor. But he liked ruffling Malia's feathers. Enjoyed her obvious irritation at his cold disregard and analyzed every reaction when he pushed. Enjoyed her obvious beauty and fierce confidence when she rose to the bait and argued a point, refusing to back off when she believed she was right.

Everything about the woman screamed queen. Her long, dark braids were usually twisted above her head like an intricate crown.

Smooth brown skin seemed to glow from within. Her heart-shaped face and high arched brows gave her an air of elegance and a touch of the regal. Full lips had a tendency to press into a straight line when she disapproved of something—usually most of the time around him. She was average height even with her preferred sexy stilettos, with ripe curves that her designer suits accented. But it was the way she walked and owned a room that fascinated Palmer. She was comfortable in her skin no matter who surrounded her, her gorgeous golden-brown eyes never afraid to meet his straight on with a spark of challenge. Lately, he was beginning to catch her scent in his nostrils long after she left his conference room—a mix of plum and musk that seemed to haunt him.

As time passed and their meetings became a staple of his schedule, Palmer found himself looking forward to them. The sexual energy crackled between them like a summer lightning storm, yet she refused to yield. He kept waiting to grow bored with the game and give control of the meetings back to Andrea and Emeril. Unbelievably, he became only more consumed with figuring Malia out and what exactly it was about her that called to him.

Palmer had finally decided to stop the foreplay and focus on his new goal: winning over Malia Evergreen. He wanted her on his arm. In his life.

In his bed.

He plotted out his careful course and made the decision to begin meeting her one-on-one. He'd finally gotten tired of her dislike for him but figured he had plenty of time to launch his new plan. He'd intended to show her his softer side. Charm her into a date or wrangle some personal time together. Dazzle her with his sense of humor, which he tended to have when not trying to be the Big Bad Wolf, and then ease into seduction with slow yet satisfying moves. But now she was leaving, and he wouldn't have regular access to her.

Now, everything had changed.

Palmer ignored the stab of worry that told him he might be too late and focused on Malia's presence.

Her low-timbered voice held ice crystals when she spoke. "Mr. Matterson, I appreciate your discomfort at being assigned another representative, but I don't appreciate you barking orders at me."

"You're right. Would you sit down, please?"

She blinked, obviously taken aback.

Instead of sitting behind his massive desk, he crossed the room toward the comfortable seating area where he held most of his meetings. Plush red velvet chairs and low couches surrounded a round mahogany table. He used the custom-built bar for both health shakes and the finest bourbon, depending on the time of day. The floor-to-ceiling windows allowed them full access to the view of New York City's mighty power—where buildings competed for height and Bryant Park welcomed crowds for eating, shopping, and gathering to enjoy the lush gardens. He'd chosen this spot as Endless Vows' hub for its central location, access to Grand Central train station, and the daily reminder he'd made his dreams come true. The other satellite stores scattered throughout Chelsea, South Street Seaport, Greenwich Village, and Tribeca were to welcome clients and create the fantasy-type wedding themes his company was known for. But his Fifth Avenue office was his haven—a private oasis soundproofed and created for shelter within the chaos.

Seeing Malia carefully sitting at the edge of the chair, poised for flight or fight, caused satisfaction to curl in his gut. Not because she was wary of him. No, it was her presence in his sanctuary and the knowledge he'd finally gotten her alone. They had always been surrounded by people since their first meeting. Palmer wished he'd decided to move faster, but he hadn't foreseen her changing jobs.

"Can I get you anything?" he asked.

"No." Malia tugged at the creeping hemline of her skirt. "I hope you understand Quench is dedicated to Endless Vows. I can guarantee it will be a smooth transition with Hana—she's been personally trained by me."

"May I ask what your new position will be?"

Her face tightened like she'd tasted a lemon. He tried not to chuckle at her obvious distaste in telling him. This may have been the only woman he'd ever met who aggressively chose not to like him. "I'll be with our new not-for-profit, the Quench Foundation. We identify sponsors to help local charities and organizations with funding and programs. We were recently able to donate a nice amount to Dream On Youth Center in Nyack and begin an internship program for high school and college students." Excitement laced her usual polite, detached tones, and those deep, amber eyes sparkled with a light he'd never spotted before.

Palmer dug a bit deeper. "I see. You'll be leaving advertising completely?"

"Yes. But as I said, Hana—"

"I don't care about Hana. I'm sure that will work out fine." He dismissed the new name with a quick wave of his hand, his mind furiously working with this new information. "I'm surprised I didn't receive any details about the foundation and opportunities there."

Quench was a company he'd watched explode over the past few years. Female owned by Malia and her two business partners, it was a digital empire that served women in all aspects of their lives—relationships, beauty, fashion, health, career, and money. He'd realized Quench could aid his own needs at Endless Vows, because it was a platform not solely focused on weddings. By instituting an aggressive, consistent advertising campaign, he'd been able to level up to their broad consumer base.

"We just received the final legal approval a few months ago and needed some time to set up administration. You're a valued part of the Quench family, Mr. Matterson. Once you see what an investment can do, we hope you'll agree to a donation or sponsorship."

Her spiel was courteous and all business, but he'd spotted the passion beneath it and didn't want to settle for only this part of her. Not anymore. "What will you be doing for the foundation?"

It took her a moment to answer. He sensed she hated giving him more information than required, and he'd thrown her a curveball with his interrogation. "It will vary. I'll be managing new staff, identifying and analyzing organizations in need of our assistance, and spreading the opportunity to clients interested in donating."

Gotcha.

He crossed an ankle over his knee and regarded her under heavy-lidded eyes. "Like me?"

Her lips pressed into a thin line. "Of course. I'd be happy to give you all the details about the foundation and what we can accomplish with your donation."

"Excellent."

"I'll have my associate reach out to you. Deanna is well versed in the not-for-profit sector." Malia's teeth flashed in a sharklike smile. "Since this is a new position for me and I'm still learning, I know you'd prefer working with a top-level, experienced staff member."

Oh, she was good. Frustration mixed with admiration, creating a curious cocktail of emotion. She didn't want to work with him and was trying to stick him with someone else. A slow smile curved his lips as he stared her down. "I want you."

She blinked. Shock flickered over her face before she got it under control. "Excuse me?"

"We've spent the last year building a relationship on trust. I'd like to continue it."

Her hand fisted, then relaxed. Her chest rose as she dragged in a breath. Oh, what he'd give to watch her finally lose her temper. Palmer bet it would be a glorious thing to witness.

Almost as much as her exploding with passion.

"I appreciate your kind sentiment," she replied, "but if you're even telling the truth, you'll need to trust me to guide you to the correct person who can help you the most."

Her words hit him like a slap. The fact that she didn't believe he had honor scraped raw, but he continued to press her. "I've also learned in business that relationships can trump knowledge. Let's just consider it an on-the-job training session that will push you to the next level."

Something close to horror lit her eyes, and his ego winced. "Mr. Matterson, I'll be happy to accompany Deanna for introductions and be here until you feel comfortable. It's what's best for you and Endless Vows."

Oh, she was stubborn. Palmer watched his opportunity begin to shrivel, because this woman was fierce under pressure. It was time he got more direct to see what happened.

He pinned her with his gaze. "I think you're the best for me."

Malia's jaw dropped. She tried to talk but seemed to struggle to find her words. He waited patiently, enjoying this rare glimpse of her off-kilter.

"But—you don't even like me!" The words burst in the room like a gunshot.

Regret coursed through him as he unhooked his ankle, adjusted his position, and leaned in. He'd taken his ruse too far. It was time Malia knew his true intentions.

"I like you very much, Malia," he said softly. Her name sounded rich and smooth, like butter melting on his tongue. "I have for a while, and I'm interested in not only continuing our business relationship but also getting to know you better on a personal level. I think we're more alike than you know."

A stunned laugh escaped her lips. "Funny, I think we're galaxies apart."

"I disagree. Why don't we find out over dinner?"

Her eyes bugged out and she went speechless again for a few moments. Though he'd been hopeful for a more positive reaction, Palmer waited until she found her words. Her voice came out a bit higher than usual. "You want to take me to dinner? On a date?"

"Yes. I'm asking for you to give me a chance. I know I've seemed distant, and you had no idea of my interest. I apologize. I'd like to show you a more, shall we say, charming side of me." He tilted his head and gave her a warm smile. Palmer knew he'd screwed up, but he'd never met a woman he hadn't been able to eventually convince to go out with him, at least once.

Especially when there was such an intense chemistry neither of them could deny.

Malia took a deep breath and seemed to gather her thoughts. "May I ask a question?"

"Of course."

"Is this invitation completely separate from the business of the foundation and our ad account?"

He hated that she needed to ask. "Yes. I guarantee your answer will in no way affect whatever decision I make regarding my involvement with Quench or the foundation."

"Good. That's important for me to know."

Her softening gave him a burst of hope. He lifted his hands in the air and went with honesty. "Your announcement threw me off guard. It's been a long time since I fumbled like this, but I'm hoping I'm not too late. There's a lovely Japanese restaurant I'd like to take you to if you like sushi. My driver can pick you up this Friday. Seven p.m.?"

Malia absently tapped her lip, as if considering his request. Relief poured through him. He was sure that with some quality one-on-one time, he'd be able to connect with her on a deeper level.

She slowly stood, uncurling her figure and standing tall in four-inch heels. Her body vibrated with an energy that packed a punch to his gut. Her lips curled in a glorious feminine sneer that only added to her gorgeousness. Palmer sat, helpless under the sheer ferocity of her, and knew he was doomed.

"I'm sorry, Mr. Matterson, but I decline your offer. I'm sure your ability to charm women is like a superpower, but in this case, I'm fortunately immune. I'm glad this won't affect your relationship with Quench, as you've indicated, and as much as I appreciate your stellar trust in me, both Hana and Deanna will be better suited to be your representatives. Now, I must go. Thank you for your time." She inclined her head gracefully and walked to the door.

"Malia."

Her hand clenched around the handle. She turned slowly, and he caught the bone-deep wariness on her face before it was quickly replaced with a cool, professional distance. "Yes?"

"I appreciate your directness. I'm sure both of your referrals will meet my needs in the future, and I look forward to a long, fruitful relationship with Quench."

Her shoulders sagged with obvious relief. "Thank you."

"One other thing. It was truly an honor to work with you this past year. I'd be happy to recommend your ad team to any of my clients." Respect rumbled through his voice. "Good luck with your new position. I hope the people around you know how lucky they are to have you." He paused, then smiled slowly. "Because I think you're extraordinary."

Shock seemed to hold her frozen. For one perfect moment, her golden-brown eyes locked with his, and strange things fluttered in his chest. Then she was opening the door and walking away.

She was gone.

Palmer wondered at the deep well of regret that had sunk through him. Somehow, he felt as if the loss of Malia Evergreen would haunt him for a long, long time.

Chapter Three

"I met with *him* today."

Malia stared moodily at her perfectly made veggie omelet and tried to find the words to describe her absolute frustration with the billionaire who'd been making her life miserable the past year. Seated at the familiar booth in Mike's Place with her two best friends and business partners, she prepped herself for the upcoming barrage of questions.

The restaurant was a cornerstone of their youth, half café and half diner. Roomy red booths, an old-fashioned countertop with high spinning stools, and a checkerboard floor gave it a fifties vibe. The antique jukebox belted out classic Rolling Stones, warning them all they couldn't get what they want. The scents of grease, sizzling bacon, and coffee rose to her nostrils.

Breakfast at Mike's was a twice-a-week ritual. Malia relied on their get-togethers not only to catch up personally but to discuss any issues in an environment that held treasured memories. It was the same booth they'd all congregated in years ago when Quench was just an idea and a dream. Of course, one of their crew was missing, and her empty seat still haunted Malia. Rory had been taken from them too early in a car accident four years ago, leaving a hole in their makeshift family and the company they'd created together. But they'd managed to honor Rory's memory by shifting roles and working even harder to achieve success.

Now, Quench was a multimillion-dollar media company. Besides offering in-depth articles on multiple subjects affecting women, they sponsored influential digital lectures and classes from experts around the world and had finally created their own not-for-profit foundation to help local programs and charities.

Chiara had taken on the role of editor in chief after Rory passed and was beginning to do more writing assignments. Tessa ran the beauty and fashion department and was now in charge of a new internship program. Malia had spent the past years in advertising and marketing, sharpening her sales and business skills. She loved her position but had recently admitted to getting burned out. She craved a new challenge, and with the formation of the Quench Foundation, she'd finally been able to connect with a new passion. She'd been slowly training her replacements with great results. All her advertising accounts had wished her well and happily embraced the new regime.

Except Palmer Matterson.

Chiara gave her a worried look, brows furrowed in a frown. Dressed in a polished black pantsuit, sleek red hair flipping perfectly under her chin, no one would believe she had a newborn baby and barely slept. "Why don't you look happy? You've been wanting off his account since day one. I thought you'd enjoy dumping his ass."

Tessa snorted and took a sip of her coffee. Her cappuccino-colored corkscrew curls bounced as she shook her head. "As long as you did it politely. Mr. Hot Billionaire gives us a ton of advertising dollars and can be tapped for the foundation. As you already know."

Malia rolled her eyes at the familiar taunt, knowing Endless Vows was a huge moneymaker for Quench. "I was polite. At first."

Tessa groaned. "Oh no, what did you do?"

The memory of their last meeting burned in her head with mockery. She'd been torturing herself with the image nonstop. "I was perfectly civil in the beginning, but he wasn't happy about getting a new ad rep. Demanded I see him in his office."

Chiara sighed. "He has no choice. We can't keep you locked in advertising just to satisfy his every need."

The idea of Malia satisfying the hot billionaire's every need had her squirming in her seat. God, how humiliating. Even after he'd treated her like some type of lackey, she still couldn't get his magnified sexual energy out of her head. The way he towered over her; those piercing green eyes shredding through her polite barriers; her name falling from his tongue like a hypnotic command. She despised her tendency to fall silent when faced with a shock and tried desperately to hide the weakness, but of course, he'd driven her straight to muteness with his outrageous invitation.

"Exactly," she said, finally digging into her omelet. "I pretty much said the same thing, but then he switched gears on me, which really freaked me out."

Worry gleamed in Tessa's blue eyes. "What did he do?"

"Asked me out. On a date."

Malia relished the twin gasps from her friends. She desperately needed their support, since she was trying to keep her outrage at his proposal properly fanned.

"I knew it!" Chiara said, shaking her head. "All that verbal warfare was really foreplay! He liked you the whole time. I always found it strange he kept insisting you personally show up at every meeting."

"Like a bully pulling the girl's pigtails because he really wants to eat lunch with her in the cafeteria," Tessa said with a serious nod.

Malia dropped her fork. "Seriously, guys? He doesn't like me. I became some sort of sick challenge to him, so he felt like he needed to win me over before I escaped his clutches!"

I like you very much, Malia.

His hot gaze barreling into hers. His voice pitched to a husky, intimate tone. She may have gone mute, but her heart had practically leaped out of her chest. Along with other body parts reacting unfavorably.

Or favorably.

Tessa regarded her suspiciously. "Wait—did he threaten you? Tie you dating him to his account? Because I don't care how much money he has. I'll destroy him if he was playing that game."

A shiver broke through her because she knew Tessa would make good on her promise. "No. He kind of apologized for acting like an asshole, then asked me to a Japanese restaurant with the promise of charming me."

"An interesting approach," Chiara noted.

"I asked him if his invite would affect his account, and he assured me that wasn't his intention."

"Did you believe him?" Tessa asked.

Malia shifted in the booth. "Yeah," she admitted. "I did. But he still pissed me off, so I gave him my honest answer."

Chiara winced. "How'd he take it?"

She thought over his parting words. The way he'd looked at her with respect and something else, something deep and raw that made her tummy drop to her toes. As if she mattered to him. As if he'd really meant what he said about wanting quality time with her. That she was extraordinary.

Even after she'd boldly rejected him.

Ridiculous. Everything about the man screamed arrogance and control freak. He was probably playing some game because she suddenly wasn't readily available. They'd be awful together, because she wouldn't put up with his high-handedness for an entire evening. "He was polite, said he'd be fine meeting with Hana, and wished me luck."

Tessa buttered her toast and nibbled on the crust. "So it's over. You got what you wanted and never have to see him again."

Malia ignored the strange pang of loss her friend's declaration brought. She'd been dreaming of this nonstop. Why wasn't she celebrating her victory? She forced a smile. "Yep, I'm finally free. He was asking questions about the foundation, so I'm going to have Deanna contact him."

Chiara gave an excited squeal. "That's great news! He's the perfect candidate if we can find a charity he'd like to work with. You're sure he won't push to have you represent him?"

"Not after I made myself clear I'd never go out with him."

"Go out with who?" A rough male voice cut through their conversation.

Malia looked up and smiled at Mike, Rory's dad and the owner of the café. As a single father, he was broken after her death, but they'd all made sure to keep watch over him to help soothe his loneliness and grief. After all, they'd known him since middle school. He was their substitute father and the mentor who had loaned them the initial money to make Quench into a reality. He was also overprotective and had no issue jumping into their conversations or their business if he thought he could help.

Malia smiled. "Just a client, Mike. One giving me some trouble."

His fierce frown would have been intimidating if Malia didn't know he was really a teddy bear at heart. In his grease-stained apron and jeans, Mike ran the café with a booming voice, good humor, and a deep-seated need to serve his customers. In the past year, his heart had healed from some of the holes his only daughter's loss had left behind, but Malia caught the loneliness in his pale blue eyes too many times. He needed a companion but was too stubborn to see it. "Do I need to pay him a visit and get him to stop bothering you?"

"Already taken care of," Malia answered.

"That's my girl." Mike walked away.

She ate a few more bites of her omelet, then felt her friends' matching stares. She cocked her head in question. "What?"

Tessa grinned wickedly. "You don't seem as ecstatic as I imagined. Sure you don't have the hots for your hot billionaire and you've just been in major denial?"

She practically spit out her coffee like a cat hissing after getting dunked. "He'd have to get a personality transplant first. Plus, I'm not the one who lives in the land of denial, Tessa."

Her friend drew back. "What do you mean? I'm the most ruthlessly honest person at the table."

"Oh, please. You still haven't given up on matching Mike with Emma, even though it's obvious they would never work."

Tessa looked hurt. "They're perfect together. Mike just needs a push."

Malia glanced at Chiara, and they both shook their heads. They'd become close to Emma, their retired high school English teacher, after recognizing she had a crush on Rory's father. After a few failed attempts to get them together, Malia accepted Mike might not be attracted to Emma. Their personalities seemed to clash and turn him from a gentle giant into a brusque, irritated male.

But Tessa refused to give up, saying they were hidden soul mates and needed time to adjust. Tessa was known for her short temper and tendency to say whatever was on her mind, but she also had a hidden soft heart. She championed the underdog and had pivoted the beauty department at Quench by focusing on women who lacked confidence in themselves. Emma was her new recruit, and even Malia admitted she'd seen a difference in the woman's happiness lately.

Malia reached out and patted Tessa's hand. "You have a romantic soul, babe. The man who finally sees it may crack down that last wall."

Tessa rolled her eyes. "Love is great, but sex is better. I've been telling you that forever, but you still won't listen. Find someone who can scratch your itch rather than look for husband material, because lately, anyone's gotta be better than some of the dates you've been on."

It was true. Her dating life was an epic disaster—so much so she'd literally offered her stories up for blog posts at Quench. A few had even gone viral, spouting new taglines such as THINK YOUR DATING LIFE IS BAD? CHECK THIS OUT . . .

Exactly what she never wanted to be well known for.

Chiara regarded Malia intently. "Did you have your appointment yet with the fertility clinic?"

Nerves jumped in her belly. She'd spent her thirty-first birthday trying not to panic as she officially settled into a new decade with a gap in her life she couldn't seem to fill. Yes, she loved her career, especially with her new position. She'd reignited her passion to make a change in the world. She had amazing friends and family. She was financially secure.

But she was lonely.

She craved sharing her life with a man she could love. Dreamed of being a mother and raising a family. Malia had been patient throughout her twenties. She'd laughed at her disastrous dates and reminded herself multiple frogs must be kissed to find the right one.

It wasn't funny anymore. After endless bad dates, she'd lost all her confidence, and a terrible question kept creeping into her mind.

What if there truly wasn't a man for her?

Maybe she'd never find him. Maybe she was too picky. Too set in her ways to compromise. Too difficult and demanding.

Too unlovable.

As the dating queen, she'd found fault with every single man she went out with, and her heart remained stuck behind a wall, longing to be free.

Like some twisted princess waiting for a kiss from Mr. Right.

Then another realization hit. Maybe she didn't need a man to be a mother. Sure, a two-parent relationship was ideal and the image she'd grown up with. But the longing to hold a baby in her arms was a constant ache that had gotten even worse since Chiara had her own baby. If Mr. Right never showed up, what was she going to do?

Being driven by logic had its advantages. Malia finally decided to put her destiny in her own hands. Fate wasn't going to screw her out of the opportunity to have a child.

"Yes, I got my blood test results back yesterday. My AMH level isn't the best. It's under 1.0, which is low, but not dangerously low the way I worried about." The real worry was the ovarian cysts they'd found after fertility tests, raising the odds that she wouldn't produce enough healthy eggs for pregnancy. She remembered Rory had suffered from the same diagnosis and had difficulty getting pregnant, which brought a whole new set of worries for Malia she'd never considered. She took a breath, willing her heart to steady. "I guess it confirms I was smart to freeze my eggs now, since getting pregnant later on could be difficult."

Her friends nodded, and Malia immediately sensed the wave of support and encouragement surrounding her. They'd backed her up on her decision and never questioned her intentions.

Unlike her family.

"Good. What's the next step, and how can we help?" Tessa asked.

Malia made a face. "I'm on birth control pills now to prep for the hormone injections. Once I start, I'll need to inject myself for about two weeks, which I'm not looking forward to."

"Ugh, the shots sound like the worst part. Then again, I used to dread my annual flu shot until I had Veronica and found myself begging for that mile-long needle in my spine to stop the damn pain!" Chiara said with a laugh.

Malia shuddered. "Don't even want to think of that."

"The epidural was worth it for Veronica. I know the fertility shots will be difficult but well worth it in the end. What about the side effects? Is it like having jacked-up PMS for a long time?" Chiara asked.

"Pretty much. I did some research, and women have a bunch of different reactions, so I won't know until I'm going through it."

"Did you tell your parents yet?" Chiara asked.

Hurt rippled through her. "No. I don't think I'm going to tell my sisters, either. The few times I seriously mentioned the procedure, they all freaked out on me. It's so unfair. They had such an easy time of things—all of them got married and pregnant by twenty-eight. But just because I'm still single, I don't want to have to give up on being a mom. I want to have a backup plan."

Sympathy gleamed from Chiara's amber eyes. "You have us. We'll help in any way we can."

"What she said," Tessa declared.

Malia smiled. "Thanks, guys. I better head out. We on for Scrabble at Mike's this Sunday?"

"Yes, we are!" Mike's voice boomed across the diner. "Have a good day, Mal."

"Thanks." She blew air kisses to her friends and slid out of the booth. "See you later at the office. Tessa gets the bill today for being a smart-ass."

Malia left, hearing her friend's laughter. Her spirits lightened as she made her way out to Main Street and took in a lungful of warm air. The lure of summer danced mischievously in the streets, tempting shopkeepers to move tables outside and display racks of wares on the sidewalk. With the chaos of March behind, it was time to pack up the boots and winter jackets and embrace the new season. Spring always made her think of second chances. A reset. Endless possibilities.

Her heels clicked on the concrete pavement as she made her way to her lime-green Mini Cooper. Her mind sifted through her goals for the day, and when her phone rang, she hit the accept button automatically without checking to see who it was.

Huge mistake.

"Mal! Why haven't you called Mom back about your RSVP to Pam's wedding? You know it's rude to keep her waiting so long, and then she calls me to bitch because you're never around to pick up. Not. Cool."

Malia summoned up a great deal of patience and kept her voice calm while she navigated the morning traffic. "Davinia, I told her I'd call Saturday morning, so I'm not sure why she's complaining to you.

I've been in back-to-back meetings this week. We just created a new division at the company, and I'm slammed."

The cry of her two nephews blasted over the line, and Davinia's voice rose in a shriek. "Mommy said not to touch each other, and I mean it! Now go into separate rooms right now or no TV." A crash, more crying, then a slammed door. "Sorry, it's been a day."

Malia's heart softened. Juggling two preschoolers all day was hard, and dealing with their mom's endless calls was even harder. "It's okay. I promise to scoop them up next week and give you guys a date night."

"I may forgive you, then. *May*. But only if you at least text Mom your RSVP."

Dread coiled in her gut, but she kept her tone light. "I need to hold off until the last minute. My . . . date may be busy that weekend."

Silence hung over the line. "You don't have a date, do you."

"Yes I do! I've been seeing someone, but he may be working that weekend, so he's checking to see if he can get the time off." Sweat clung to her forehead and under her arms. She tried not to babble—it was her tell when she lied.

"Malia, what is *up*? Are you a closet lesbian?"

She choked out a gasp. "No! Not that there's anything wrong with it if I was."

"Not saying it's wrong. I'm saying this bullshit you keep giving us for every event is getting old. You say you're dating, yet you haven't brought anyone to a gathering in forever. Mama's sick with worry you're going to be a rich spinster with a bunch of cats. And when she worries, she calls me to share her worry, and I'm dragged down into the pits of hell."

Malia knew that as the oldest, Davinia got the brunt of their mother's anxiety, but her other three sisters weren't much help, either. They were the first to gleefully back up her parents about Malia's nonexistent love life. She'd become the black sheep of the family where having a family was the goal. "I told you I'm seeing someone steady now. I'll make sure he gets the time off." She tried not to wince at the lie.

"Oh, you better. And he better be good, because even Pam said everyone's getting tired of kicking the bouquet to you."

Humiliation burned. It was a ridiculous conversation to have in the current era of #MeToo and women's rights, but her family remained stubbornly traditional and unapologetic about what was expected. Malia wasn't the youngest daughter, and she was still unmarried and single. A double whammy and a complete disgrace. "I told you I'll bring him, and I'll call Mom on Saturday."

"Fine. Next Sunday is family dinner. Aliya has an announcement to make, so your ass better be there."

"Oh no."

"Oh yes, but don't tell her I said anything. You know she loves a good surprise."

Another baby. Great. And now that her cousin Pam was getting married at twenty-five, Malia would be the talk of the party. People would stare sympathetically as she'd be the only one on the floor to catch the bouquet other than the flower girls. Hell, they'd probably get hitched before Malia would.

"Davinia, I gotta go. Pick your night and I'll come over to watch the boys."

Her sister began yelling again, so Malia just clicked off.

Her good mood crashed and got swallowed up like a tsunami had hit. She couldn't put herself through another torturous family event. Somehow, she had to find a date for this wedding. A date that would look legitimate enough to keep her family preoccupied and buy her time. If she could dazzle them just once, they might be satisfied enough so she could spin some stories about a deepening relationship and then they could break up later. When it was appropriate.

She just needed to find a guy. Any guy willing to put up with a million questions from her big, nosy family without the guarantee of sex.

She was so screwed.

Chapter Four

Palmer walked out to the private terrace, wiping his face with a towel, and looked out over the city.

The view was magnificent at night, with thousands of lights exploding from the skyline and setting off Central Park like a natural centered jewel. But he preferred it now, in the early morning, when the sun was struggling to rise and a new day offered endless opportunities. It gave him hope. Lord knew, he needed some.

A painful smile twisted his lips at the thought. It had already been two weeks, and he couldn't seem to stop thinking of Malia. In his entire life, there'd never been a woman he couldn't either impress, seduce, or gain forgiveness from. His sister Christine always called him spoiled, because with four sisters, he'd been learning how to charm women since toddlerhood. But it was one of the few assets he had growing up around a throng of females who liked to boss him around. He considered it more as survival of the fittest. Malia just happened to be the first one his skills hadn't worked on.

He stretched his sore muscles from the intense workout he'd just finished. Punishing his body with weights and CrossFit hadn't worked. He was still obsessing over Malia, even though he'd promised to stop if she rejected him. Sure, Palmer hadn't thought the possibility existed, but she'd been clear.

She simply didn't like him.

The thought stung. If only he hadn't leaned into his role of asshole CEO and allowed her to see who he really was. But there was nothing more he could do. Blackmailing her to spend time with him in the name of work would only cement his bad reputation and make things worse. Best to push onward until another woman caught his eye. One who reciprocated his attention.

Palmer turned and retreated inside, ready to start the day. He showered and dressed, listening to the drone of news in the background. His penthouse was in a prime location, furnished with modern, sleek furniture; all the amenities required, such as a gym and pool; and twenty-four-hour concierge service. But lately, he preferred to stay in his main home outside the city, where he was technically more alone but felt less isolated. Towering over New York City was an amazing feeling, but he hadn't shared the view with someone special in too long. He wondered what Malia would think of it.

Shaking his head at the pathetic thought, he headed out, chatting casually with his driver, who adeptly managed the jammed streets to get him to his favorite coffee shop on time. The Zibetto Espresso Bar had the best espresso to get him fueled, plenty of counter space, and the buzzing energy of customers who knew exactly what they wanted. He was meeting his eldest sister, who'd insisted on a face-to-face encounter.

Never a good sign.

He ordered a café latte and cornetto, then spotted Veronica at one of the tables. Dressed in navy-blue yoga pants, a T-shirt that said Drinks Well with Others, and sneakers, she looked a bit worn around the edges. Her honey-brown hair was caught up in a loose ponytail, and her face was makeup-free, emphasizing large brown eyes. Her grip on her coffee was like a shipwreck survivor clutching a life raft.

Palmer greeted her with a kiss and dropped in the seat across. "Hey, how are you?"

"Crappy."

"You look great."

She snorted. "I haven't slept decently because of these damn hot flashes, but I decided to get up early for a yoga class since Christine's been bugging me to do more self-care. I fell asleep during corpse pose, and the teacher had to wake me up because I was snoring and drooling on myself. Needless to say, I didn't make any new friends there. Plus, I think I'm fat."

Palmer shook his head. Veronica was the most like him—ruthlessly organized, an overachiever, and hopelessly direct. It was the other three who called only to lead him on one conversation puzzle after another, filled with tidbits of gossip, speculation, and inane chatter. Veronica always told the truth and didn't like surface niceties like the rest of the world. "You already lost ten pounds and don't need to lose any more—you're perfect. And yoga is for underachievers. You'd do better with kickboxing. Here, have some of this. You're probably cranky from no breakfast." He broke off the end piece of the pastry and slid it over.

She hesitated, then took it. "Maybe. I notice you didn't mention the menopause."

He winced. He didn't love talking about female body mechanics with his sisters, but Veronica was especially fierce about men being educated. She felt they had a responsibility to be comfortable around such discussions, and as her only brother, he'd been her first student. "Maybe you should go on hormones after all. I read this article I can forward that said there's very low risk."

"No, I'm not putting anything fake into my body. I've got a meeting with a holistic practitioner next week, which may help. But I appreciate your willingness to discuss." Her lower lip twitched in a smile. "Wanted to give you a heads-up on a few things, and you haven't been returning my calls."

Palmer rolled his eyes. "Once."

"Twice. Doesn't matter, I needed a coffee break before my day begins."

He squared his shoulders and took a sip of the steaming brew. "Okay, what's going on?"

She already looked more relaxed after a few nibbles of the cornetto. "Christine has been bugging me to volunteer with her over at the Children's Hunger Initiative. I can't make it with my schedule, Jane is out of town, and Mom said one of us needs to step up since she's doing her part to help in the world. Georgia volunteered you, so you're up next."

He gritted his teeth. "I'm running a company here. I have no time to volunteer. Why don't I cut them a check?"

"We all have lives, dude. Chris wants a warm body and not cold cash. Deal with it."

Palmer held back a groan. Once Christine recognized a need in the world, the entire family was helpless under her passion to fix it right now. And that usually involved volunteering, every single one of them. His mother allowed the bossiness, citing that Chris was helping save their souls, but Palmer knew Mom had just given up because nobody won an argument with her. Chris preached flow and kindness, but she was more ruthless than all of them when she had a purpose. "Shit. What do I have to do?"

Veronica shrugged. "You need to meet her in Verily tomorrow night. It's a charity that helps feed underprivileged kids. I think she said they need help prepping for a meal outreach."

His day tomorrow was packed with meetings and two weddings to check on. He knew he was screwed but tried anyway. "What if I said no?"

His sister simply laughed. "Go ahead, but get ready for a call from Mom."

Palmer shook his head, trying not to get pissed off that even she realized he was unable to stand up for himself. "Fine."

"A smart decision. I'll text you the address." He glared at her as she continued. "Now to the second thing: you're getting set up for another blind date."

Irritation ruffled. He rubbed his head and muttered a curse. "I told them I was done. No more setups—I can find my own women. Plus, they're horrible at it."

"So are you." Veronica wiped her mouth and gave a sigh. "The new victim is Jane's coworker who saw your picture and thought you were hot. She's going to accidentally run into you to cement a connection."

"Tell me where and I'll just avoid it." It was the wince that made his stomach lurch. "No. She didn't."

"She did."

Steam rose from his cup and his ears. "Are you kidding me? Jane told her where my favorite coffee place was?"

"And she told Mom about the setup plan. She's all for it so she can save you from your lonely, wifeless, kidless life."

"Dammit, I'm going to kill her!"

It was happening again. Something about the spring season brought out his family's mating tendencies, and since he was the only single one left, they all turned their attention on him. Palmer shuddered at the thought of what was ahead. Endless setups that bombed immediately. Stalkers who pretended to bump into him, citing his family's connections or his business, as if that gave them an instant right to know his personal life. Mom's sad faces and worried calls about him getting older and having too many regrets. Christine's ridiculous belief in Wiccan love spells to allow the universe to offer up the woman who'd change him forever. It was all too much.

Palmer stood up. "I'll take care of it, Veronica. Thanks for letting me know. I better get going."

She rose from the chair and picked up her purse. "Me, too. Oh, don't forget to RSVP for Barbara's wedding. You're bringing a date, right?"

Disbelief cut through him. "I'm the one planning it! Why would I need to RSVP?"

Stubbornness clung to her voice. "Endless Vows is doing it—I'm sure you're not personally picking out the napkins, dude."

Palmer grabbed for patience. "It's our cousin, so I'm personally involved. She's not waiting to hear the name of my date."

"Actually, she is. Mentioned it to me yesterday and asked if I knew her name so she didn't have to create the place cards as 'Palmer' and 'Guest.' Everyone's going, and I'd advise you to show up with someone good. And not one of those too-perfect, skinny-ass women who's obviously a fake escort. They've seen through that ruse before. Remember, Christine can spot immediately if you're attracted to someone. She's got scary juju."

He seethed. Yeah, he'd tried to ask associates or casual friends to pose as his girlfriend in the past, but their youngest sister was half witch and immediately called him out. "Fine. I'll work on it. For now, tell Barbara using 'Guest' is fine and completely appropriate."

"Sure you don't want to go with Jane's pick? She should be here any minute."

"You used to be my favorite sister, but you're dropping fast." Palmer turned and stalked out the door, her laughter ringing behind him.

If anyone knew he was secretly ruled by a bunch of female tyrants, he'd be humiliated. No matter how many times he told his family he wasn't interested in marriage, they pretended he was kidding and forged ahead on finding him a wife. They just couldn't accept or believe he didn't want the package he sold every day of his life, especially after all his sisters were happily in love and had welcomed a bunch of babies into the family. His nieces and nephews were one of the best things about his life, but he'd never experienced the need to have his own children.

His family didn't care, though. On his thirty-fifth birthday, they decided his time was officially up and they'd begun wife hunting. At first, it was humorous and a nice distraction. But since he'd turned forty a few months ago, it had begun to be a painful exercise, causing fights and tension and driving a wedge between them. Palmer just didn't understand why they couldn't leave him alone to live his life in his own way.

He was happy exactly the way he was.

~

Malia walked onto the grounds of the Children's Hunger Initiative. It was a local charity in Verily, a quirky town close to Nyack, and housed in an abandoned restaurant. Close to the schools and within walking distance of a host of motels, the not-for-profit was small but passionately committed to serving the population of forgotten or struggling kids and families.

She dragged in a breath as excitement danced in her belly. Deanna was drowning in applicants and had declared Malia ready to begin taking on her own accounts. They'd thoroughly vetted the grassroots charity, and it was finally approved. Malia was excited about how to both help and expand the program by matching it with a donor. Today she'd finally get to meet the rest of the team, get involved in some hands-on work, and then finalize details with the founders during their business dinner.

Xander and Laura—the brainchildren and owners behind the charity—were at the door to greet her. "I'm so glad you could come!" Laura said with her usual enthusiasm, her pixie cut, nose ring, and sharp chin reminding Malia of a mischievous fairy. Her outfit consisted of denim shorts, T-shirt, and Keds sneakers, making her look about fifteen. She was balanced perfectly by her husband, a burly, bearded man with kind eyes and a preference for plaid and flannel. Since it was a warm spring evening, he'd settled for jeans and a black-and-white checkered shirt. A cap declaring him a Nets basketball fan was pulled low over his brow.

Xander pumped Malia's hand with a smile. "Honored to have you. It's been touch-and-go for a bit here, and having the foundation take us on has given the place new hope. Looking forward to discussing the plan."

"The Children's Hunger Initiative is the exact type of program we're looking for," she said, taking in the space. "Looks like you have a solid group of volunteers."

Tight groups were working together at tables, sorting groceries into bags. People drifted in and out of the kitchen with trays of hot food, dumping it into pots and labeling various items. The energy seemed high and positive, and each volunteer was focused on a specific duty, lending control to the overall chaos.

"Let us take you around and introduce you," Laura said, tucking her arm into her husband's.

She chatted with various individuals from the community—some regular volunteers and others doing local community service. Everyone was warm and seemed eager to help in any role. The industrial-size kitchen was impressive, with pantries holding varieties of boxed foods and two refrigerators packed with produce, fish, and meats.

"Fridays, Saturdays, and Sundays we put out hot meals for families in the community," Xander said. "Our numbers keep growing, but our budget is tight. We do the best we can but would like to offer more variety and larger portions."

"Hopefully we can help you with that," Malia said.

Laura waved her hand in the air. "Holiday weekends can be hard for the kids, so we're combining outreach with a mini food expo. Tonight, we recruited some extra people to do prep. We work with some local restaurants, but we've been short on cooks, especially to make desserts for certain occasions. Kids need to feel like they're not ostracized, and distributing cupcakes now and then goes a long way."

Malia liked their perspective. Too many charitable organizations were stringent with what they believed the poor should be able to eat, but everyone had a right to enjoy well-prepared food and treats. By the time the tour was over, a certainty had settled within her that hadn't been there for a while. She was exactly where she should be, with a new job that not only fulfilled her but gave her a passionate purpose.

"Oops, one of our volunteers looks a bit lost," Laura said with a laugh. "Be right back."

Malia chatted with Xander, who gave her free access to their operation. "Jump right in, and any of our people will answer questions or show you what the process is."

"Thanks. I'd love to stop at all the stations and do some hands-on work. You seem to have some wonderful volunteers."

Xander nodded. "Some of them were recipients years back. The world is hard out there, but kids deserve a safe shelter and a full belly. The more people work together, the closer we can get to our goal."

Emotion choked Malia's throat. She opened her mouth to agree, but Laura came up behind her and interrupted. "Xander, look who's here! This is Christine's brother. He came to help out tonight."

A gravelly, rich voice rose in the air, as familiar as the spicy clove scent that wrapped around her like a hug. "Sorry I'm late—traffic was bad. Unfortunately, my sister got held up, so she won't be able to make it."

No. No, no, no . . .

"We understand. She's been such a great help to our program. We were thinking of giving her a commission for her recruitment skills," Xander said with a grin. "I think we've met almost all of your family. Oh, Malia, this is Palmer Matterson, the owner of Endless Vows Bridal. His sister Christine is one of our core volunteers."

Trapped in a bad dream, she slowly swiveled her head around and fell into the endless sea-green depths of his eyes. The familiar breathlessness gripped her as she took in his appearance and steeled herself against the punch of sexual energy. God, the man looked sexier in denim than Armani. How was that possible?

Dark-washed jeans hugged his powerful thighs, and she could only imagine what his ass looked like. An aqua button-down shirt was open at the collar and showed off sinewy, muscled arms. The color warmed his skin and gave his eyes an intense gleam. Leather loafers clad his feet. Thick gray hair fell a bit mussed over his forehead, beckoning her fingers to comb through the strands.

Palmer's full lips quirked, as if he'd known to find her here, though his eyes flashed surprise before turning to satisfaction. She hated the flare of response that flamed between her legs at his obvious interest. Yet, what mortal woman could fight the purely animalistic attraction he radiated? It wasn't her fault. At least her brain was in charge, and running into him here wouldn't change her resolve.

"Fortunately, I've had the pleasure of working with Malia for a while. She was my ad representative at Quench, but I lost her when she moved to the foundation."

Laura clapped her hands. "That's wonderful! Malia is here because the Children's Hunger Initiative has been approved as a charity for the foundation."

Malia tried clearing her throat to get her voice back. "Yes, it's nice to see you, Mr. Matterson."

"Palmer. We're not here on business." He studied her face with a hunger that threw her off balance, as if he were desperate to hear his name from her lips. "And I'm delighted to see you again."

The warmth in his voice caused Xander and Laura to glance at both of them curiously.

Malia fought off a blush and tried not to panic. "Well, I better start making my rounds. I'll let you know if I have any other questions." She forced a smile and walked away as the back of her neck prickled.

Of all the places in all the world, he had to show up here? She never would've thought him to be hands-on at a charity. Palmer seemed the type to not want to wrinkle his good suit. Was he doing it for the press? But who'd be here to write about it?

Malia shook off her thoughts. It didn't matter. She was here to do a job, and Palmer wasn't going to distract her.

~

She was here.

Every nerve in Palmer's body tingled as he tried to concentrate on Xander's spiel. He was led into the kitchen to meet some of the staff, then put to work sorting and filling boxes with healthy snack foods such as granola bars, peanut butter, seeds, and nuts. He went on automatic while his brain frantically tried to decide how to use this amazing coincidence to his advantage.

When Christine canceled on him, he'd been ready to strangle her but refused to quit on his commitment. He figured he'd work hard, make a donation, and please his mother, who he had no shame admitting he adored even as she drove him mad. But running into Malia here changed the stakes. He had to find a way to talk to her. Maybe he'd ask Xander if he could join her on a task—any excuse to be in her presence. He didn't care anymore that he was acting like a needy puppy, desperate for her affection. Once his stare met hers, and the heat shimmered between them in all its sexual glory, he'd been a goner. Pride had nothing left on him.

He was about to leave his station to find Malia when the main cook, a guy named Al, exploded. "You mixed up the flour and sugar again? Come on, man, this is the second batch you screwed up."

Palmer turned to see what was going on. Al was scowling at the kid next to him, who looked completely intimidated by the cook. Palmer couldn't blame him. With a clean-shaven head, huge muscled build, and tat sleeves on both arms, Al filled up the room with his presence.

"I was supposed to be putting boxes together, not stuck in the kitchen," the kid whined. Seeing the boy's long brown hair, lanky build, and acne scattered on his face, Palmer figured him to be about sixteen. His phone was lighting up every second, and he seemed more interested in seeing who was texting rather than baking. "Plus, it's my last community service, Al."

"I don't care if it's your first or last, all you have to do is listen. I gave you the rundown twice, but you're attached to your phone. I won't have these kids eating a bad dessert."

"Shirley was supposed to do this."

Al gave a grunt. "Shirley's granddaughter got sick, so she's not here. You are."

"I'll do it."

They both swung around to stare at Palmer.

He walked over and nodded. "I can bake. You can do my job stacking snacks in boxes," he said to the kid.

"Thanks!" The teen scurried over, obviously relieved to get out of Al's firing range.

Al shook his head. "Sure you don't mind? I'm drowning over here, but I don't want to bother Xander. He's got enough going on."

"Looks like you're handling it like a pro," Palmer said, taking in the simmering pots and organized kitchen utensils. "And I like to bake."

Al handed him an apron. "Thank God. There's your stuff. We're a bit low on inventory, but we need about fifty more cupcakes to pack up for tomorrow. Frosting is in the cupboard to your right. There's vanilla and chocolate. Sprinkles, too, if you wanna get fancy."

Palmer was already settling into the deep calm that overtook him whenever he was about to bake. He loved everything about the process, from the rhythmic mixing and measuring to watching how multiple ingredients created something magnificent that made people happy. He winced at the idea of canned frosting, though. No way. He'd make his own if they had enough staples.

Lining up what he needed, he got to work and fell into a comfortable pace next to Al. "You work as a chef?" Palmer asked.

Al grunted. "Nope, just a cook. I work for a restaurant-bar in Connecticut called My Place. I know Xander from back in the day, and when he mentioned he was short staffed for this weekend, I decided to come and help him out."

Admiration cut through him. "That's a nice thing to do."

"It's a nice thing he does for the kids. I know what it's like to be hungry."

Palmer gave him a side glance, but the man didn't seem embarrassed or regret the comment. "Tough childhood?"

"Hell yeah. My parents' refrigerator held beer and the freezer had vodka. Peanut butter was my best friend when I could get it. I was a kid who wanted to be in school because I got fed and it was safe." Like a maestro, he moved from pot to pot, scooping and chopping and cooking in a graceful dance. "Weekends sucked. Who knows what could have changed for me if I'd known a place like this existed. To get food and some school supplies and a damn cupcake? To know someone gave a shit? People don't realize that's a big deal when you're a kid."

His words struck hard, and Palmer really heard them. It had been strained for Palmer growing up with a big family and not much money, but there was always something to eat, a safe place to sleep, and people who loved him. It had been a long time since he thought of the others out there who hadn't been so blessed. "Yeah, you're right," he said slowly, keeping his focus on the batter. "It's easy to forget when you have so much for yourself."

"Yeah, we all do it. What do you do for work?"

"I run a wedding planning business."

"No shit. That how you know how to bake?"

"Nope, that was just from growing up with four sisters who wanted me well versed in feeding them."

Al gave him a respectful nod. "Nice to have you in my kitchen."

"Nice to be here."

They settled in to work, occasionally exchanging small talk, and Palmer let the scent of sugar and the hypnotic whirr of the mixer take over. Sooner than he expected, he'd baked and iced fifty cupcakes.

"These smell amazing," Laura said when she came in to check on them. "They look like they're from a professional bakery!"

Palmer grinned. "It was nothing. I just followed the box."

Al shot him a look but didn't say anything.

"We're so grateful. Al, we're running out with Malia to discuss the foundation, but we'll be back soon. Carol is out front if you need anything."

"No problem."

Palmer spoke up. "I've been trying to set up a meeting with Deanna regarding the foundation, but our schedules haven't matched up. Seems like an interesting opportunity to get involved with."

"I don't know what we would've done if we hadn't been approved," Laura said quietly. "Now we're just hoping for a donor to sponsor us." Suddenly, her gaze sharpened as she looked at him. "Palmer, would you like to join us for dinner? It may be a good opportunity to learn about both organizations. I'm sure Malia won't mind."

"Mind what?" Malia asked, walking into the kitchen. She stopped short when she saw him. Satisfaction curled in his blood when her pupils dilated, and she quickly turned away to hide.

Too late.

"I invited Palmer to come to dinner with us! He wanted to know more about the Quench Foundation and our charity. Don't you think that's a great idea?"

She froze for a second, then lifted her gaze to his. Palmer gave a slow grin as he waited for her response, knowing she was backed into a corner.

"Of course, but only if he can fit it into his busy schedule. Deanna was looking forward to meeting him."

His mother would adore her sass. She'd always told him he needed a fierce woman to challenge his cockiness. Seems Malia fit the bill. She was subtly warning him right then and there to politely decline. But fate had stepped in, and he wasn't about to squander this opportunity. He hadn't gotten to the top of his game by being polite and playing by the rules.

"I'd love to go."

Chapter Five

Oh, she was going to kill him.

Malia sipped a glass of pinot grigio and tried not to glare at the man across from her. Xander and Laura had taken them to a small Italian restaurant with cozy tables, low lighting, and a sense of intimacy. It reminded her of a place she'd go on a date, looking to cuddle in the corner, feast on delicious pasta, and get a bit giddy.

Instead, she was trying to keep her focus on work without getting sidelined by Palmer's game playing. She had no idea why he wanted to join them, but he was in for a surprise if he thought he'd blow up her business dinner. So far, Malia had managed to politely ignore him while she kept her attention on Laura, Xander, and the ways the Quench Foundation could help the Children's Hunger Initiative.

But it was as if he was enjoying her ignoring him. Like it only added to his sense of pleasure and satisfaction. He regarded her with a lazy ease, buttering his bread and sinking his teeth into the crisp crust. His attention was resolute, and she had a feeling he was picking apart every word of the conversation, looking for further knowledge on how to handle her.

Even worse? He smelled like all her weaknesses in the world. Sugar, chocolate, and sin. The Big Bad Wolf had been baking cupcakes, pretending to be a sheep. Why did that have to turn her on?

"How do you match an investor with a charity?" Palmer asked smoothly, tilting his head. He held his wineglass like James Bond held his martini, tapered fingers in a loose grip but always in control. She wondered if he touched a woman like that in bed, with both delicacy and passion.

Malia tried not to glare. "When a donor signs up, we try to match them with a charity they feel a purpose and passion for. It's an opportunity to get beyond the simple act of writing a check and become personally involved in the organization. Kind of like a benefactor. There are various payment programs—either monthly, quarterly, or sponsoring a particular project."

"But sponsors have no say in how we run our organization, correct?" Xander asked with a frown.

"Absolutely not, and that's clearly in the contract. Money does not equal a say in how you run the Hunger Initiative, and both parties must agree."

Laura sighed. "Good, that was my main concern. We want sponsors to be passionate about the organization but not be able to control the funds."

"Understood. Another advantage with smaller local organizations is the immediacy of the funds you receive. It doesn't need to be channeled through a large board or levels of bureaucracy, so you'll see results faster," Malia said.

"What are some of the things you are looking to expand in your program?" Palmer asked curiously.

Xander leaned in. "We need to hire a full-time program coordinator to take over the endless admin tasks for us and help with our volunteers. We need to increase our food supply to serve more of the kids. But the most important thing is the backpack program."

Laura nodded. "Too many kids don't get what they need on the weekends. Many stay home while their parents work and are starving by

Monday. We want to begin donating food-filled backpacks to schools on Fridays so kids have something to eat for the weekend."

"I know some of the bigger school districts have instituted this type of program, but none are currently offered here locally. It's a huge void we can fill, but it will take an influx of money to make it happen," Xander said.

Malia tapped a note on her phone. "That's an item we can approach an interested investor on. I have a few contacts that may fit. Let me send you some websites to check out."

"That'd be great," Laura said, squeezing her husband's arm.

"I'm interested."

Malia forged on, ignoring Palmer. "I'm also ready to share all your financial history, recommendations from volunteers, and what the prime benefits of the Hunger Initiative are, so we're on the final step now."

"I'm interested," Palmer repeated.

Malia paused and stared at him. "What?" she asked dumbly. Laura and Xander glanced at each other in confusion.

He laid his hands flat on the table and spoke firmly but quietly. "I'm interested in becoming an investor for you."

"Oh!" Malia shook her head. "Of course. I know you're working with Deanna, but I'd be happy to speed things up if you want to sign on. I'll get you everything you need via email."

"No, you don't understand. I want to invest in the Children's Hunger Initiative."

Shock barreled through her. She wanted to warn him not to joke around, but he was obviously serious about the offer.

Warning bells clanged in her head, but Laura was already excited, her blue eyes lit with hope. "I can't believe this," she whispered. "You're like an angel."

Palmer laughed. "God, no. I wouldn't have even known about you if it weren't for my sister, and Malia, of course. I must admit I'm a bit ashamed. I've never been involved directly with a not-for-profit, and this is the first time I've felt the need. I love what you want to do for the kids and your vision. I also love the team you already have behind you. I'd be honored to help."

Ah, shit.

Malia blinked and tried to wrestle control of the situation back without being the bad guy. He hadn't filled out any forms! He hadn't even met with Deanna! How could he suddenly agree to such a commitment without careful research? The man was a machine when it came to business—there was no way he was doing this because of his heart.

"Um, Mr. Matt—Palmer, it's a wonderful offer, but you know no specifics about the program yet. Even if I thought you could be a match, you should meet with Deanna first to make sure this is for you. I don't want to raise Laura and Xander's hopes right now because you're feeling impulsive."

Suddenly, that hot male gaze was digging deep, shredding barriers with a shocking heat that held her frozen in place. An edge of temper crusted his voice. "I don't do impulsive. I happen to trust you wouldn't vet an organization that wasn't worthy, and I liked what I saw tonight. When I make a promise, I stick by my word."

The warning hit her full force, but his devastating smile softened the blow.

He continued. "You can sign me up so we can move forward. Trust is important to me, and I trust you, Malia, to take care of me."

She managed to tamp down a squeak as those words poured over her like creamy caramel on a sundae.

"Oh my gosh, it was like fate that you came by tonight when Malia was here and I invited you to dinner," Laura gushed. "What do we need to do now?"

Malia tried to remain professional. It usually took months to court a sponsor and match them up with a charity. Yet, in a few moments, Palmer had offered his support without any official meeting or discussion. She needed to think quickly, without showing her doubt regarding his seriousness. "Well, I'll sign Endless Vows up and we'll draw up the contract. I'll share the financials and breakdowns with Palmer and create a plan to move forward. Sometimes, these things take time depending on how the investor works."

Palmer spoke up. "I work fast. If you give me a dream time schedule, we can make it happen."

Laura and Xander beamed.

Malia gnashed her teeth at his outrageous promises and tried not to explode. Forcing a smile with too many teeth, she said, "We'll all do our best."

Palmer quirked a brow, looking amused. "Why don't we meet this week in my office?"

Anger bubbled in her veins. How dare he hijack her business meeting! She'd had a careful plan to present to her clients, and he'd blown it up with his need to play savior. Oh, his arrogance made her want to scream. Instead, she forced herself to remain calm. "I'll talk to Deanna. She may want to jump in."

He lifted his hands in mock surrender. "I understand. Whatever you think is best, Malia."

Bastard. Now he was playing the sheep role in front of Xander and Laura and making her look like a hard-ass for not wanting to meet with him.

She was saved from having to respond by the ringing of a cell phone. Laura answered it with an apology, then murmured a few words before turning to them. "I'm so sorry, but we need to get back. There's a few items that we have to oversee before tomorrow, and some volunteers have left."

"Of course," Malia said, reaching for her purse to pay the bill. "We'll head out with you."

"Absolutely not," Xander said firmly. "Stay here and finish dinner. It will be a great opportunity for you to talk over the contracts and get some things done. The meal is on us—we're so grateful for both of you."

Her eyes widened with panic. "Oh, no, I don't think—"

"Thank you, that's quite generous," Palmer smoothly interrupted. "I'd love to stay and talk more with Malia."

"Wonderful," Laura said, sliding from her seat. "Order anything you want, the chef will put it on our tab. You've simply made our dream come true." Blinking with emotion, she took her husband's hand, and they walked out of the restaurant.

Silence fell.

Malia took a few precious moments to gather her composure, then looked up.

Palmer stared back at her, sea-green eyes filled with heat, elbows on the table, fingertips resting together in a kingly manner. "Would you like to order?"

A humorless laugh escaped her lips. "Why are you doing this? Do you realize how important this money is to Xander and Laura? You can't play games just because you're used to winning in the boardroom and need some entertainment."

Ice replaced the heat, and shivers raced down her spine. "I'm not interested in playing games with you or the foundation. And I don't lie. Ask me anything and I'll give you the truth."

Oh, she wasn't about to back off from that invitation. "Fine. Why are you suddenly interested in donating?"

"Because Laura and Xander are good people and passionate about helping others. My sister speaks highly of the organization and its volunteers. And because tonight I realized I take things too much for granted. What I have. What so many others don't. It's just like you explained—this is more than handing over a check. I can truly watch change happen and be involved in it."

His words threw her off. Sincerity rang from his tone, and he met her gaze head-on. Malia shifted in her seat and decided to forge on. "Why did you wrangle an invite to dinner?"

"To be with you and hear a bit more about the foundation."

She hated to ask the next question but knew it was important to move forward. "Are you suddenly eager to donate because you think you can force me to spend time with you, or is it truly to help Xander and Laura?"

"Both. I'm honestly excited about the Hunger Initiative and intend to donate even if I never see you again. If you want Deanna to take over, I won't fight you. But when you walked in and I caught sight of you, I was suddenly happier than I've been all week." She caught her breath, but he continued. "I never expected to see you again, Malia, but once I did, I realized how badly I missed you."

His words seared through her and left her unable to answer. A man had never looked at her the way he did right now, with such hunger and intention, as if she were the answer to all his questions. It was a heady feeling, and it took a few moments to regather her composure.

"I'm not sure what to say. I have a responsibility to the foundation to do my job, and I don't want to mix personal with business. We have a strange . . . history."

"I understand. Again, if you want Deanna to step in, I intend to sign a contract and work with Laura and Xander no matter what. But I'd like to ask you for something tonight."

Malia squinted with suspicion. "What?"

"Stay and have dinner with me. Give me a chance to get to know you, and vice versa. Afterward, you can walk away if you're not interested, and I promise not to bother you again."

She studied his face in the candlelight, the shadows flickering over his carved features. The fullness of his lips and slight stubble hugging his jaw. The high brow and jeweled eyes intently holding her gaze. The way he seemed to be waiting for her answer, as if it honestly meant something to him. "I said no to your invite before."

"Yes, but it was as if fate gave me a gift. I don't waste them."

Oh, he was good. The mention of fate again and his smooth words had the desired effect. Goose bumps broke out on her skin, and suddenly, Malia was tempted. This ridiculous physical chemistry might finally die if she gave them a chance for a real conversation, because even if he seemed like the hero of the moment, underneath, he was an arrogant asshole. Surely, those traits would burn bright if she gave herself over to deep dialogue. She'd walk away after dinner, and Deanna would take over. She had nothing to lose, right? After this, he'd finally leave her alone.

"Just one dinner?"

Palmer inclined his head. "In order to make the most of our time, I propose two rules."

She gave a short laugh and sipped her wine. "Now there are rules?"

"We promise each other full honesty. And we're both free to ask any questions."

She was suddenly intrigued by the terms. Palmer was a man who aroused curiosity, and she'd be able to indulge without worrying about their business relationship. To speak freely sounded like a welcome relief. "Okay, but I don't intend to confess my deepest, darkest secrets. Also, nothing either of us says will affect Quench or the foundation, right?"

"I give you my word."

"Then let's order."

Chapter Six

Palmer smiled and raised his hand for the waiter. Malia went with branzino grilled with olives and capers, and he ordered classic lasagna. Wineglasses were refilled and they were left alone.

She wasted no time diving in and taking control of the conversation. "I always wondered why you sat in on our advertising meetings. Seems it would have been better kicked to Andrea and Emeril. Your time is valuable."

"I learned early on it's best to be involved in some capacity with all levels of the business. But I admit, once I knew you were capable, I showed up because I wanted to see you. You . . . intrigued me."

Malia blinked. This truth thing could get a bit heavy. Maybe she'd stick to the business part of his answer. "I believe delegation is a key to success. Too much constriction at lower levels prohibits creative problem-solving and employee confidence."

He grinned, seemingly pleased with her answer. "Business 101. But I've dug deeper into studies and found that a successful CEO brands their vision on every part of the team. I make sure I sit in on a meeting in every one of my departments weekly so I'm abreast of what's coming. I also believe in knowing as much about my employees as possible. That's what creates bigger vision and trust."

She couldn't help but give a mocking laugh. "Interesting."

Palmer cocked his head. "Oh, you must elaborate. That word piqued my curiosity."

The wine warmed her blood and gave her an edge of recklessness. "Because I truly doubt you know any of your employees. I think your theory is based on the need for control rather than being armed with information."

He leaned back and studied her under heavy-lidded eyes. "Andrea has worked with me for five years now. She has a degree from NYU, and I hired her as an intern in the creative department. Now, she runs it. She has a girlfriend, Amy, and they plan on getting married next fall. I've had them over to my home for an engagement celebration dinner. They're both vegetarian, have three rescue dogs, and plan to honeymoon in Hawaii."

His fingers absently tapped the table, showing off his sinewy wrist and simple silver watch. He'd tucked away the Cartier rose-gold time-piece he usually wore in the office. A cloud of white powder clung to a patch of his shirt, softening his usual polished look. Right now, he seemed more accessible. More human than a powerful, polished CEO. She realized how much she preferred this side of him.

Palmer continued. "Emeril is fiercely ambitious and prefers being in the background rather than taking on a leadership role. He's single, adores literature, and owns an impressive vinyl collection. He's eaten the same lunch every day since he began at Endless Vows—turkey on rye, with cheese, tomato, and no mayo. Friday nights are reserved for clubbing or dating, and he sees his family every Sunday morning for breakfast. He likes to be on call and feel needed, so I push him a bit harder because he excels at his job. Loyalty is Emeril's greatest gift, and I make sure he's happy at all costs."

It didn't seem so much a speech as the truth. She imagined him taking the time to get to know the details of who he worked with, and found something inside her soften.

"Yes, I have hundreds of employees, and many I don't know as personally, but I do my best. The backbone of a company's success relies on both a successful CEO and the team that does the day-to-day work. I don't regard them as numbers, Malia. They're people, and knowing how to motivate and satisfy each individual remains my responsibility." Palmer deliberately dropped his voice to a soft, intimate pitch. "That being said, you're right about one thing. I do like control. But only in certain situations."

Her body exploded like a true traitor, and Malia scrunched up all her muscles to fight the instinctive need to reach across the table and touch him. Every part of him screamed male domination and sex. The low purr of his voice, that hypnotic gaze glittering with hunger, even the scent of sandalwood and sugar urged her to rip off his clothes and . . . mate.

She was a woman who enjoyed sex but never had an issue denying herself for a good cause. If she felt a business relationship could be compromised, she simply didn't allow herself to go there. Sure, she'd experienced some butterflies and attraction in the past. She loved orgasms like most females, although admittedly her vibrator was a bit better than her previous lovers. But she'd never responded on such a primitive level to a man like this.

The worst part? He knew it. The arrogance pulsed from his aura in shocking waves, as if he'd been biding his time and finally decided to turn up the heat. Even now, staring at him a bit mute from his speech, she wondered what his hard mouth would feel like over hers. Ached to run her fingers through his magnificent mane of hair and muss it up. If she didn't get her act together, this entire meeting would end up in the worst place possible right after dessert.

In bed. Without a contract for the foundation.

Malia cleared her throat and reeled her hormones in. "I'm glad to know you take an interest in your employees. Running a wedding agency must require you to have sharper skill sets in communication and emotion. How did you get into the business?"

His gaze narrowed, and she wondered if he'd push her. Palmer's last comment had sharply veered their conversation into intimate territory. She may have agreed to his rules, but she wasn't about to offer her body on a silver platter just because she was crazily attracted to him.

"I'm surprised you didn't read one of those articles on me. It's funny how the world regards a man taking on a mostly female-centered industry. They want a juicy story to go with it."

"Oh, I did. I just know it was a lie," she said easily.

This time, he looked surprised. "You didn't believe my motto of trying to make the world a more beautiful place in the midst of ugliness? My explanation of everyone's right to have a wedding of their dreams, no matter the cost?"

She rolled her eyes. "No. It was an awful, canned response, and the writer should have seen right through it."

His laughter was real and robust. She liked the sound a bit too much. "You're absolutely right. My true answer is too boring."

"Which is?"

"I have four sisters and suffered through each of their weddings. I became an expert on every ritual that can be created around love. I went to college to study business, positive I'd run a multimillion-dollar corporation one day based on money, stocks, or sales. I never questioned my talent. My problem was I kept getting dragged into wedding disasters until my only goal became building a damn bridal place my sisters could count on to get what they needed."

Fascinated, Malia stared at him, his casual confession only emphasizing the innate confidence he seemed to naturally own. "You have four sisters?"

"I do."

She shook her head in surprise. "I never would have guessed. You hold a lot of male energy."

Oh no. The stupid comment flung out of her mouth before she was able to snatch it back. But his voice held no smugness when he spoke. "You need to generate all the testosterone possible to grow up with one shared bathroom."

Her jaw unhinged. "One?" she screeched. "And you didn't murder each other?"

White teeth flashed and showed Palmer's crooked front tooth. "It got close. My parents' bathroom was rationed out as a reward and withheld in punishment. They were always savvy with discipline."

"Sounds like my parents," she muttered, remembering when Daddy nailed shut Davinia's window after discovering she was sneaking out at night. Then he'd punished everyone for keeping her secret. Tattletales were encouraged in the Evergreen household.

"How many siblings do you have?" he asked.

"Three sisters, all older."

"I'm the baby, too. Whoever said the youngest was spoiled rotten must've been the oldest."

She laughed. "Yes! All I got was leftovers, orders to do it myself, and endless comparisons to my siblings."

"How about being fourteen and surrounded by tampons, birth control pills, and lingerie drying on all possible surfaces?" His face was pure suffering. "It was like growing up on a battlefield. Once, I ate the chocolate bar my sister was saving, and when my girlfriend came over, Georgia showed her an old pic of me in my underwear."

"Aww, I'm sure you looked cute."

Palmer glowered. "She told my girlfriend to look carefully, because I hadn't grown up much in certain areas. Then she slowly looked down, stared at my crotch, and patted me on the head with a smile. Needless to say, my girlfriend never returned my calls after that."

Malia shuddered with horror. "That's evil."

"Georgia always was. Still is. She got married with a Halloween theme. Appropriate."

She laughed, relaxing into his banter. "I'm surprised you'd want to forge a career in a female-centered industry after all that."

"Well, I thought of opening a secret fight club, but I like weddings better. They make more money, too. Plus, I feel like I'm able to see other opportunities under the wedding umbrella."

"Like shoes."

He nodded. "Exactly. I intended to launch a variety of new products, but a few years ago, I realized the core of Endless Vows was off track. I'd gotten too big, I guess, and sacrificed what some smaller agencies were able to give."

"It's hard to spot weaknesses when there's so many moving parts," she said slowly. "To own up and want to fix them is part of business."

"I lost a big celebrity to Sunshine Bridal in Cape May and realized their team was ripe to steal a lot of my business. So I tried to poach their wedding planner to work for me. Unfortunately, he was loyal and turned me down."

"Imagine that." The name and location tugged at Malia's memory. "Wait—was it Gabe Garcia? One of my cousins was married in Cape May and used Sunshine."

Palmer stared at her in shock. "That's him! You're telling me I lost a wedding for my own ad rep's relative to that guy? That's inexcusable."

She chuckled. "It was a second cousin, so not that close of a relative."

"Well, at least Gabe inspired me to tweak the way I put my teams together for the bigger clients. Once that was fixed, I was able to concentrate on other things."

"More shoes?" she teased.

He studied her for a few moments in silence. Malia didn't expect him to answer, but when he did, her heart thumped painfully, realizing he was confiding something not many knew. "Perfume. I bought a supplier and finally lined up some brilliant chemists. I want the fragrance centered around the emotions for a wedding. A scent that encompasses all the excitement, hope, and dreams of a future together."

Her head spun a bit, so she took a sip of water. Palmer was surprising her. She'd never expected such openness, from his family to his new venture. He'd run their meetings in a clinical manner with little emotion. But perfume and weddings throbbed with romantic themes. He seemed able to discuss them with an open confidence that was completely unexpected.

And swoony.

Crap. This getting-to-know-you conversation was diving into the danger zone.

"That's a tall order," she said lightly.

"It is. But I like a challenge."

Her breath caught, and suddenly, that gaze narrowed on her with intensity. As if he'd decided to get serious.

She wanted to kiss the waiter when he interrupted. Their plates were set down and water refilled. Malia grabbed her fork and dug in, moaning at the gorgeous lemon flavor balanced with the salty olives and capers.

She looked over as Palmer regarded his plate and began to murmur under his breath, head bowed. When he was done, a spot of red appeared on his cheekbones. "Sorry, habit."

A strange affinity swept over her. "Were you saying grace?"

"Yeah, it was drilled into us since we were young. We may not have had money for luxury items and big vacations, but our table was always full." A shadow crossed his face. "Working in the kitchen today with Al, I realized it was wrong for me to forget that many people never had the shot I did."

His gesture touched her, bringing back treasured memories of her siblings gathered around the table, being admonished for digging in before saying thanks. "My parents taught me the same, but I'm embarrassed to say I forget sometimes."

He waved a hand in the air. "Don't give me credit. I do enough bad things to make up for it."

She laughed. "I bet you do."

"Back to our original conversation. It's my turn."

"For what?"

"Questions."

She hated to admit her stomach twitched nervously. Malia had dozens of other things she wished he'd answer. This dinner had piqued her curiosity to know more about the man he'd been hiding during all those Thursday meetings. Giving him too much information about her seemed like a bad idea. It would only strengthen a connection she specifically intended to sever.

Malia gave a casual shrug. "I'm not that interesting, but go ahead."

"Are you seeing anyone right now?"

Her belly dipped. He got straight to the point. Those sea-green eyes pierced past her shields and warned her not to lie. "No."

"Why not?"

Off guard, she tilted her head. "Because."

Disappointment flickered over his features. "A cop-out. Go deeper."

She got ready to lecture him. Her personal dating history was none of his business. Instead, she found herself blurting out the truth. "I haven't found anyone I could love yet."

Savage satisfaction reflected in his gaze. "Better. Is love important to you?"

A searing pain tore through her at the raw question. To find her person seemed like a dream right now. The doubts had begun to take root inside, and there wasn't enough weed killer to extinguish the awful, secret fear that she was unlovable. "Yes. Isn't love the goal for anyone in a relationship?"

"Not always. Sometimes, it's sex. Money. Companionship. Friendship. The world is a lonely place, Malia. Never underrate comfort."

A jolt hit her body. He spoke like a poet. She needed to remind herself he still retained the coldness of a CEO running an empire. Did both sides war with one another, or had he melded them together like a hidden seam? The question ruffled her irritation.

"I'm not naive, Palmer. People may seek all those things you mentioned, but underneath, I believe we're all looking for connection. That's love. You just wrapped it up in convenient terminology."

He jerked back, obviously startled. "I like the way you see things."

She nibbled on the end of a crisp green bean. "What do you mean?"

"The way you speak and see the world. How you interpreted our search for comfort as love. Yet, you're ruthless with negotiations and show no soft side when it comes to business."

Her brow arched. "I could say the same for you."

He stared at her for a few moments. "I made a mistake."

Malia stiffened, not sure where he was leading. She focused on her plate. "I doubt it. Endless Vows is at the top of its game."

"No, I mean with you. I should have stopped playing games a while ago, when I knew I was interested in more than business."

She froze. Refused to look up and deal with his scorching gaze and what she'd find there. "I don't know what you're talking about. We played no games."

"Yes we did. Pretending if we didn't touch each other, the sexual chemistry between us wouldn't exist. Bantering with negotiations and clever innuendos to mask the curiosity we had about the other."

"That was called simple dislike," she said lightly.

"That was called connection. You deny it?" Palmer's husky voice stroked her ears like a caress.

She rallied and slowly looked up. The light of challenge rammed her head-on, and Malia realized he was a game master, knowing how to maneuver the delicate balance of getting what he wanted while appearing nonthreatening. She refused to cower. "Yes."

"Lie," he said softly. "You broke the rules."

Her belly tumbled into free fall at his sexy drawl. This man was like quicksilver, and she couldn't keep up. "I think we should change the subject."

"I don't. I've been driving myself crazy with what-ifs, but what I keep going over and over is why. Why don't you like me?"

Her hand clenched her fork. Her heart beat frantically against her chest as her words came back to haunt her. "I simply don't think we'd be compatible."

A slow grin curved Palmer's lips. "Oh, you'll need to give me more than that. Here's your chance, Malia. All the things you've wanted to say to me over the past year, you suddenly get a free pass."

The opportunity to blurt out all her opinions and irritations suddenly seemed too good to miss. She believed he wouldn't hold it against her, and once he knew her true thoughts, maybe he'd finally leave her in peace. This was going to be satisfying. "You have a big ego."

Why did he look pleased with her insult? Those broad shoulders lifted in a shrug. "Of course I do. I built a company from the ground up, and now it's a multimillion-dollar enterprise. Thousands depend on me for their salaries and benefits. Brides and grooms depend on me to give them the dream of a lifetime. Don't you think it'd be a problem if I didn't have an ego?"

"Confidence is different from ego. It's obvious you think you're the most important person when you walk into a room."

Palmer seemed to consider her words instead of defending himself. "Hmm, let's shred that statement down for a better analysis. First off, confidence is an innate part of ego. You need to have some sort of ego in order to retain a healthy confidence in yourself, so the two go hand in hand. Would you feel comfortable going into surgery with a doctor who doesn't command the room? Who allows his interns or assistants to run the consult while he humbly steps back because he's afraid you'll think he's egotistical?"

The question almost made her stammer. "Well, no."

"Exactly. I use my confidence to lead. I use my team wisely, but it's important everyone knows I'm in charge for a very solid reason. If I show weakness, it trickles down the line. You can have a healthy ego and not be an asshole."

Malia squirmed in her seat, hating that he'd managed to twist her words to suit his argument. "Yes, but running a business should be a team effort. The surgeon knows that without an anesthesiologist, the patient will suffer. They need to treat them as a partner."

Those jeweled eyes sparkled with satisfaction. The energy tightened and hummed around them as they both leaned in, engaged in a debate they each seemed to want to win. "An excellent point, but I do honor my team and take their opinions seriously."

She snorted. "How? I've only witnessed commands, demands, and *ass*-umptions you're always right."

"I'm a bit pushy," Palmer admitted. "It can definitely be harder for the more reserved employees, so I hold a biweekly think tank."

"What's that?"

"Every person gets a say. We pick a topic, gather in a room, and I hear their honest feedback—the good, the bad, and the ugly. No recriminations and no filters. Those sessions have given me some of the most successful programs at Endless Vows. I do know how to listen, Malia." His deep-timbred voice rumbled with intimacy. "I do the same with my partners. I'm sorry I didn't get to show you that side of me, but I can do better."

Holy crap, this is too much. Malia's skin felt itchy and tight. Her nipples pressed against the lace of her bra in a demand to be freed. What was happening to her? She needed to get back on track and stop this ridiculous seduction from his words and sexy voice.

Somehow, he'd won that round, and he didn't seem like such an asshole anymore.

Dammit.

"Next objection?" he asked mildly, pushing his plate to the side.

Malia fortified herself with another sip of wine. "You're obviously a workaholic. Endless Vows is your main priority. I'm looking for someone who can put me first." She shook her head. "I've had enough dates with men attached to their phones and early departures where I was left at the dinner table."

Sympathy flickered in his eyes. "That's awful."

"It is until a huge deal is on the line, or a big client. Then it's just business. I'm dedicated to my own career, but lately, I've wanted to focus on other things. Things I've put on the back burner for too long."

"Relationships?"

"Healthy relationships," she said drily. "There's a difference, believe me."

"Malia, the idea of those men leaving you alone at a restaurant because they can't take care of their shit makes me sick. You don't deserve being second best on a date, in a relationship, or even on a phone call." The fierce way he spoke the words made her insides shake with need. As if he meant it. As if he understood the humiliation of consistently being second or third choice. Her long string of endless dates over the past few years held some doozies, but it was the quieter ones that died on the vine that haunted her the most. It seemed she was never worthy to be chosen. Mothers, jobs, friends, even pets always took precedence, until she began to believe she was too needy.

Palmer made it seem like it was a natural request to be a priority, even a natural demand.

But he was smart and could easily try and fool her. The man was too smooth and desperate to win once again, whether it be their argument or her conceding and giving him what he wanted. Men just didn't think like that anymore. At least not the ones who were interested in her.

"Easy to say, I guess. Harder to put into action."

He studied her like a predator assessing his dinner. "Give me a chance and I can prove it."

A reluctant smile fought to surface. "You're persistent."

"Another fault?"

"No."

"What's left, then? Anything else that we need to air? I'm sure I have some terrible traits left to pull apart."

It was impossible to deny her reaction to this virile man who seemed to rattle her walls. But Malia didn't have time to waste on a short affair. No doubt he'd be a drool-worthy distraction, but with her plan to freeze her eggs, and the next few months being prickly at best with all her bodily changes from the hormones, entertaining a few interludes with Palmer wasn't a good idea. Her heart had been bruised a bit too much, and she wanted to concentrate only on controlling what she could—getting her fertility in order and giving herself a hard reset. Not getting involved in an intense affair with a man who was larger than life.

She laughed, but the sound seemed to hold a touch of sadness. Why was she feeling like this, almost regretful she'd discovered he wasn't the ogre she'd believed? It would've been so much easier to have never seen this softer, charming side of him. But even though she enjoyed his company, and her body lit up like a firecracker in his presence, Malia wasn't about to embark on this journey. It had disaster written all over it, and she was tired.

She needed to protect herself. Best to shut and lock this door between them before he focused on changing her mind.

Malia squared her shoulders and got ready for the final confrontation. "You've managed to shoot a lot of holes in my perceptions. I guess it's time to admit you may not be as bad as I thought."

"Excellent. Are you free Saturday night?"

The waiter eased over and cleared their plates. The candle on the table flickered, throwing the hard angles of his face into shadow. She wondered what it would be like to study him at her leisure, without worrying about getting caught. The knowledge she'd never get to touch him, even once, caused a strange flare of grief to rise.

Malia quickly stamped it out. "I'm still not interested in dating you. You're not my type."

Instead of showing irritation, he grinned. "You haven't given me a chance to change your mind. I could very well be your type."

She blew out a short breath. "Look, I can't suddenly change gears and begin dating you after a year of dislike. This is the first time we've had a real conversation. You're a bit . . . too much. And honestly, I think you'd end up bored with me rather quickly. It's better if we move on and stick to business."

"I can make you like me." Palmer's voice dropped. "I can make you like a lot of things."

Their gazes locked, and suddenly she was caught up in a storm of emotion. The softly spoken promise seethed with sexual undertones, and hunger blazed from his eyes, unbanked and unapologetic. Her body softened, warmed, and longed. Malia fought for composure at the chemistry crackling between them, giving him valuable ammunition.

Her throat tightened. "Palmer—"

"My turn. I want to say a few things, and then I promise we'll go back and hide behind percentages and figures and all the things that make sense. Over the past year, I've not only grown to like and respect you, I've begun to crave more. On Thursday mornings, I wake up early because I can't wait to get to work and see you. I love the way you never back down from a negotiation and fight for your opinion at all costs. I love the way you glare at me when you don't think I'm looking and mutter under your breath things I can only imagine aren't endearments."

He placed his hands on the table and leaned forward. Masculine command oozed from his pores, and Malia could only stare back helplessly, caught in a whirlwind of blistering heat.

"I ache for you all the time. I dream about being in your company for hours and dissecting every single fascinating thought in that amazing brain of yours. I fantasize about your lips opening under mine and the taste of your tongue and the feel of your skin. I want to hold you in my arms and know all those walls between us have finally come down. I want to know your dreams, your fears, and your heart. I want a chance for all of that, Malia, but you won't give it to me. So I'll have to be content with telling you my truth and hope to God you hear these words before you go to sleep at night, until I haunt you like you've done to me."

Eyes wide, frozen in place, heart galloping in her chest, Malia watched as he reached across the table and lifted her hand to his mouth. Pressing his warm, firm lips against her open palm, she felt the imprint of the caress brand her sensitive skin. The breath stuck in her lungs.

"Don't ever say you'll bore me again." Palmer slowly dropped her hand, sat back in his chair, and regarded her intently.

The waiter reappeared. "Will that be all, sir?"

"Malia? Are you ready to leave?"

She stared helplessly at him. Her thoughts raced, as jagged as her heart. She'd never heard words spoken about her with such passionate intensity. To her. It was too much to process, but she felt the desperate need inside to respond, to let him know she heard him.

For one wild moment, she was ready to blow it all up. Agree to go out with him. See what unfolded and take a chance on this mysterious, infuriating, arrogant man who'd managed to charm her over one dinner.

Instead, she nodded. "Yes. I'm ready."

Was that a flicker of pain in his eyes or just her imagination? She tried to pick through the rubbles of emotion, but the energy had already changed between them, snapping her back to reality.

Palmer walked her out and waited until she opened her car door. "Thank you for dinner, Malia. I'll never forget it."

Then he disappeared into the night, good as his word.

She got in the car, started the engine, and wondered why she was full of regret.

Chapter Seven

Malia settled herself at the Quench conference table with her laptop and waited for Deanna. She was a bit early so she could snatch a few moments of quiet and eat her granola bar. Work had been nonstop all weekend, but she wasn't complaining. It was nice to be caught up in a new endeavor again that spurred on a creative need for work.

The next year would be critical in getting the foundation up and running smoothly. Pitching new clients and taking on more local charities was important, but they also needed to make sure the endeavors they'd taken on so far were growing successfully. Malia loved being involved in such important tasks, driving her to put in longer hours because of the payoff.

Her thoughts immediately flashed to Palmer and their intimate dinner together. He'd managed to surprise her, with both his sudden offer to fund a charity after one meeting and the driven way he pursued a date with her. The man was outrageous. And attractive. And now she could add charming to the list, because she'd seen all that magnetism in person, coming at her full force. No wonder he was so successful. It was almost impossible to say no.

Yet, she'd managed.

That annoying inner voice, occasionally ruled by FOMO, whispered, *But why?* Why not take advantage of his delicious body and indulge? Why say no to an affair when she was forging ahead with her plan to freeze her eggs?

Malia figured that by taking charge of her fertility, she'd be able to let loose more and stop looking at every date as a potential husband. But she sensed Palmer could not be easily managed. His very aura overtook a room and overwhelmed it with magnetism. She was much more comfortable with the regular Joe. One who didn't run a huge company and get his picture in the papers. One who'd allow her to run the show.

Hey, at least she was honest about what she wanted.

She nibbled at her Kind bar, expertly multitasking between spreadsheets and memos, falling into a familiar rhythm. Tessa and Chiara meandered in, surprising her.

"What's up, girl? Thought you were at the other office today," Tessa said.

"Figured I'd stay here since we had our morning meeting. Deanna will be here shortly. Trying to get some prep work done."

Chiara nodded, setting her oversize water bottle on the table. "I'm happy with the way things are going at Quench. I was worried we'd take a bit of a hit since we've been focused on the foundation, but I was wrong. It's as if our team picked up the slack."

"I think they want more responsibility," Malia said. "With the new hires and upcoming internship program, we'll be more flexible about our roles. I like that."

"Me, too. We've come a long way since the beginning," Tessa said.

They all looked at each other, and the moment was bittersweet. Rory was missed every day, but Malia was proud of what they'd done since her death. The company was even stronger, and she believed it was because they refused to let their friend's dream fail.

Malia glanced around the room and remembered when they'd bought the old purple Victorian house to begin their start-up company. It had no heat and crumbling paint and needed a total renovation, but Mike had cosigned a loan, and they'd transformed it into the headquarters of Quench. Now, the house had a big addition, crystal chandeliers, fancy-ass bathrooms, and a bunch of offices converted from bedrooms. The silver-and-purple color scheme was carried throughout, and they'd invested in gorgeous, lush accents to create an atmosphere of luxury. Watercolor canvases and black-and-white vintage photos on the walls, silvery shag area rugs, beaded lamps, and a carved mahogany conference table with leather chairs for all.

Malia loved the quirky modern atmosphere of working in a converted home, but the team had been growing, so they'd secured an additional space to work on the foundation. Luckily it was right down the road, and they'd snapped up the house/accounting office at a deal. Malia figured they'd work on a color palette and design later—right now she was happy enough with the formal conference room and few offices that were already set up for work space.

"How was your consult with the Children's Hunger Initiative?" Tessa asked. "We didn't get to see you for Sunday Scrabble."

"Is Mike feeling better?" Malia asked.

Chiara nodded. "Yep, just a cold."

"Good." Malia nibbled her lip and hoped she'd be able to communicate the least amount of information to avoid drama. Her friends were like her sisters on steroids—they wanted to know all the details of her life. So far, she'd successfully avoided telling them about dinner with Palmer, but it was time to face the squad. "Friday was good. Xander and Laura are excited about expanding the program. Oh, and we found a donor that very night, which worked out well."

Chiara gasped. "That's incredible! Who is it? A volunteer?"

"Actually, it was Palmer Matterson. I guess his sister is a volunteer and he showed up to help, then decided to sign up for the foundation. We had dinner that night." She didn't miss a beat. "Chiara, how's Veronica doing? You know I'm always up for babysitting duty when you need it, since I'm her godmother."

"Co-godmother," Tessa corrected. "Now back it up. I've never seen such avoidance in my life."

"Agreed." Chiara leaned in with a shred of ruthlessness. "Mr. Hot Billionaire was at the Hunger Initiative volunteering and decided to get involved? Then took you to dinner?"

Malia tried to pretend it was nothing. "No, Xander and Laura asked me to dinner, then invited Palmer. Over dinner, Palmer asked to be part of the foundation so he could donate to the Hunger Initiative, which is wonderful news. He'll be working with Deanna."

Chiara and Tessa shared a meaningful look. "Oh, this is good," Tessa said. "What are the odds you see your nemesis at a charity event? It's like fate or something."

"Did he ask you out again?" Chiara demanded. "Tell us now or it will be worse later."

Malia stared at her friends with rising frustration. They wouldn't let this go until she confessed. Trying not to blush, she kept her voice steady and neutral. "Fine, but I'm saying all of this under duress, and I think you are the worst friends in the world."

"Duly noted," Tessa said. "Did you make out?"

"No! Laura and Xander got called away, so we finished the dinner alone. Once again, he informed me he was interested in dating me. I thanked him but said no. I think we've settled things, and he shouldn't be bothering me again."

I can make you like me.

A shudder worked through her. The fierce promise in Palmer's eyes still haunted her. She'd never had a man look so intense regarding gaining her company. It was a thrill to her ego. Unfortunately.

"Oh, this is good." Tessa rubbed her hands together. "You're deliberately underplaying it, which means he actually got to you! All this time you thought he hated you, but it was just like I said. His assholery was all foreplay."

Malia buried her face in her palms. "You did not just say that. How can you run a female-centric company and say something so chauvinistic?"

Someone patted her shoulder and she figured it was Chiara. "It's okay, babe. We all know Tessa devoured Harlequin romance novels for breakfast for too many years. Sometimes, it comes out in all the wrong ways. Her faves were the boss/secretary trope. I think she still wants to be ravished on a desk, so you're living her dream."

Malia raised her head, laughter helplessly bubbling out at Tessa's mean glower.

Tessa gave a humph. "Very funny. Guess you're living the trope of falling in love with your best friend's widower and a secret pregnancy."

"It wasn't secret. I told all of you," Chiara said.

Good. If they fought, maybe she could sneak out and deal with this later.

Tessa turned and jabbed a finger in the air. "Let's focus on the real issue here and recap. Malia and Hot Billionaire have meetings filled with banter and sexual tension. Malia dislikes him for his control-freak ways and arrogance and tries to dump the account. He gets desperate and confesses his feelings for her, asking her to dinner. She says no. Fast-forward a bit and they both meet randomly at the charity and end up at dinner. Hot Billionaire signs up for the foundation and asks her out for the second time, desperate for her company. Malia says no. Am I correct so far?"

"I hate the way you're communicating my experience, but yes. Technically, you're right. And why do you have to call him Hot Billionaire? It's Palmer. He's not that hot."

Her instant blush caused her friends to giggle.

"Lie," Chiara sang. "Why are you denying he's getting to you? Why won't you just go out with him? Is he single?"

"Guys, you're not understanding. For this past year, he's tortured me. Now, he suddenly wants to change gears and date me, and I'm supposed to just fall into line? No. Plus, he's a bit too much for me. I want an ordinary guy."

Tessa blinked. "What the hell is an ordinary guy?"

Malia cut a hand through the air. "You know, someone with a regular job who's low-key."

"Hmm, interesting. How about someone who actually shows up, buys you dinner, and wants to listen to you? You haven't had a decent date in forever, dude. I think you're being narrow minded. There's nothing wrong with giving the man a chance as long as you're interested. And I think you are. The woman doth protests a lot."

She glared. "It's *the lady doth protest too much, methinks*. No wonder we only got a B on that Shakespeare report in high school—you suck."

Chiara cleared her throat and jumped in. "Malia, remember what you said to me when you decided to freeze your eggs? You said it would give you the opportunity to be free. Instead of feeling that ticking clock, you wanted to have fun and date whoever and sleep with whoever without worry. Isn't Hot B—I mean, Palmer—the perfect guy to begin with?"

Malia hated when her words were thrown back at her. For the past few years, her dating matches had revolved around men she felt would be good for her. She'd said no to any types online who didn't seem ready to settle down, yet each date she did go on had ended in disaster. Relying on friends and family wasn't a big help, either. She'd even tried to date Chiara's husband's best friend, Ford, but there had been zero sparks.

Was Chiara right? If this was the first time she'd experienced such a strong reaction, was she being stubborn about throwing away the opportunity?

"He's still a Quench client," she finally said. "Even if I did date him, it has all the components to end badly and affect Quench and the foundation. Plus, he won't be interested once he hears my fertility plan. I start injections soon. I won't be fit to date."

"I don't think so," Tessa said. "You're both professionals, and work is a normal place to date and fall in love nowadays. He's not your boss, just a client. And if you scare him off, fine, but something about this guy tells me he doesn't surrender easily. I think you should go for it and stop analyzing things so much. Aren't you tired of trying to figure things out all the time?"

God, she was. She gave a sigh and patted her head, the braids feeling a bit too tight today at her scalp. Sometimes, she wished she could just give a good scratch, but there was no way she was ruining her hairstyle. "It's the only way I know how to be," she admitted. "Believe me, Tessa, if I could be more WTF like you, I would."

Her friend reached out and squeezed her hand in support. "Sorry, I didn't mean to give you a hard time," Tessa said. "I just want you to take a leap. You've been driving this route for so long, you're forgetting what it's like to take a side road."

A laugh escaped. "I prefer using Waze and not getting lost."

"Remember, my side road brought me to the love of my life," Chiara said.

Her friend's journey had been rocky. Falling in love with Rory's husband and getting pregnant had shaken all their foundations, but watching the beautiful family they'd made and the love they shared made it all worth it.

"Okay, okay. I'll think about it."

"That's all we're asking," Tessa said. "We got your back no matter what. You deserve it all."

Malia stuck out her tongue even as her heart softened from her friend's words. "Now you're just buttering me up so you can have material for your makeover and matchmaking column."

"Maybe."

They all laughed as Deanna came in. "Sorry I'm late. What's so funny?"

Malia sighed. "Nothing worth repeating."

Her friends nodded, chatted a bit with Deanna, then left. Yeah, they always had her back. And they were usually right.

But not this time.

Side roads might be tempting, but she'd end up missing the destination if she got stuck in the mud. Malia intended to stay away from Palmer Matterson, get her injections, match up his money with the Quench Foundation, and live happily ever after without looking back.

Deanna slid into a seat, flipped open her laptop, and shot her a dazzling smile. "Girlfriend, I almost dropped to the floor when you told me this weekend you got a match already for the Children's Hunger Initiative. You're like the leprechaun who followed the rainbow to a pot of gold."

Malia laughed. She'd known immediately Deanna would be the perfect hire. She'd come from a bigger not-for-profit in Manhattan and knew the ins and outs of growing a start-up successfully. Her heart was caring, her mind was sharp, and she didn't seem intimidated by anyone's role or position, treating everyone exactly the same. She wore a sleek cream-colored suit, which emphasized the smooth ebony of her skin, wide eyes, and classic features. Her hair was cut short in a bob that showed off her long, slender neck. They'd become fast friends through the endless hours of intense training, and Malia felt like she was blooming under Deanna's tutelage.

"Honestly, it was more luck and opportunity than skill. I just happened to be there at the right time."

"No such thing as luck, but I do believe in fate," Deanna said, her fingers clicking madly on the keys.

A shiver raced down Malia's spine. All this talk about fate was beginning to freak her out.

Deanna continued. "Palmer's literally the perfect client, with gobs of money to spend and a cause he's personally involved in. It's harder to sell when they're looking at a brochure of the charity, but since he was on premises and met everyone, he's hooked. Now, I've sent you the steps to follow and the finalized contract. I'd recommend you have a meeting to go over the financial options and clauses, have him sign, and then we can go directly to funding."

Alarm bells clanged in her head. "Wait—aren't you meeting with him? I'm still too new to take on such a big client."

Deanna shot her a concerned look. "Malia, this is your baby. You're ready to take on clients now, and honestly, I'm slammed. I really need you to step up for me on this and close it. Plus, you already bonded with him and have a working relationship. Trust is key when working with large amounts of money. He trusts you."

Malia blinked and let the shock hit her full force. No. This couldn't be happening. Deanna was using the exact words Palmer had. There had to be a way to get out of this.

"Um, what if I took over some of your other duties and you do this one? I promise to take on the next client. I just feel like I need a bit more time."

Deanna patted her hand. "I hear you, and I know how scary it is when you're afraid of screwing up something you're passionate about. But this is your time, Malia. I want you to go through all the steps with a client, from initial consult through contract through follow-up. Endless Vows is perfect for you. You need to trust me. I'm better served right now if you do this for us."

She wanted to close her eyes in defeat but didn't want to worry Deanna. Forcing a smile, she dragged in a breath and nodded. "I understand. I got this. No worries."

Relief flashed in Deanna's brown eyes. "I know you do. You're ready, and I'm here for any backup you need. Now, let's go over everything for the meeting."

Malia listened intently even as a dim chant echoed through her head like a mantra.

You are so screwed.

Chapter Eight

This time, when Malia walked into Endless Vows, Cassandra pointed her directly to Palmer's office. "Go right in, Ms. Evergreen," she said with a smile. "He's been waiting for you."

The room change caught her off guard. Palmer was known to hold only certain meetings in his office—one-on-ones and those where he wanted to dazzle clients. All other business fed into the massive map of private and shared meeting areas.

She refused to hesitate, though, and didn't miss a beat as she opened the door and shut it behind her.

"Hello, Malia."

That deep, husky voice knew all the hidden places to stroke, and immediately her body peaked, ready to play. Palmer was standing in front of his desk, arms crossed, hips shifted to the left. Versace today, and his slim form wore it well. The smoke-gray suit matched his thick, unruly hair, and instead of making him look old, it just gave him an extra dose of virility, emphasizing his lean, muscled body. The tie was narrow and purple. His engraved diamond cuff links flashed when he moved. He was the epitome of sexual power neatly wrapped in civility. Her spit dried up as she tried not to stare.

Thank goodness she'd worn her armor again, anticipating this reaction. Her bra was plain cotton and extra padded. Her underwear had not a scrap of lace or special design. The pantsuit was a severe Ann

Taylor in cocoa brown, even though it was spring and she craved color. The shoes were missing the signature red sole and had a thick heel. Her braids had been pulled back in a simple bun.

To get her point across, her entire demeanor screamed WORK and held not an ounce of attention. She could only hope he got the message. At least she hadn't deciphered any smugness in his tone when she'd called to arrange the meeting and announced she'd be his liaison for the Quench Foundation, not Deanna.

Malia gave a nod of acknowledgment. "Hello, Palmer. I'm looking forward to signing you with the foundation. Will your financial manager be joining us?"

"No, I've already run the project by him, but this isn't something I need him to sit in on."

"I see." She made a point to look around. "Would you like to go to the conference room?"

His lips quirked in a half smile. "I think we'll be comfortable here, it's more intimate. I've cleared my morning so we can take our time."

She blinked and studied his face, searching for signs of double entendre, but he looked innocent, pointing to the smaller round table in the corner of his office—which was more like a luxury suite to Malia. The floor-to-ceiling windows seemed as arrogant as the view—a sprawl of Manhattan below them in its mighty glory. The thrust of buildings toward a misty skyline reminded anyone looking that if you can make it here, you can make it anywhere.

Besides the majestic desk positioned right in front of the intimidating view, the room boasted a full wet bar, a square sitting area with couch and chairs, and a large bookcase overflowing with worn leather and fabric covers. She wondered if Palmer had read any of the books. He didn't seem like a man who'd display rare books solely for the sake of appearances, but she didn't know him well. She stamped out the odd flicker of longing that sprang up, the stir of interest to be the woman who knew all his hidden secrets.

Malia opened her briefcase and set out a fat folder filled with paperwork, along with her laptop.

"Would you like an espresso? Cappuccino?" he asked.

Usually she declined, but a shot of caffeine would be welcome to keep her focus. "Cappuccino would be nice, thank you."

He strolled across the room. She waited for him to ring his receptionist, but instead he busied himself by the wet bar, and soon the sounds and smells of brewed coffee filled the air.

"I didn't notice you had an espresso machine there."

"My office is my haven. Many times, I prefer to do things by myself to keep away an endless parade of interruptions. Also, it helps me not get lazy, as my sisters say."

"Were you the one who got stuck fetching things and serving them all the time just because you were born last?"

"Of course. I remember my oldest sister, Veronica, got in trouble because she had me refilling her wineglass when I was eleven years old."

Malia grinned. "I said the F word at three, and my sister got grounded for a week."

His laugh was robust and music to her ears. She wondered if he laughed regularly or if he was in serious mode too much. "We needed some breaks to go our way." He set the coffee in front of her with a perfect froth of steamed milk and sprinkle of cinnamon. "Sugar?"

"No, it's perfect. Thanks."

He watched her take the first sip, his gaze focused on her lips, and she tried to ignore the sudden crackle of electricity between them. Sliding gracefully into the seat beside her, he shot his cuffs and settled in. The scent of his cologne drifted in the air—a mix of spice and cloves that made her want to take a bigger sniff.

Clearing her throat, Malia prayed she'd be able to do her job without distraction. "I've pulled all the financials and the proposals for the backpack program and new hiring. First, I think we should go over the contract, then delve into each point so I can answer any questions."

"Good. Show me what you got."

She slid over the stack of printouts. Nerves jumped in her belly as she questioned whether she was ready, but Malia took a breath and trusted her gut. She knew the material. Deanna would have never thrown her into the deep end otherwise. "Let's begin with section 1."

Malia fell into work mode. He listened without interruption, occasionally asking her to clarify a point. "Is a three-year term standard or negotiable?"

"Well, we'd rather avoid a yearly commitment due to the effort of repurposing a whole new program. But if that's a make or break, we can certainly accommodate."

Palmer cocked his head. "I thought the same. I'd be happy to sign for five years. I think it gives all parties the security to move the organization forward."

He managed to surprise her. Again. She nodded and made the change. "I agree. Thank you."

They moved on. He murmured under his breath, his concentration absolute. Time ticked. Papers shuffled. The keyboard clicked as he advanced to each tab. She sipped the rest of her coffee and tried to keep her own face calm. Tried not to show him how nervous she really was on her first big nonprofit presentation alone. Deanna had taken her through each scenario and warned her most executives needed time to process and ask endless questions before deciding on contributing.

"I'm happy with the terms. Can I see the final numbers for the new hire and backpack program? The spreadsheet is cut off."

"Sorry. Right here." Malia turned her laptop and he leaned over to look at the screen. Their shoulders brushed, and her breath skittered. The slither of fabric over his hard thigh when he adjusted and moved closer made her heart beat. She licked her lips and kept her attention on the figures in front of her.

"In order to properly fund without cutting corners, you'd need a million dollars." She looked up. His gaze drilled into hers.

Her heart stopped, then beat madly in her chest. Malia refused to flinch and kept her voice calm. "That's correct."

Palmer studied her face intently. "I have questions."

Her belly twisted. "I assumed." The quick arch of his brow made a laugh slip from her lips. "Sorry."

"I'm not. It's nice to know you have breaks in your armor sometimes."

She jerked back. "Me?"

"Malia, you're one of the most confident women I know. It's hard to know what you're thinking. That's another reason I enjoyed pushing a bit during our meetings—to see your real emotions come out. Even if it was mostly irritation."

His words stunned her. She never thought of herself as distant or guarded. Did she really give off that impression, or was it just him? Was that a reason why she was bombing with so many dates? "I'm not like that," she said a bit stiffly. "I'm just trying to do my job."

Concern flickered in those jeweled eyes. "I didn't mean to insult you. Do you know how many referrals I've given Quench over the past year based on your interactions with me? You're an excellent salesperson—one of the best."

Suspicion piqued. "Sure."

Palmer threw back his head and laughed. "You're asking me to fund a program for a million dollars. I'd say that's successful."

"You haven't signed the contract."

His eyes danced with humor. "Simply a technicality. I'd like your breakdown on this. How do you see the program developing over time? The final result? Xander and Laura are too close, and I'm too stuck in the business part. You see things we wouldn't." He leaned back and crossed his arms in front of his chest. "Pitch me."

Excitement bubbled in her veins. The challenge and passion of her vision were clear, and she was being given the stage to reveal it to him. Malia gave a slow smile. "I will."

Time faded away as she took him through the development of how his funds would be used and the way the Hunger Initiative would look within five years. After, they fell into the discussion, going easily back and forth to sharpen her ideas. She liked the way he listened to her suggestions. Most men didn't hold the space—they just waited for their turn to talk. Palmer seemed to see the bigger picture rather than concentrate on tiny segments he could control. It was interesting to watch his perspective develop until all the pieces fit together, maybe not right away, but eventually.

They both collapsed back into their seats at the same time. She twisted right and left to stretch out her back. "I think we solidified the proposal," she said, pleased. "I'll confer with Xander and Laura and get you a clean copy to send to your lawyers."

"Good. I like where we ended up." He regarded her intently. Awareness rippled between them. "I see now why you're a better fit for this job. Your skills were wasted with advertising."

She bristled at his arrogance. "As much as I appreciate the compliment, I was happy with advertising for a long time. It served its purpose, and I found it challenging."

"I think you'd succeed at any job you put your mind to." He got up and retrieved two bottles of water from the cooler. "But passion doesn't come often. We're lucky if we can integrate such emotion into our career. I'm glad you made Quench work for you rather than the other way around."

She was struck again by the way he viewed things. Not black and white. Palmer saw all the gray and didn't seem afraid of it.

Palmer twisted off the cap to one of the waters and handed her the bottle. "Your founding story says you created the company with your best friends. How did that develop?"

Malia smiled. "In a booth at a diner called Mike's Place. One of my best friends, Rory, announced she wanted to do something big for women and believed the four of us had the skills to pull it off."

The memory pulled at her with bittersweetness. "Her dad, Mike, gave us a loan for the office. Our first business plan was written on a legal notepad."

"And look where you are now." Respect shone with his sharp nod. "Well done."

The rush of pleasure from his approval took her off guard. "Weddings are your passion, then?" she asked curiously.

Palmer returned to his seat. "Making people happy is important," he clarified. "Helping others achieve a dream—whether it be a wedding of a lifetime or the hope of a new beginning. Each couple sees it differently, and the challenge is to satisfy whatever their perspective is."

Doubt trickled through her. He chose his words carefully, answering her questions with thought. She wished she didn't like talking to him. She wished she didn't have a million more questions she craved to ask. But was this just another game? A way to show off a fake idealism to seduce her because he wanted to cross her off a list of conquests?

Malia watched him take a sip of water, his tanned throat muscles working. "That's a perfect answer."

One brow arched. "You don't believe me?"

"I don't know." She gave a half shrug. "Does it matter?"

"Yes. It matters a lot." His jaw clenched. "It's important you trust me."

A half laugh escaped her lips. "Why? I trust you enough to work with you for the foundation. I think we'll make a solid team, and I'm excited to watch the Hunger Initiative blossom."

A strange intensity shimmered around him, making her want to get up from her chair and back off. "You don't understand, Malia. I want much more." Masculine demand weaved through his gravelly voice.

Instead of pissing her off, he was turning her on, and that was the worst embarrassment of all. She focused on gathering up her loose folders. "We discussed this at dinner, Palmer. There is no more than our business relationship."

"Look at me."

Her head swiveled around without thought. His eyes locked with hers, and heat steamed between her legs.

"Ask me anything."

She blinked. "Excuse me?"

"Right now. Any question you want, and I will tell you the truth."

It was ridiculous. Juvenile. Malia didn't want to play these games, and it was time to gracefully exit. But the bookshelf seemed to mock her with all those fancy books stacked in neat piles. And in that moment, she wanted to know the answer more than she wanted to walk away with her head held high. "Fine. See all those books on your shelf?"

He nodded, obviously puzzled. "What about them?"

"Did you read any? Some? All? Or are they simply props?"

Malia waited for him to stumble or delve into an explanation. Maybe to defend himself and point out he'd read a few and liked to collect rare books for a hobby. What she didn't expect was for his face to clear with a deep understanding that seemed to bond them together even tighter. He seemed almost delighted by her probing question. "I should've known you'd ask something that clever. God, you're an amazing woman."

She held her jaw tight so it wouldn't drop open. "Nice distraction."

With an easy stride, Palmer crossed the room and plucked a book from the shelf. His large hands cradled the small volume with care, as if it actually meant something. "Kurt Vonnegut is my favorite author. This is a rare edition of *Slaughterhouse-Five*, my favorite book."

She tilted her head, considering. "Why is it your favorite?"

"So it goes." At her puzzled look, he seemed to think about what he was going to say. "The book explores a lot of themes such as death, unfairness, and the exploits of the innocent in the world. Basically, we have a mess on our hands, but we have no real control over it. We must move into an acceptance and grace of our circumstances and find a place for the chaos. My favorite quote from the book is 'So it goes.'

Whatever will happen, shall happen." A shadow crossed his face; his eyes darkened with a flash of pain she wanted to linger on and analyze, but it was quickly swallowed up and gone. A sad smile curved his lips. "Death is part of existence. I learned a lot from Vonnegut. Have you ever read him?"

Malia shook her head, then considered the man holding the book to his chest. "What about the others?"

"I've read them all. Dickens. Tolstoy. Austen. Wharton. Fitzgerald. They were my friends through my youth, stuck in my hand when I was bored because I didn't have fancy video games like my friends. My mother told me to climb a tree, ride a bike, or read a book. Television was limited. She was extremely strict." A flush of red hit his cheekbones. "There's popular fiction, too, of course. I'm no snob. I love horror. Especially vampire books for some reason."

Her throat tightened, and she was suddenly fighting the impulse to go to him, slide her arms around his neck, and pull him close. Kiss the flush on his cheeks and then his lips. Would he taste like cinnamon from the flavored gum on his desk? Would he dominate her with his fingers and tongue, or seduce her slow and gentle?

Palmer rocked back on his heels, obviously feeling awkward, and in that stunning moment, Malia felt as if he'd given her a true piece of himself not many glimpsed.

She stood up and cleared her throat. Wrapped her arms around her waist to keep from giving in to her initial impulse. "I like books, too. Have a ton of them in my place, stacked up in the basement because I ran out of room. I don't like to give them away, because each one owns a part of me, and I feel bad separating from it. Stupid, right?"

"Not at all."

"And vampires are cool."

His grin took away the vulnerability, and he was back to his magnetic, confident self. "They are." He paused. "You believe me?"

"Yes. I believe you."

She had to get out of there.

Malia turned, hurriedly packed up the rest of her stuff, and shot to the door before Palmer had time to stop her. "I'll get you the materials by tomorrow."

"Good. I want to move quickly. I think we should meet again this week once the contracts are finalized."

Alarms clanged in her head. "Oh, that's not necessary. We can Zoom or email."

"I prefer in-person meetups, especially with such big stakes."

She felt his stare hot on her back but refused to face him.

"I'll come to you. Friday?"

Horror hit. She fumbled with her briefcase. "No! Um, no need—I don't really have the facilities yet to properly meet with clients. I can take the train to you."

"All we need is a table and chairs. I'd like to see the headquarters anyway, of both Quench and its foundation. See who I'm working with."

She snuck a glance back in hopes of convincing him. "Palmer, it's really not necessary for you to make such a trip at this point. We can wait until we have more pieces in place."

"I want to, Malia." His gaze caressed her face, moved downward, and resettled. Her body flamed as if he'd touched her. "I'll see you Friday."

She walked out in a daze. The whole meeting played out in her brain on repeat. And Malia wondered where she'd gone so wrong.

Chapter Nine

"Boss, we got a problem."

Palmer turned to Emeril, but his gaze still held flashes of Malia. Malia, in her beautifully cut, reserved brown suit. Malia, with her braids neatly tamed and fiery amber eyes firmly banked. Malia, who dazzled him with fresh ideas, unafraid to challenge his opinions. Malia, who boldly accused him of being a phony judging by the books she believed he hadn't read.

He was falling for her a bit more every moment they were together, and she could not care less. His ego took a hard beating in her presence. She'd been horrified when he forced another meeting later in the week, obviously anxious to keep as much distance as possible between them.

He'd been horrified himself. Palmer had never used business as an excuse to push his company on a woman before. Yet, as she poised for flight, he gave in to his desperation and finagled a meeting so they'd get more time together.

Of course, a million dollars was on the line, and he had every right to require additional time. But he needed to move carefully and make sure she knew his interest in her was completely separate from Quench Foundation business.

Palmer twisted a silver pen in his hand, morosely staring at his computer. What was happening to him? She had put him under a spell, clouding his big brain and his little brain, until he became a puppy dog, thirsty for attention. He was no longer a hormone-ridden teen but a man with a multimillion-dollar company, a man who'd had previous relationships and great sex. Yet, Malia made him feel as if no one ever existed before her.

"Boss? Did you hear me?"

He blinked the image away and tried to focus. "Sorry. What's up?"

Emeril took a few precious seconds from his consistent phone tapping and frowned. "What's wrong with you?"

Palmer straightened in his chair and dropped the pen. "Nothing. Tell me the issue. I'm running behind schedule today, so I have little time for distractions."

The cold snap of his voice didn't deter his valued right-hand man. In fact, Emeril leaned in to peer at his face like he was a new museum exhibit. "You're behind because you refused to end the meeting with Malia. How'd it go?"

"Fine." He stared boldly back, practically daring Emeril to challenge him.

The man suddenly burst into laughter. "You have a crush!"

He rose from his chair and sputtered. "Get out of my office. You're fired."

Emeril ignored him, clapping his hands together in a rare form of enthusiasm. "My Lord, she's got you in a tangle. I haven't seen you like this since . . . well, never. I'm guessing she's not feeling the same."

Shit. Emeril lived for gossip but could keep a secret like a foreign spy. He'd also become a friend in the years he'd worked for Palmer, which gave him an awful advantage. "Give me time," he muttered.

"I wondered why you were such an ass with her all the time. I suspected you liked her, but you were so terrible and rude and uncharming, I figured it was the first time in my life I was wrong. But I wasn't." He preened with satisfaction. "You should have come to me for advice."

"This is not *Romper Room*. Can we just drop the subject and get to the disaster you can't seem to solve by yourself?"

Emeril gave him a hurt look. "This one's above my pay grade. The Donovan wedding is this weekend, and our planners ran into a problem."

The wedding united a superstar celebrity couple who fell in love on a television sitcom while the world watched. They were young, impulsive, and hard to please, but he'd picked his top team, and they were finally getting it done this Saturday at the American Museum of Natural History. Seemed the groom's dream was to be married with a gigantic dinosaur skeleton in the room. Palmer was grateful that was one fantasy easy to fulfill in the playground that was New York City. It was a front-page affair with a huge buildup, and Palmer tried to keep a close eye on it.

He cocked his head. "How bad?"

Emeril tightened his lips. "Bad. We've got a code red situation. Pandora is having second thoughts."

Sympathy warred with a sense of disaster. "Press?"

"Nothing. Right now, she just told her grandmother, who told the planners, who told me."

"Did they try to talk to Pandora?"

"Not yet. They wanted you to know first."

Good. He'd trained his planners for these types of disasters but always preferred to take care of them personally if he could. Malia might call it one of his control-freak tendencies, but it was his company, and the couple's happiness was his ultimate responsibility.

Possibilities scrolled through his mind, and within seconds, he'd analyzed several scenarios. "Groom?"

"No clue, but the grandmother says if she can't calm Pandora down, the groom's going to get the call."

"Any idea if it's cold feet or something bigger?"

Emeril, as usual, was razor sharp. "Definitely cold feet. She suffers from anxiety. Usually her grandmother can talk her down, but so far, no luck. What do you want to do?"

This was the wedding of the century. He'd dealt with his fair share of runaway brides, but Pandora had never struck him as having any doubts—it was obvious she and Garrett were madly in love. If she truly didn't want to marry Garrett, Palmer would do his job, eat some of the costs—cancelled weddings never got fully refunded—and move on. But Pandora deserved someone who cared about what she wanted rather than someone worried about the bottom line.

Once the press got ahold of the story, Pandora would be trapped. He'd watched too many people be forced into a decision because the world was watching. He needed to get to her and figure out what she truly wanted before the whole thing blew up. "Tell the team to stand down. Call the grandmother and tell her I'll be there within the hour to talk to Pandora. Have Dr. Rose on standby in case she needs some counseling or wants to talk to a professional."

"You're the best professional I know, boss," Emeril said. "Is this lucky number thirteen?"

Palmer winced, already grabbing his phone and heading out. "Why do I keep you around again?"

"Because no one else can put up with your shit, as Malia would say?"

He cut the man a glare and strode out the door. "You're fired!" he called out.

"Yeah, tell someone who cares."

Palmer swallowed a smile and headed downstairs to the car.

It was showtime.

~

"I can't do it. I'll make a terrible wife. We'll get divorced and blow up our careers. I need to let him go before it's too late. I love him too much."

Pandora paced the luxurious suite of the Plaza, her famous coal-black curls spilling down her back and bouncing with each turn. Her already high voice had peaked to extremes, and her breathing was shallow as she kept repeating all the reasons getting married would be a mistake.

Her grandmother, a spry eighty-three-year-old of Italian descent, shot Palmer a worried look. He had realized the first time meeting Pandora's family that Maria Lucca was the true matriarch, and her granddaughter was the light of her life. He loved watching the close relationship between the two and the way they'd planned the wedding so carefully. Maria had vetoed the dinosaur and preferred the classicism of the New York Public Library, but Garrett had won this major battle and given up the rest to the bride and Palmer's team.

At least it wasn't like she had found Garrett cheating or decided she didn't love him. Palmer knew he should be able to fix this and come out ahead with thirteen saved weddings, but he needed to dig deep and focus.

"Darling, Garrett loves you on the deepest level, even your flaws," Maria said. "You're allowing yourself to fall into a tizzy. Did you wear your Italian horn today? Did you cross someone who gave you the evil eye?"

Pandora shook her head. "No, Nonni, it's not that at all. One day, he's going to realize I'm not who he believes I am, and he'll leave me and my life will be over. Isn't it better to break it off now under my control? If I wait, he'll destroy me!"

Maria blew out a breath. "That is ridiculous! Where do you get these ideas, my child? Were you watching that *90 Day Fiancé* show again?"

"No!" Pandora wailed. "I need to call him. Tell him the wedding's off."

Maria held her head and swayed back and forth, whispering some type of chant in Italian. Pandora was gearing up for a dramatic breakdown, whipping herself into a frenzy Palmer had to head off. His only weapon right now was to shake things up and hope it all worked out fine in the end.

"I think that's a good idea," he announced.

Pandora stopped pacing and stared at him in shock.

Maria gasped, her dark eyes filled with distress.

"What did you say?" Pandora asked.

He lifted his hands, palms up. "Listen, you make a good point. No one knows what the future holds when you say your vows. What if you're *not* right for him? What if he wakes up one day down the road and realizes he can trade up?"

Her eyes widened and she took a step back. "That bastard! I'd kill him!"

Palmer nodded. "Exactly. There is no certainty in marriage. That's why I never did it. Better to let other people get hurt, right? You're smart, Pandora. This way, you'll have all those perfect memories and nothing will get ruined. You can move on and keep from getting hurt."

Allowing Pandora to follow through with her plan seemed to throw her off guard. "I'm doing this for him, you know. I mean, I'm not the one questioning my feelings or commitment." Tears sparkled from her amber eyes. "The real truth is—I'll never be good enough for him."

"Pandora—"

He cut off Maria before she could jump in. "Probably right. I've seen him around you, and he's kind of perfect. Not many women are special enough to truly satisfy him."

Pandora stomped over and jabbed a finger at Palmer. "Are you kidding? Do you know what I do for that man? For his birthday, I took him to a professional racecourse so he could drive one of those cars because it's on his bucket list. I write him love notes at the studio and leave them in secret places. I get along with his juvenile friends and love his slobbery, ugly dog. I cook when he's tired and listen when he's sad, and I'm the only person in the world who can love him the way he needs!"

B-I-N-G-O.

Maria seemed to catch the game and gave a deep sigh. "But is that enough? Like Palmer said, maybe you were right all along. Cancel the wedding, break it off, and move on. You'll never get hurt or have to worry."

Pandora stared at her grandmother with her jaw unhinged. "Nonni, how could you say this to me? I thought you loved Garrett?" Her lower lip trembled. "I thought you said we were soul mates."

"You are, my darling. But you need to be strong enough to believe it yourself. To fight for him. Marriage is not for the weak."

"I'm not weak!" She threw her shoulders back and glared. "And I am not canceling this wedding! Palmer, you better have everything ready, and it better be perfect. I've had enough of this talk—I have a million things to do. Capisce?"

He arranged his expression into benign acceptance, as if he had no idea what was going on. "Of course, I'm sorry to even have mentioned it. It will be our secret."

"I should hope so. God help us if such dramatics got out to the press at this stage. Did you confirm the security for J.Lo? And that the Okavango Blue Diamond special exhibit will be available for guests? Who doesn't love a giant diamond? My guests will love it."

"It's all taken care of, Pandora." Palmer allowed himself to smile. "I promise, your wedding will be perfect."

Her aura seemed to relax and hum, no longer belting out sharp jabs of panic. He said goodbye and let himself out.

Climbing in the back seat of the car, Palmer chatted with his driver before hammering out the text to Emeril.

Number thirteen put to bed.

A thumbs-up emoji came through.

He relaxed against the cool leather, looking out the window as they crawled down a crammed Fifth Avenue, feeling good about what he had accomplished.

If only he could fix his situation with Malia as easily.

Chapter Ten

"Malia, someone's here to see you."

She looked up from her brain fog and blinked at Kelsey. The girl was dressed in one of her funky outfits, which accented her plus-size curves—a rainbow tie-dyed dress with heeled pink boots—and it took Malia a few moments to focus. As Chiara's assistant, Kelsey worked her magic at the office to keep everything running smoothly. Right now, her face was flushed and her eyes sparkled with excitement.

"Who? My next appointment isn't for another hour."

Kelsey brushed her purple bangs to the side and gave a deep sigh. "Palmer Matterson. God, Malia, he's so handsome! I mean, if I were into guys, I'd date him in a heartbeat. He said he liked my hair and that when I decide to get married, he'd fight to be the one who gets to plan it."

She buried a groan. "He's not supposed to be here until two—at the other building!"

"He apologized for being early but said he wanted to meet Chiara and Tessa before they left."

Malia narrowed her gaze with suspicion. "How did he know they were leaving?" She'd pushed the man off when he asked to meet with her friends, chalking it up to nosiness, and agreed to meet him at the Quench Foundation offices instead. It was a way to compromise because she refused to bend and give him a tour of Quench's corporate headquarters. Quench was her safe place, and they rarely met big clients at the office anyway, preferring to meet on the client's territory. They protected their space from negative energy at all costs.

Or from dangerous, sexy men who wanted to take over.

Kelsey bit her lip. "Well, he called and was so nice, asking if they'd be in, so I told him any time before one p.m. would work. Should I have told you? I'm sorry, he said he was meeting with you anyway, so I didn't think it was a big deal."

Colorful curses floated to her lips. "Why am I surprised? He's like a damn bull, forcing through any barriers to get what he wants." Annoyance skated through her, along with something else, something she refused to acknowledge. "I guess I have no choice. Are Chiara and Tessa on their way?"

"Oh, we're here," Tessa announced.

Her friends squeezed through the narrow doorway and stood by her desk. Malia wanted to hide her face in her hands at the knowing looks they cut her. "I'm sorry, guys. I told you he was a pain in the ass. For some reason, he's insisting on meeting you."

Chiara grinned. "We got you, boo. This is a perfect time to pump him for info the same time we take his check. But I gotta say, from what I saw, he is one fine specimen of a man."

Tessa licked her lips. "Damn, I love a man who knows how to wear Armani without having Armani wear him. And that hair? A young George Clooney combined with a hot Taylor Kinney."

Kelsey nodded. "Very sexy."

Malia glanced at all of them in shock. "Get it together! Remember, he's trying to impress you for some weird reason. Don't fall for it—inside he's evil." But even as she uttered the words, the denial sprang up from within. Once, she'd believed it, but spending more time with Palmer had softened her stance. There was definitely more to him than met the eye, but she didn't want her friends to see anything but his manipulations.

They all shot her doubtful stares, which pissed her off since they needed to be on her side.

Kelsey bounced away to escort him in, and Malia had only a few moments to refocus. She hurriedly neatened her desk. "He may ask a bunch of questions for recon. Don't answer him or get intimidated."

Tessa waved a hand in the air and settled into the chair. "Like I worry? I just want to take a peek at his ass."

"You can't ogle men in a business environment, babe," Chiara scolded, sitting next to her. "It's all shades of wrong."

"Sorry. It was only in my role as Malia's friend. I need to make sure the man is equipped to handle her for their upcoming affair. She's waited long enough for someone decent."

"That's different, then," Chiara said. "I'll be making sure he's not narcissistic. Malia can handle some arrogance, but a guy admiring himself in a mirror would drive her batty, even during a short affair."

"I am not having an affair with Palmer Matterson," she hissed. "Now, would you two please focus!"

The husky drawl hit her ears right before his presence hit her sight. "Good afternoon, ladies. I hope I'm not causing any . . . problems."

Horror washed over her. Her cheeks flamed as his gaze caught and held hers, amusement flickering in those sea-green depths, confirming he'd heard her response. She didn't know who she wanted to kill more—her friends or Palmer.

Tessa jumped to her feet, practically purring. "Of course not. I've been wanting to meet you for a long time as one of our most valued accounts. I'm Tessa Harper."

"And I'm Chiara Kennedy. It's nice to meet you."

Palmer shook their hands, his face wreathed with a warm smile that made Malia's heart do a bit of a tumble. She hadn't noticed the creases around his eyes when he smiled big, or the way those full lips softened, a contradiction to the sharp angle of his jaw, a lovely combination of hard and soft that had her staring a bit too long.

"No, it's my pleasure. I didn't want to inconvenience either of you, but I told Malia I wanted to meet the team behind Quench. I've been a fan for too long."

It could've sounded cheesy coming from anyone else, but with Palmer, the words came out with sincerity.

He swiveled his head and gave her his full attention. "Hello, Malia. How are you doing today?"

She forced a stiff smile. "Fine. Sorry, I had no idea you were coming early when we made our appointment. It may take me some time to gather up the finalized papers I'd promised."

He waved his hand in the air and gave another dazzling smile. "I never meant to throw off your schedule; this is strictly a social call. I wanted to thank all of you for the past year and everything we've accomplished at Endless Vows. Sales were up, and I saw a direct correlation with our advertising with Quench as one of the reasons."

"Please take a seat," Tessa said. "We're glad you've been pleased with our services. I think you'll find the foundation to be another opportunity to make a difference."

He sat and leaned back comfortably, as if he was gearing up for a chat rather than a business meeting. "So far, I'm impressed. What made you want to start the Quench Foundation? Financials show you're just reaching a new level of profit that can easily be reinvested rather than take on the not-for-profit sector."

"We created Quench so we could help women in the community," Chiara said. "But I think if a company like ours begins to focus on greed, or selfishly gobbles up more than its share, it begins to lose its original intention." She glanced over, and Malia nodded in agreement. "The foundation is an opportunity to use Quench to give back on a bigger scale. We don't want to be defined by a narrow lens from social media and allow our success to trap us."

"Chiara was inspired by her husband's work at the Dream On Youth Center," Malia added. "She saw how too many places suffered because they weren't trendy or social-media savvy."

"That was our first check we distributed as the Quench Foundation," Tessa said with a snap of pride. "And we all agreed it was the best use of our funds we could imagine."

Respect glimmered from Palmer's gaze. "I wish more companies had this type of vision. The results would be extraordinary for the world. I'm embarrassed to say I never even thought about that type of concept other than handing over a few donations on behalf of Endless Vows." He gave a shake of his head. "I can't imagine if you all had decided to get into the wedding business. I would've gone broke years ago."

They laughed on cue, but Malia noticed her friends seemed charmed. Tessa would normally be on the lookout for a patronizing tone, and Chiara despised false compliments. Neither seemed suspicious of Palmer yet.

"Palmer and I are meeting at the foundation's offices at two p.m.," Malia said, trying to take control of the conversation. "He's now an official donor and matched with the Children's Hunger Initiative."

"Malia's been a crackerjack at her new position." He stared at her with his usual razor-like focus, and the air seemed to charge around them. "I'm glad I didn't lose her completely. We work well together."

Chiara jumped in. "Yes, she told us you were upset to lose her on your advertising account. Didn't trust anyone else to handle your needs, though her replacement has a high level of experience."

"We all wondered about the reason, especially since Malia mentioned you liked to give her a hard time," Tessa added. "It all seemed quite contradictory, so we were curious."

Malia watched in growing horror as her friends leaned in to circle him like a vulture. She opened her mouth to avoid disaster but found she'd gone mute—her usual reaction when thrown off guard.

Palmer never missed a beat. "You're right, I had been giving her a hard time." His voice softened, growing deeper, and his gaze never left Malia's face, as if he was talking only to her. "It's rare to meet someone so sharp, who's not intimidated by me and my position. Sounds ridiculous, I know, but the more stubborn I became on certain points, the harder she fought to topple me. I got caught up in the game but forgot to keep my eye on the prize."

"What's the prize?" Tessa asked.

He smiled real slow. Her breath stalled out. "Malia, of course. Not that she's a tool to negotiate with. To be honest with both of you, I admit I have a crush. Unfortunately, she doesn't feel the same." He paused, and the pulsing silence hummed with anticipation. "Yet."

Oh. My. God.

This was not happening. Yet, she felt trapped by his glowing eyes and sexy declaration, unable to move or speak.

"I knew it," Tessa said with satisfaction. "Next time, don't try pulling a girl's ponytail to get her attention, Palmer. It works better if you're just nice."

"Lesson learned the hard way."

Chiara gave a little sigh. "I'm glad you value her talents, but you're going to have your work cut out for you. Between your past behavior and the series of bad dates she's been on lately, you'll need to be patient."

He arched his brow, his tone ringing with conviction. "Those men were beneath her. She deserves to be treated like a queen."

Malia squeaked, but still no words emerged. It was like starring in a *Twilight Zone* episode and not being able to change the channel.

"Damn right," Tessa and Chiara chimed in together.

"If she gives me a chance, I can promise that. In the meantime, Chiara, I wanted to ask about Veronica and how you're doing being a new mom. My oldest sister's named Veronica—lovely name."

Chiara lit up. "Thank you, she's almost six months. And yes, it's a challenge, but so is anything worthwhile. I think it's important she grows up in a household that not only tells but shows how hard work can morph dreams into reality."

"Do you have pictures?"

"Yes!" Chiara grabbed her phone and handed it over.

Palmer made approving noises and asked her several questions that showed how well versed he was with child-rearing. Malia took it all in, unable to grasp the entire strange exchange.

"Veronica had so much trouble breastfeeding and pumping when she was at work. I didn't like how some of the lactation consultants made her feel guilty about not doing enough. I hope that's not an issue for you," Palmer said.

"So far, I've been okay," Chiara answered, "but it's funny you said that. I was going to do a series of articles about pressuring women to do certain things for children, whether it's breastfeeding or co-sleeping or creating organic baby food, in order to keep them trapped in a false sense of competition. The mommy judgy culture is creating a toxic atmosphere."

"My sisters all said the same thing when my nieces and nephews were young. Let me know if you need help reaching out to anyone—I have a lot of contacts I can tap into."

"Thanks."

Palmer turned to Tessa. "I heard you're dealing with a new internship program. Does this apply to a certain demographic or age?"

"I'm concentrating on college-age or high school students who need some help with focus and experience. Most have no idea what type of jobs are really out there."

"Can I refer someone to the program? My niece is a senior and she's got an amazing photographic eye, but she has no idea how to make it into a job."

"Of course! I'm having Magda, our photographer, do small training sessions I think would be helpful. I can send you the information if you're interested."

"Magda's running it?" Malia asked, grateful to get her damn voice back. "Isn't she a bit unfriendly to be communicating with kids?" Their photographer was insanely talented, but she was also temperamental and held a cutting honesty that threw many off. She didn't like animals or children, so it was a surprise Tessa had tapped her to help with the internship program.

"Oh, she loves teens because they're not phony," Tessa answered. "I had my own doubts, but it was like she found her people. I think in her soul, she's a pissed-off nineteen-year-old who has so many lofty dreams of life, she's endlessly disappointed."

"Fascinating perspective," Palmer said. "I'd like to meet her. I'm always looking for someone with a fresh vision to do some work for Endless Vows." He threw up both hands and grinned. "Not to poach, just to give her more opportunities."

"Feel free to ask her. Malia can hook you two up," Tessa said.

Palmer beamed. "Thanks, I appreciate it."

Okay, enough was enough. It was like the mutual-admiration club having tea together. This was not what she'd imagined when her best friends and business partners met the man who'd made her life miserable the past year. Time to shut it down.

Malia jumped up. "I think we should head over to the foundation headquarters, don't you?"

Palmer cocked his head. "Of course. Do you think you can give me a quick tour of Quench before we go? Kelsey was so knowledgeable; I'd be happy for her to accompany me if she has time."

"Oh, I'll take you," Tessa said. "That'll give Malia time to gather up what she needs. Come on."

"I'll join you," Chiara said, standing up. "I'm so glad we finally got to meet."

"Me, too. The architecture of this house is amazing. Who had the vision to turn this into offices?"

"Our friend Rory spotted it first, but we were all involved in the renovation project. Do you know Mike from the local diner in town? Oh, we should take you there for coffee afterward if you're free," Tessa said, chattering on as they walked out the door and left Malia behind.

Palmer turned his head and winked at her. "Be ready in ten."

Then they all disappeared, leaving her alone at her desk, her thoughts completely scattered from the scene she'd witnessed.

Traitors.

They'd turned on her within seconds of meeting a billionaire with a handsome face and a tight ass.

Malia was in this fight alone.

Too bad she didn't even know what she was trying to win anymore.

Chapter Eleven

"Well, that was quite a spectacle. Are you proud of yourself?" Malia asked Palmer.

They'd reconvened at the new building and were currently settled at her desk. He had the nerve to look hurt as he shot his cuffs and settled comfortably across from her. His spicy scent distracted her as much as the intense scrutiny of his gaze. "I have no idea what you're talking about."

"Sure you don't." She crossed her arms in front of her chest. "You deliberately set out to charm them into liking you."

His grin held a boyish tint of mischief. "Have you ever considered that was the real me? People do like me, you know. A ton of them."

"Sure they do. You read up on them, didn't you? Knew exactly what questions to ask so they opened up and lowered their defenses."

"You're hurting my feelings. Everything I asked you'd previously told me about them. I listen to everything you say, Malia. More than you know."

She jerked back, refusing to feel guilt. He'd probably ordered a full dossier on everyone at Quench before deciding to even work with them. No man listened to her that closely, unless it was about money or if he wanted something specific. Palmer was just telling her what she wanted to hear.

His short laugh took her off guard. "You don't believe me. Who did a number on you? Was it one specifically or the whole damn lot?" He was angry. His lips tightened, and he stared back at her as if she were a complicated puzzle he didn't know how to solve.

A thrill jolted through her at his intense male focus. She'd never been that important to anyone before. Still, it was too dangerous to enjoy. He'd already snuck under her walls, won over her friends, and secured regular weekly Quench Foundation meetings when she'd tried to quit his account.

If only she could figure out what he really wanted.

"You give them too much credit," she finally said.

"No one broke your heart?"

Malia thought over her past and the endless line of men who had never made a lasting impression. The familiar cocktail of disappointment and guilt had become a bit easier to swallow lately, especially since she'd tucked it all aside to focus on her future as a mother. "I wasn't that lucky." Malia turned to him and cleared her throat. "I thought we'd first talk about your level of involvement with the Hunger Initiative and what you're comfortable with. Most of our top sponsors have minimal contact due to their busy schedules, but we always encourage the team to open their doors whenever you'd like to volunteer or attend any meetings."

"I'd like to be hands-on with this," Palmer said. "Serving the food. Meeting the kids. Eventually, delivering backpacks. This means more to me than a check. I hope the goal here is to make sure these kids get fed no matter where they're located. God knows, before they can hope to have a decent education, they need their stomachs full and a safe place to stay."

Malia watched him as he spoke. The passion vibrating in his voice touched her. She was happy to take money for the foundation in whatever capacity, even if it meant a huge tax break for a billionaire looking for a write-off, but she hadn't expected Palmer to care so much. "Then let's make it happen one kid at a time," she said softly.

Palmer smiled.

They spent the next hour working and finalizing the paperwork. Finally, Malia lifted her head. "It's official. You're a part of the Quench Foundation, and your charity will begin to receive the funds immediately. Congratulations."

"Thank you. I'm grateful I can finally help in a way that will make a difference." His green eyes blazed, and a missile of heat hit her core. "Speaking of which, why don't you show me this famous Mike's Place. I'm sure we both skipped lunch. We can celebrate."

For an impulsive moment, she almost agreed. But the thought of him crossing another boundary and sitting in her booth, talking with Mike, and laughing with her friends was too much. Too personal. "Sorry, I have tons of work to do. I hope you understand."

His frown said he didn't believe her, but the insistent buzz of his phone caught his attention. He muttered something under his breath and picked it up. "I'm sorry, Malia, I have to get this."

"Of course."

She waited for him to walk out of the office, but he pressed a button on his phone and a feminine voice came over the speaker. "Palmer! Barbara said there's a terrible problem with her reception dress. Remember she's supposed to start slow dancing and then rip off her train when the DJ switches to that fast Justin Bieber song? Well, she went for the final fitting and the dress is a disaster. It doesn't fit, and they said there's no way to guarantee it will be done in time because the fabric is special ordered and needs to be sent away. They even hinted it wasn't their fault because she gained weight! Barbara said she left you two messages today, but you never called her back, so I had to track you down so our cousin doesn't have a complete breakdown. Are you listening? Are you there?"

Malia watched in surprise as he dragged a hand through his thick hair, leaving the strands sexily mussed. Suffering lined his hard features, but his voice held nothing but calm. "Georgia, I've been in meetings all day, and this is a detail you do not call me about. Remember our last discussion? What did I tell you?"

Hard breath blasted over the line. "Don't talk to me like a child, little brother. I can still kick your ass. I agreed not to call you over minor details, but this is a catastrophe. She's our first cousin, you are in charge, and our entire family will look bad because you were the one who recommended the bridal shop! I thought you ran a wedding empire!"

Malia couldn't help it. She clapped a hand over her mouth to stop from giggling.

He caught the gesture and rolled his eyes in apology. "I'll talk to my team, who can handle this snag without my interference. Which is what we discussed before—that my planners take care of any issues. This is the third time you've interrupted my day in hysterics. What if I did that to you in your classroom? How happy would you be if your principal had to cut in during your kindergarten lessons because your brother was in a frenzy about something ridiculous?"

"Oh, please, stop being so dramatic. I'm educating the future of the world here, not throwing a party."

"I'm hanging up now."

"Fine! You've been so pissy lately. Which leads me to my most important question: Did you get a date yet for the wedding? Jane said her coworker hasn't seen you at the coffee shop even though she goes every day—are you avoiding her?"

"I drink tea now. Caffeine is bad for my growth."

"Real cute. Well, don't worry about Jane, because I found the perfect woman—she's the new substitute here and super cute. You'll love her."

"No! I have a date already, thanks so much."

"Who is this new date of yours? Don't think Christine won't know if it's a setup—you know she's the witch in the family. Plus, Chris said her friend Kate is a matchmaker and wants to sign you up with her company, Kinnections Matchmaking. That has to be worse than going with my pick!"

"Bye, Georgia. I'll talk to you later." Palmer clicked the phone, sat back in the chair, and let out a deep breath.

Malia bit her lip. "I guess that was your sister?" she finally asked.

"You'd be correct."

She bit down harder to stop more giggles. Listening to his side of the conversation was like being dragged into her own family dynamics and the most ridiculous dialogues of all time. "Where's Georgia in the pecking order?"

"Second. There's Veronica, Georgia, Jane, and Christine. Then me."

Curiosity piqued. "Do they call you a lot?"

"Yep. Some more than others. And lately, more than usual because of our cousin's wedding, which I'm planning, though I would've gladly paid anyone else to take on that job."

"Did they really say she gained weight and can't get the dress?"

"I have no idea."

The laugh burst from Malia's chest and exploded. She just couldn't help it. Palmer's male suffering gave off an adorable air, especially since he was so patient with his sister.

He tapped his fingers against his knee and regarded her with a lifted brow. "I see you think this is quite funny."

"I'm sorry," she gasped. "It's just, I don't know too many other people who have to deal with this stuff. My sisters always call me about the stupidest things, yet they never seem to listen."

"Ah, but do they try to set you up all the time? Do you know how many interventions I've had to dodge? I've lost more of my favorite coffee shops and gyms than you can believe to avoid female stalkers."

She gave a snort. "Bet I got you beat. A few weeks ago, I was minding my business, ordering a protein shake from my favorite juice bar, and the guy behind the counter takes my credit card, swipes, and asks if I'm the Malia related to my sister Zinnia. When I say yes, he tells me he made us dinner reservations for Friday. I, of course, am confused, and learn that he's a student in my sister's accounting class. Apparently, she told him we'd be perfect together and that she'd make sure I showed up. She literally set up a date without even telling me or knowing him on a personal level."

"That's not too terrible. Was he a decent guy?"

"He's much younger, works full-time at the juice bar, and made reservations at the local pizza place."

Palmer winced. "Studying for a PhD?"

"He was on his third attempt at trying to gain a bachelor's in business management. My sister hinted to him that I ran my own company and would be happy to finance his education if we hit it off."

"Yeah, that's bad."

"I liked that juice bar, too. I haven't found a decent replacement."

"It's like they're all over, hiding in bushes, doing recon on our daily activities, just to get us a date."

"Why are they so against letting us decide who and when? Are they that happy, they want to share the sanctity of marriage?"

"Or are they that miserable?" Palmer questioned.

Their eyes met and they both grinned. A sense of mutual understanding flowed between them, adding to the natural physical chemistry. She hadn't expected all this. Not now. Not from him. It was time to begin pulling back or she'd be on a slippery slope.

She began to rise. "I better get back to work."

He hesitated. Something in his eyes flickered. "Malia?"

"Yeah?"

"I'm in a situation, and I think you could help me."

She sat back down and tried to ignore her racing heart. "What do you mean?"

"This wedding. My entire extended family will be there, and all of my sisters are married. Since I lost my father, my mother has become doubly obsessed with me settling down."

Genuine sympathy squeezed Malia's lungs. Losing a parent was a nightmare of hers, even though she knew it was part of life. "I'm so sorry about your dad."

"Thank you. Unfortunately, my mom's been focusing all of her attention lately on me. I really need to bring a date to this wedding."

"I'm sure that won't be a problem. You're rich, and some would say pretty to look at." He flashed her a smile at that, his teeth ridiculously white with that slightly crooked front tooth. "Grab someone you trust."

"It's not as easy as you think. I've done that several times before, but Christine senses when there's no connection and rats me out to the family. That makes it even worse. I need to find someone I'm naturally attracted to so it doesn't look fishy. Someone who can pose as my escort and get me some needed breathing room. Someone like—"

"Hell no." She put up her hands as if to ward off the rest of his sentence. "Absolutely not. We're strictly business partners."

"Malia, hear me out. Please. One weekend. One wedding. My family is wacky, but they're also super nice. They'll adore you and won't give you a hard time. You pretend to crush on me, we spend a few hours eating and drinking and being merry, and it's over. I can do the rest myself."

She stared at him in disbelief. "You can't be serious. First of all, they'll batter you afterward, inviting me to dinner, asking when you'll get serious—they'll never back off, Palmer. They'll get too invested."

"No, because I'll spin a simple story that you work out of town and we're in a long-distance relationship. I just need to give them something to believe in. Do you know the last time I didn't have to suffer through a summer without them meddling in my love life?"

"Wait—when was your last girlfriend?"

"Two years ago."

She blinked. "You haven't dated in two years?"

Palmer threw his shoulders back and straightened up. "Of course I've dated. Casually. There just hasn't been anyone I wanted to see again after the first few dates."

Deep understanding unfurled from his confession. Who would've thought he was in the same position as her? Still, that was no reason to go along with his plan. "I can't pretend we're in a relationship! It'll be too awkward, and I'll screw up and make things worse."

"No you won't."

"I can't, Palmer. I'm sure you'll find someone else to fit the bill."

"You're perfect," he drawled.

His words hinted at a deeper meaning, and she fought off a shudder at the silky caress of his voice. The idea of spending a whole night with him, his hands on her, forced to pretend they were intimate, would be a literal nightmare. The way he pinned her down and studied her at his leisure was both sexy and terrifying. She wasn't comfortable with him burrowing beneath the surface of what she intended to show him.

Malia responded on her own gut level, ready to shut him down for good. "I'm not."

They stared at one another, locked in a battle of wills.

"What if I offer to do you a favor, too. Anything you want. All you need to do is accompany me to one small social event."

"One small event? It's a family wedding, and if your relatives are even slightly like mine, it will bring out the batty in everyone. I'll be subjected to inquisitions, stares, comments, and general abuse."

"I will guarantee your safety." Arrogance oozed from his pores.

She shook her head with a grunt. "Sure, like you control your sisters' behavior?"

Palmer paused. "I can sometimes."

She threw up her hands. "My answer is no. I don't need a favor from you, and you have plenty of time to find a nice girl who you want to take to bed so you can avoid Christine's intuitive gift. Try Craigslist."

"I don't want anyone else." He regarded her with intent, tapping his finger steadily. His shiny timepiece crusted with diamonds gleamed in the light. "You don't know, do you? How you've gotten under my skin? It's been two years since I've felt like this about a woman."

Tension and something else sizzled between them. Malia admitted being wanted by this powerful man stroked her ego . . . and other places. She struggled to keep her focus on all the reasons this was not a good idea, stunned by the level of intensity burning in his gaze. Men didn't look at her that way. Like she'd be tasted, savored, and swallowed whole. Her skin tingled with anticipation. "Stop talking like this."

"Maybe it's overdue. I waited too long to make my move and let you hide. Why won't you give me a chance to show you how good we could be together?"

Her ovaries exploded with need, and that's when she realized all she had to do was tell him the truth. He would finally stop with this ridiculous goal of pursuing her, and she could get on with her life. Though it was heartbreakingly personal, she felt it was the only way. She'd been denying their attraction, and Palmer knew it was a lie. Her excuses were becoming weaker, and even this man deserved honesty.

"You wouldn't want me at this wedding, Palmer. I'm going through something right now you don't want to be a part of. Trust me."

His face paled, and suddenly, he leapt from the chair to kneel beside her, hands on her knees. "Are you sick?"

"Oh God, no! Nothing like that."

His body sagged as if in relief. "Good. You scared me."

"Sorry." When he didn't move, she cleared her throat. "Um, you can get up now."

"I kind of like it here." With his staggering height, they were eye to eye. Close enough for her to see the cutting edge of his jaw, the high arch of his forehead, the full lips slightly parted as he released a small breath. Her fingers itched to touch the thick waves of hair falling across his brow. His scent wrapped around her like a hug. "Now, tell me what you've been holding back."

If she leaned forward a few inches, his mouth would be close enough for a kiss. Hunger zipped through her body, a reminder of how long it'd been since she was held against hard muscles, touched with greed, or ravaged by lips and tongue and teeth. Her palms dampened. Her thighs clenched. "I'm freezing my eggs."

A frown creased his brow. "I don't understand. Does this have to do with a pregnancy?"

Feeling horribly vulnerable, she shifted in her seat and wished he'd give her space. Those ten fingers burned through the thin fabric of her skirt. If he slipped over an inch and upward, he'd practically feel her wet, burning heat.

Malia swallowed, feeling a bit dizzy. "No. Well, a future pregnancy. I'm beginning the process of freezing my eggs so I can have a baby one day on my own time."

"Okay. Is there an issue that would prevent you from getting pregnant? Is that what you're afraid of?"

Her cheeks heated. Why was she telling him this? Yet, she found herself answering. "I found out I have some ovarian cysts, so it makes my odds lower. But mostly, I got tired of worrying over a timeline I can't control. This way, I get to choose when I become a mother, and if I don't meet my future husband soon, I'll do it on my own."

A mixture of emotions flickered across his face. Half of her felt sweet relief—this was the easiest way to get him to run. "Jane went through fertility issues with her husband. Did you begin the shots?"

She stared at him with surprise. "Not yet. You know about the process?"

He nodded. "Jane shared a lot with me. Two weeks of hormone injections, regular checkups, an ultrasound, and then they grab the eggs, right?"

"Pretty much, unless there's an issue. I'm hoping it will go smoothly."

"Then what's the plan? Afterward?"

She kept waiting for his horrified reaction, but he seemed matter of fact. Why was he still here, kneeling next to her? Simple curiosity? "Then I control my options. I can wait, or I can decide to forge ahead as a single mother. Maybe finding a forever love isn't meant for me. I refuse to allow fate to decide for me."

Respect shone from his jeweled green eyes. "I'm not surprised you're someone who goes after what she wants—just like me. But I admit, I didn't expect this obstacle."

Malia let out a breath. Finally. "No hard feelings. I'm sure you understand now why I can't be your escort."

Palmer tilted his head as he studied her. "This doesn't change my attraction toward you, Malia. Or my not so humble need for your assistance at my cousin's wedding. I do know when you begin the shots, things can get a bit rocky. Jane had some emotional breakdowns from the hormones. And the process triggers some deep feelings. You went over this stuff with the doctors, right?"

What was he trying to do? Where was the male distaste or fear over her bold announcement? Why did he seem more concerned with her mental state, as if he actually cared? "Why are you acting like this?" she asked suspiciously. "To prove a point?"

He gave a snort. "Damn, you really don't trust me at all. Okay, at least that's a place we can start. I can deal with that." Slowly, he unfolded his length to straighten, but she had little time to feel relief. His words were sharp, direct, and seared past too many of her careful barriers. "I'm not afraid of you or what you're about to do. Too many women marry someone they don't love because they're desperate to have a family, and it ends up in disaster. When you fall for someone, it will be for the man he is, and you'll never let him forget. That's the type of loyalty I'm looking for, Malia. The kind I'd like to inspire one day."

She fell mute, unable to analyze the whirling tornado of emotions ripping through her.

His lips lifted in a half smile. "But for now, we can help each other. You'll need major support these next few months, and I intend to be there. That will give us plenty of time to figure out what we can be to each other. I'll forward you the invite so you can block it off on your calendar."

"I'm not going with you to the wedding!"

Palmer gave her a slow, satisfied grin that made her heart stutter. "I think you will. Because you know what I'm going through, and a part of you feels bad for me." He winked. "The other part wants to see how good I look in a tux."

He strolled out the door with his head held high and his tight ass on display.

Malia didn't recover her voice for a long time. When she did, she tested it out on a scream of frustration.

Damn him for being a little bit right.

Chapter Twelve

5:00 a.m.

Guess that was the best he was going to get today.

With a groan, Palmer got out of bed and donned his workout clothes with automatic motions. He'd had a hell of a weekend and passed the last few days in a blur of work. Pandora's wedding was a complete success and, once again, cemented Endless Vows as the best in the business.

Even more important, he'd gotten a glimpse of the couple's joy when they first introduced themselves as a married couple. The way their hands and gazes entwined stirred a curiosity inside he'd never experienced before. Probably just weariness from his nonstop schedule.

Palmer headed into his private gym and began stretching, his mind slowly coming awake. He'd always embraced work—the more, the better. There was something intensely satisfying about growing his business and the talented team he relied on to continuously challenge him to keep things fresh. Each time he spoke with a satisfied couple, he felt as if he'd given value back to the world.

But lately, he couldn't stop thinking about Malia instead of work. Her face never seemed far from his mind, especially when she was admitting her secrets and showing a hint of vulnerability. Palmer sent her the details on his cousin's wedding but had received a cursory response that she would see him at their regularly scheduled Quench

Foundation meeting. He knew she wanted to go back to their initial relationship and keep him at a safe distance.

He didn't intend to let her.

For those brief moments in her office, she'd been real with him. He treasured the trust she'd shown. Did she really believe she was so easy to walk away from and forget? Did she think he'd get spooked by a woman making choices about her future with strength and passion?

A trickle of unease caught him by surprise. Obviously, her main goal was to get married and have children. It might not be the path Palmer was committed to, but he was someone who focused more on the present. He supported a five-year business plan but preferred to live his personal life organically. Love couldn't be controlled. If Malia experienced the honesty of a true relationship without fake promises of the future, Palmer was positive it would be enough for now.

He'd just need to be more delicate about the journey. Once she began the shots, he'd need to back off and offer support and friendship. Seduction would come later, when the foundation was firmly built. He had plenty of patience. No reason to skip the necessary steps that would make their physical intimacy even stronger.

Something told him he and Malia could create an explosion together.

He hit the treadmill first for his run, then switched over to weights, keeping his reps short and focused.

Having her be his escort to this wedding was key. Besides the one-on-one time, they'd be forced to level up in order to act like a couple. The more time they spent in each other's company, the more Palmer realized she was fighting her feelings for him with all her effort. For some reason, Malia was afraid to fall for him.

Was it her fertility journey she was protecting? Her need to focus on herself rather than a relationship? Or was she simply scared to try again after so many dating disasters?

He finished up his workout and glanced at his watch. Chiara and Tessa had invited him to Mike's Place, but it was obvious Malia hadn't wanted him there. Yet Palmer sensed if he allowed Malia too much space, she'd push him right out of her life. Plus, he wanted to meet Mike, who was like a second father to the group and had helped fuel these women's dreams.

He knew they met there every Monday morning for breakfast. Doing a quick calculation in his head, he decided he had time to head to Main Street before his busy day of meetings. Eggs and bacon sounded better than his regular protein shake.

He hit the shower and headed out.

~

Chiara forked up a bite of blueberry pancakes and asked, "Have you decided when you're beginning your shots?"

Malia took a sip of her coffee. "Yes, I made my appointment for the end of the month. I wanted to make sure I've got a handle on the foundation work." She made a face. "I'm kind of freaking out about the injections. If anyone told me I'd voluntarily stick myself with a needle on a regular basis, I'd never believe it."

"I'll do it," Tessa said with a grin.

Malia threw her napkin across the table. "You'd probably enjoy it."

"Does it go in your ass?" Tessa asked.

"No, my stomach." Malia gave a quiver. "I have to attend this shot school first, where they show me what to do and which shots happen when. It's intense."

Her cell shook with demand and interrupted her. She glanced at the text.

I need to know your plus one! What's his name?

Dread gathered in her core. The deadline had officially arrived, and she needed a victim fast. She'd been desperate enough this round to call Ford—Chiara's husband's best friend—but he was going to be out of town for some sports radio conference. She flipped the phone over and decided to ignore her sister's text for now.

"Hello, ladies." Malia looked up and smiled as Emma slid into the booth with them. She regularly dined at Mike's for breakfast and had begun joining them occasionally.

"Hi, Emma. How was your weekend?" Malia asked.

The teacher pursed her lips in thought, and Malia wished Tessa could give her a session on how to do makeup. She wore garish orange lipstick, and a bit of white powder clung to her face, giving her a too-pale tone. Chunky glasses slid a bit down her nose. Her outfits consisted of long skirts and thick sweaters, anything that clothed every inch of her body. And, of course, her hats were legendary and mostly awful. Today she sported a hunter-green suede with a wide brim, forcing her to peer out from under it.

"I won my Scrabble tournament at the local Barnes & Noble. Oh, and I met Abagail for tea and scones—she's quite lovely."

As they'd gotten to know Emma, all of them realized how isolated and lonely she'd been. Tessa encouraged her to join the local senior group, and now Emma seemed to have a more active social life.

"Any men?" Tessa asked with a teasing glint.

A blush brought color to Emma's cheeks. "Maybe."

Malia laughed with the rest of them. "Tell us the gossip," she encouraged.

"Well, his name is Arthur, and so far, he's very nice. He doesn't like Scrabble, which is disappointing, but he does enjoy cards, so he's been teaching me poker."

"Oooh, a bad boy. I love it," Tessa said.

"Stop!" Emma shook her head. "Enough about me. I want to know first how Veronica and her mommy are doing."

Chiara whipped out her phone and displayed the adorable chunky baby with her mouth smeared with cereal. A tuft of red hair sprang up from the center, and she was making a face that was YouTube worthy.

"She's on cereal!" Emma said, studying the picture. "And I see she can't decide whether or not she likes it."

Chiara laughed. "Oh, she loved it after a few tastes. Sebastian was a wreck, though. Kept thinking she was going to choke, so he was hovering like a true helicopter dad."

Malia's hormones tingled at the obvious adoration in her friend's voice. Chiara had gotten it all. She was madly in love with both her husband and baby. Fierce need shook through her body. She sipped more coffee to try and drown it.

"Are you showing new baby pictures without me?" Mike yelled, stomping over to the booth, stained apron tied around his waist. He peered over the table for a peek.

Chiara rolled her eyes but was smiling. "I sent this to you immediately in video format. She's so mad about you, her first word may be *papa* instead of *dada*."

Instantly, the man lit up like a Christmas tree. "That'd be great. I got her another I Love My PopPop shirt I can drop off later." He looked at Emma, and the sound of his voice flattened. "Oh. Hi, Emma. I'll get you tea."

"Thank you." She stared at the table instead of him. "Did you have a nice weekend, Michael?"

He made a snort. "Mike. Sure. I worked, and then the girls came over for Scrabble."

Malia caught the skitter of hurt cross the woman's face. She'd been invited once to the house to join them for Scrabble, but it had been so awkward, Mike told them not to invite her anymore. Emma's obvious crush had been painful to watch, especially since Mike refused to acknowledge her, even going as far as to be a bit rude. There was an odd chemistry between them, as if Mike resented Emma for something, but he wouldn't share.

"The usual, right?"

"Yes, please."

He disappeared, and a short silence came over the booth.

Tessa blew out an impatient breath. "I cannot believe you are still allowing him to get away with that behavior. Next time, put him in his place."

Emma's eyes widened behind her thick glasses. "Oh, I can't. He's family. I'm not."

Chiara spoke gently. "You're important to us, too. He's a good man, but we still don't agree with the way he ignores you."

"That's very sweet. I'm so grateful for you girls."

"I think you should focus on Arthur and learning poker," Malia said.

Emma tilted her chin up. "Maybe I will. Maybe I'll even have a real date on my birthday this year."

"When's your birthday?" Tessa demanded.

"Next week."

Tessa jumped up in her seat. "Well, I have a perfect gift. Why don't we go to the spa? We can get our nails and hair done. Maybe a body wrap. Indulge a bit."

Emma twisted her hands together. "Oh, I don't know if I'd like someone touching me. But last time I got my nails done and that was fun."

Malia immediately cut in. "Then how about a new haircut and a manicure? It would be from all of us as a gift."

"Yes, we won't take no for an answer," Chiara said.

Mike appeared in front of them with Emma's tea and pancakes. "Who won't take no for an answer?"

"It's Emma's birthday next week, and we're taking her to the spa. Don't you think that sounds nice?" Tessa said, her voice full of sharp warning.

Mike blinked, seemingly having no clue why Tessa seemed mad. "Sounds real fancy. You should like that." His judging look took in the woman's outfit. "Maybe go shopping, too, for a new thing to wear."

Emma stiffened.

Malia closed her eyes as Mike left.

Emma cleared her throat. "I think I would like to get my hair done," she said firmly. "Thank you so much for the offer. Now, Malia, I wanted to ask about freezing your eggs. What's the next step for you?"

Malia allowed Emma to steer the subject away, knowing how Mike's comment stung. Being consistently rejected would begin to affect any woman's ego. "Once I begin the shots, if I burst into tears, ignore me."

Emma patted her hand. "We'll do no such thing. We'll just hug you."

Chiara nodded. "We're here for you no matter how emotional it gets. This is such a brave, strong thing to do, Malia. Are you still keeping it between us?"

"Yes. When I'd first mentioned the idea to my family, Mom actually said it would deter men from wanting to ask me out because they'd feel pressured knowing my eggs were just waiting there."

"That's ridiculous." Tessa waved her French-manicured nails in the air. "They don't understand the struggle. I think it will be the opposite. Men will practically flock to you because there's no more worry or desperation about finding the perfect one."

"Speaking of men, how did your meeting go with your hot billionaire?" Chiara asked, brows lifted. "All I can say is, *Yum.* Plus, he's charming. Rich. And totally into you. Why aren't you interested in him again?"

She thought of their last encounter. He'd forwarded her the wedding invite with the tagline, Can't wait to see you. She kept replaying his offer over and over. One date to help someone who had the same exact problem she did.

Just like she did. The thought hit her like a freight train.

She glanced at her phone, mind spinning. "I told you already, he's not my hot billionaire," she said automatically. "Palmer and I would be a disaster together."

"I must disagree on that one," a drawling voice cut in. "I'd be happy to be her hot billionaire anytime she's ready."

No. No, no, no.

Heart hammering, Malia slowly looked up in growing horror. Palmer towered over her, a sexy grin curving his lips, pale green eyes gleaming with satisfaction. That razor-sharp gaze focused only on her, confirming the shocking words he'd just uttered.

Shivers exploded down her spine. He made it clear with every gesture that she was the one he wanted and refused to back off.

If only she weren't beginning to love how it made her feel.

Chapter Thirteen

"Eavesdropping is rude," Malia wrung out, hating that her cheeks were aflame.

"Just innocently walking past and heard my name." He turned to the others. "Good morning, Chiara. Tessa. And I'm sorry, I don't think we've met. I'm Palmer Matterson."

Emma kept blinking as if she was afraid he'd disappear. "Emma Primm. Lovely to meet you, Mr. Matterson."

"Palmer, please. Or Malia's *hot billionaire*. Either will do." Mischief danced over his hard features, giving him that adorable bad boy look.

Everyone laughed merrily.

Malia wished she could sink down under the booth. "Very funny. What are you doing here?"

"I heard Mike's was a great place for breakfast, and I was in the area."

"You live in Manhattan. You drove over an hour for pancakes?"

"No, only about twenty minutes. I have a full day ahead, and you know what they say about breakfast."

"It's the most important meal of the day!" Emma chimed in, staring at him with a tad of hero worship. "Palmer, why don't you join us."

Alarms clanged in Malia's head. "Um, there's no room in the booth, Emma. Sorry."

"We'll drag a chair over—Mike won't mind," Chiara cut in.

Ignoring Malia's warning glare, she jumped up and began moving one of the chairs, but Palmer quickly took over, settling it at the end of the booth so he looked like the king to his queens.

Unbelievable.

"Thank you so much."

"Who's this?" Mike demanded, his inherent nosiness driving him straight over. "You girls seem to be making a lot of new friends lately."

"Palmer Matterson. You must be the famous Mike. Chiara, Tessa, and Malia say the nicest things about you, and I heard you make the best breakfast in the county. I wanted to check it out myself and meet you in person."

Oh boy. Mike preened with male pride at the stroking. "How nice! Glad to have you—what would you like?"

"Coffee, eggs scrambled, bacon, rye toast."

"Sounds good, coming up. Um, how do you know everyone?"

Palmer grinned. "I'm Malia's client. Gave her a hard time for a while, and now I'm trying to show her I'm a nice guy so she'll go out with me."

Malia squeaked with outrage. She felt everyone's gaze hot on her face. "Don't say things like that," she hissed. "We're strictly business partners working with the foundation."

"You're donating to the Quench Foundation?"

Palmer nodded at Mike's question. "I'm working with the Children's Hunger Initiative. Malia's been invaluable. I thought I'd be weighed down with paperwork and too many details, but she's made it both easy and fun. She's an amazing woman."

"Damn straight. Nice suit."

Palmer shrugged. "A bit pretentious but necessary in my role. I own a wedding agency."

Mike studied him for a few moments, then grinned. "A man comfortable in his own skin. I like that. I'll get your eggs." As he turned to leave, he gave Malia a look. "Not sure why you won't give him a chance, Mal. This one doesn't seem like he'd treat you as disposable. You deserve a win."

She shook her head and glared at the seated king. "You're unbelievable. Have you no shame?"

"Not for you."

Tessa looked delighted. "Dayum! He's straight out of a romance novel!"

"Not the kind I read," Malia said.

"Ouch." But Palmer didn't seem bothered in the least. Mike dropped off his coffee, and he immediately sipped the black brew in obvious pleasure. "Emma, tell me about yourself. You look like a teacher. English?"

"Oh my goodness, yes! Well, I was. I'm retired." He drew out the woman, who normally didn't chatter, until she looked at him with something close to adoration.

Maneuvering the conversation politely, he touched on Tessa and Chiara, then turned to Malia. "Did you have another doctor's appointment this week? You never mentioned when you were beginning the shots."

The collective gasp around the table was the final nail in Malia's coffin. "You told him?" Chiara asked, obviously in shock. "He knows?"

"I'm sorry, was I not supposed to mention it?" Concern flickered in his eyes. "I assumed your closest friends knew."

Fisting her hands, Malia fought to get control of the train wreck this conversation was becoming. "Of course they know. I'm not starting the shots until the end of the month."

"I can't believe you told him," Tessa muttered. "You really do like him."

"Stop! I told him because we're working closely together, and he needed to be aware I may be a bit off my game for a few weeks."

Palmer's lifted brow confirmed he'd caught her lie but wouldn't call her out. He set his coffee cup down and regarded the group. "I'm honored Malia trusted me with this. It won't go beyond this table—I won't make the mistake of mentioning it again."

Everyone shot him a look of respect. His words made her insides go a bit mushy. Palmer was frustrating, arrogant, and controlling, but he seemed honestly concerned about her. His consistent pursuit still surprised her, but the man kept showing up, even when she turned him down.

It was getting harder to pretend she didn't enjoy his company. The more she got to know him, the more she liked. The more she craved.

Mike delivered his breakfast, and Palmer continued to dazzle them through the meal until Malia admitted it was a lost cause. He'd officially turned everyone against her.

"I have to head out," Chiara said, sliding out of the booth. "Palmer, it was good to see you again."

"I'll go with you," Tessa added, and Emma quickly agreed. The mass exodus and big grins shot her way made it obvious they wanted to leave them alone.

After the goodbyes were said and they left, Palmer returned the chair and slid into the seat opposite her. "I really like them," he announced, his white teeth crunching on his bacon. He ate with the same focus he approached anything, and it was damn sexy. She wondered if he'd bring all that focus to the bedroom.

"Ah, I'd like to know that thought," he said.

She pushed her own plate away and snorted. "You never will."

His laugh was hearty and zinged her nerve endings with a pleasant buzz. "Now I'm considering it a challenge."

"Is that how you see me? As a challenge? Is that why you're so focused on winning me over?"

The laughter faded. Pale green eyes shimmered with intensity. "No, Malia. A challenge implies once it's won, the person loses interest. I'm looking for more."

She blew out a breath, needing to get on the same page. "I'm planning to be pumped up on hormones so I can have a baby, Palmer. Doesn't that freak you out?"

"No. I mean, as long as you don't want to have a baby next week. You're planning for the future—that's smart."

"What are you looking for? Have you ever been married? Engaged?"

He tapped his fingers against the Formica table. "No."

She waited for more, but he didn't offer. "Have you ever wanted to?"

Regret crossed his face. "No. I believe in relationships that are honest and real and bring another level to life. But as for marriage and kids, I've never sought that out."

She hated the flicker of grief that caught her off guard, but it was a clear sign that he wasn't meant for her. Maybe it would be easier this way. She could retreat behind that information and keep herself safe.

Palmer groaned. "I can see you hiding already, shrinking right in front of me. Dammit, I'm asking you to just feel your way through this with me. I want you—physically, emotionally, mentally. I can't get you off my mind. I want to worship you and make you happy. Get to know you in every way possible. All you have to do is say yes and give me a chance."

Her body shuddered with need. She grew wet between her thighs, thinking of him worshipping her in all sorts of fantastic ways. God, she missed sex, missed the deep connection with a strong male body, missed being held and pleasured. Maybe he was right. Freezing her eggs was supposed to give her the freedom to make reckless choices until she found the right one.

But Palmer Matterson scared the living hell out of her. He was too . . . dangerous.

She swallowed. Time to focus on what she really needed from him. "I was thinking about your proposal regarding the wedding."

He leaned in. "You changed your mind?"

"I'm thinking about it. But I'd need something from you."

"Anything you want."

She hesitated, thinking about her sister's text message. Was it a good idea? She kept refusing to date him and open that pathway, but how could she text her sister back and say she was going solo? She couldn't handle the humiliation. She'd officially run out of time, and this was her only option.

"I'd require an additional favor." Palmer's wolfish grin made her shake her head. "No, not that!"

"Damn."

"A function has come up, and I find myself in a similar situation as you." Malia squirmed with discomfort but spit it out. "I need a date for a family event."

His grin should have been mocking, but it looked genuine. "Your family's driving you nuts, and you need to shut them up with a pretend boyfriend."

Her pride tanked and there was nothing left to do. "Yes. I ran out of time to find a suitable companion. So I'll come to your wedding if you play my plus-one."

"What's the event?"

"My cousin's wedding."

He chuckled and shook his head. "Our lives are running parallel. Why didn't you tell me when I was on my knees, humbly begging for your assistance?"

Malia bristled and tried to salvage some of her ego. "Because I had a date lined up, but it fell through. You're my last hope."

His eyes glittered, and his voice was whisper soft. "Lie."

She couldn't look him in the face. "Look, it's none of your business. You either need my help or you don't, so that's the offer."

"I'd be honored to be your plus-one, Malia." The intimate way he said her name gave her goose bumps.

She crossed her arms in front of her chest and glared. "Stop being so nice. We're pretty much blackmailing each other so we don't have to deal with our siblings."

He quirked a brow. "I'd rather think of it as helping each other out while we explore our connection."

"This is a business deal, pure and simple. I'm still not interested in getting involved with you."

He winked. "Not yet. But once I pull out the big guns, I promise you'll be dazzled."

She couldn't help it. Her gaze dropped.

His rich laughter stroked her ears. "That too, but we'll start slow."

Heat crackled through her like an electric shock. His eyes darkened, sensing her rioting hormones. Oh, she was acting ridiculous. Like Emma tripping over herself with Mike.

Malia cleared her throat and wrestled back the conversation. "I'll forward you the invite. It's in May."

"Ah, two cousin weddings, back-to-back. We're going to have fun."

"I think we should go over the rules."

That seemed to give him pause. He studied her thoughtfully. "What type of rules?"

She snapped into business mode. "Rules dictating our behavior. We also need to educate the other on some primary family dynamics and knowledge. The more facts we're armed with, the smoother both evenings will go."

"Hmm. Never thought of rules before, but I guess prep work isn't a bad idea. Should I compose flash cards?"

She squinted with suspicion. Was he teasing her? "This is serious! You can't show up and fake it. Your charm won't be enough to convince my sisters you're real. They're already suspecting I'll hire an escort."

"Did you try that one, too?"

She patted her braids and looked away. "Once."

"Me, too. Disaster. That was the worst summer of my life—they all thought I was dating prostitutes from a high-class agency. My mother wept on the phone and begged me to go back to church." He shuddered. "I went legit after that."

Malia couldn't help her chuckle. "Me, too. He was so obviously out of his element when Zinnia grilled him. Just kept smiling and nodding like she'd accept that as answers. Then she googled his picture and found he was fresh from an agency. I'm still making up for that one."

"How are two attractive, successful, intelligent people this desperate to find a decent date?" he asked. "If we swiped left, would things be easier?"

"Lord, no. Tried that, too. I had no idea it meant you wanted a straight hookup. I just wanted a decent dinner conversation."

Palmer laughed again, and she relaxed, enjoying this easy side of him. Even though he looked hot and intimidating in his sharp black suit and red tie, hair slicked back neatly, right now it felt like he was in jeans and sneakers, hanging with her over breakfast.

Malia shook herself back to reality. "Rules," she reminded him.

"Sorry, right. We should create cheat sheets and meet to quiz each other. We don't have much time."

"No need to meet, we can do it over email."

"I disagree. Cold facts on paper are different from sharing face-to-face. Besides, we need to get comfortable with each other's company."

She hated to admit it, but he was right. "Fine. Each of us should create a family tree. Go over the highlights of our siblings and parents."

"What about us?" he asked. "We need to know more about each other."

Nerves shredded her belly. She waved her hand in the air. "I don't think so. If we focus on talking to our families, they won't have time to give us a full grilling."

"Are you kidding? Malia, my sisters are going to drag you off and ask you a million questions. You have to be prepped to answer them."

She stuck out her lip stubbornly. "I'll talk about work. About the Children's Hunger Initiative. About how we met through advertising. About our companies. There's plenty to keep them fed."

He tapped his fingers faster. "Oh, you think so? Let's do a practice run. If you can answer these, we'll be good to go."

This was stupid. "Go ahead."

"When was our first kiss?"

She opened her mouth to answer, then shut it.

He continued. "How long have we been seeing each other? What was our first date? What was the last wedding I worked on? What hobbies do we share together? What are our favorite restaurants? Do you come see me in Manhattan or Piermont? Describe each of my places and which you like better. And that's just for starters. Sure, they'll ask about work, but they're more interested in what we're building together. Are you prepared for that?"

No. Panic hit. Was this a good idea? Maybe she should just give up and go single. Take the beating and deal with it like a grown-ass woman.

As if he sensed her defeat, Palmer slid his hand across the table and captured hers. The touch of his skin made her jerk from the shock. Malia looked up, caught in the drill of those fiery green eyes.

"We can do this. Together. Gain ourselves a bit of peace from the endless pressure. Do this with me, Malia."

Warm, strong fingers stroked her palm with slow, deliberate motions. She glanced at their entwined hands, so innocent looking, but knew this man had a sexual power over her that would take all her will to deny. They'd be together for two events, pretending to be intimate. Could she handle it?

The challenge in his gaze stirred Malia's own competitive spirit. Yes. She'd finally be able to quell her family's concerns. It was a win-win. She just needed to keep her focus and her panties tightly on.

She pulled back, her skin still tingling. He looked slightly mournful from the loss of her touch but allowed her the space. "Fine. We'll meet and share information about our families and each other."

"Good."

"But there's one additional rule I'm requiring."

"What?"

"No serious touching."

"You have to be kidding me."

Malia shook her head. "I'm not. No slow dancing. No public displays of affection. We can hold hands, but no kissing or inappropriate hands on my body parts." Feeling relieved and back in control, she waited for him to argue, whine, or try to convince her otherwise.

Slowly, he propped his elbows on the table and leaned in. His gaze raked over her, filled with determination and raw hunger. "Sure about that, sweetheart?"

Her belly dropped to her toes. The breath caught in her lungs at the smoldering heat suddenly blazing from his aura. "Y-yes."

His whiskey-rich voice was like a shot of sex. "I won't break a promise. So if you eventually want me to touch you, you'll have to ask me nice and proper."

Steam rose from the center of her thighs. Her body went hot and cold with the image of being forced to beg for his touch, a crazy alpha move that turned her on so much she was afraid she'd combust right in front of him.

Bastard.

Her throat barely managed to work. "That won't be a problem."

A hint of a smile lifted his lips. "Another challenge?" he murmured.

"No," she said with a bit of temper. "Remember, for me this is strictly to get my family off my back. I'm not interested in an affair, relationship, or one-night stand with you."

"Duly noted." Instead of seeming concerned or pissed off, he acted pleased with himself.

What kind of Jedi mind tricks was he playing on her? And why did she care? All she had to do was stick to the plan and the rules, and she'd get everything she needed from him.

He reached for his wallet and left money on the table. "I have to head out."

"I can pay."

His warning glance made her put her purse down. "Not with me. I'll write up my list and send it over. How's this weekend for a meetup? My place—seven p.m.?"

"How about here instead?"

A frown creased his brow. "We'll be going over personal stuff. My place will be more appropriate—I'll have dinner for you and send my driver." When she still hesitated, his face softened. "Malia, I gave you my word. I won't make you uncomfortable."

"I know! Okay, fine. Your place. Wait—which one?"

"I'm at the house on weekends."

"Noted."

Palmer's quick grin eased some of the tension. "I see you're studying already. Soon, you'll be an expert on me."

"Could be pretty dangerous," she teased. "I'll know all your weaknesses."

"Right now, I only have one." His gaze drilled, probed, and drove his meaning straight home. "See you Saturday."

He left, his words drifting in the air like a threat.

Or a promise.

Chapter Fourteen

When the driver dropped her at Palmer's house, she realized the extent of his wealth.

Malia should have asked for an additional million for the foundation.

The multitiered mansion was set on a rise that looked out over the Hudson River. Timber beams and glass crisscrossed in an architectural orgy of modern and rustic, complete with a massive wraparound porch with cedar flooring and carved wooden rockers. Various floating decks with magnificent french doors were built into the structure.

Nerves fluttered in her belly when he greeted her. She hated feeling like this was a first date rather than a recon session to fool his entire family. But Palmer eased her tension with a warm smile and welcomed her inside.

"Your house is stunning," she said.

He beamed. "Thank you. A buddy of mine built it. I love the hustle of the city, but I also crave some privacy away from the madness. I used to go upstate for vacations where my parents would rent a cabin, and I always loved that type of home. So he built me something that combined it all."

Malia took in the interior with a greedy gaze, admiring the high loft ceilings, circular staircase that looked handmade, and the open concept layout that combined all the rooms into one large space. Warm Tuscan colors gave off a masculine vibe, but her jaw dropped at the kitchen.

It was a baker's paradise. A butcher-block island cut straight through the space, outfitted with eight leather stools. Two Wolf ovens took up one wall, and a massive refrigerator was set into the cabinets so there was no break from the flow of wood. She'd never seen so many appliances and accessories—espresso maker, food processor, a stack of hand-painted mixing bowls, a pasta and bread maker—all lined up like marching soldiers ready to do his bidding. The rich scents of garlic and sizzling bacon hung in the air, making her stomach growl.

"Do you cook?" she asked in astonishment, making her way deeper inside his unusual man cave.

"Of course. Baking is my specialty, but I can produce a decent dinner."

"You bake? I thought you only did those cupcakes because Al was desperate."

His laugh rumbled from his chest. "He was, but it's also a hobby of mine. I thought of being a pastry chef for a while. Being in the kitchen calms me, especially when the air smells like sugar and comfort." He was a drool-worthy sight in dark jeans and a casual green T-shirt that made his eyes ignite on a whole other level. His hair was damp and combed back from his forehead, but there was a slight wave at the back that hinted at a stubborn cowlick. His feet were bare. He pulled out a seat for her at the counter and held up two bottles of wine. "Red or white?"

She dropped her laptop case at her feet and slid onto the stool. "Red, please."

He poured her a glass, and she took a few precious moments to resettle herself. Already, she was learning new details about Palmer that fascinated her. Hopefully more bad qualities would come from the process to help balance things out.

"I hope you eat pasta?" he asked.

"There hasn't been a carb I haven't worshipped."

"Good. I make a killer carbonara sauce, so we're having that with some rigatoni and a simple salad."

"Sounds delicious. I figured we were doing takeout."

Palmer made a face as he began expertly chopping peppers and olives on the cutting board. "I'm a bit spoiled when it comes to food. Once I began making money, that was what I put most of it toward. I began shopping at those fabulous Italian delis, the fish market, and Whole Foods."

"Was your mom a big cook?" Malia asked curiously.

"She did a decent job, but you can imagine raising five kids was a handful. We always had a hot meal, and she taught me there's no leftover that can't be transformed into culinary greatness." Pride edged his voice as he spoke about his mother. "When Dad lost his job, we hit some hard times for a while. Unemployment ran out. We almost lost our house. Mom went back to nursing to keep us afloat, and as we got older, she switched to full-time. Things were righted, so we got lucky." A shadow passed over his face. "Many aren't."

"I don't hear of too many people coming from large families anymore," she commented, sipping the wine. It tasted of blackberries and spice with a rich finish that was delicious. "They bring a whole set of challenges."

"Yeah, they also teach you intrinsically about selflessness. I learned early on that nothing was truly mine. We were required to share—none of that labeling or hiding treats." He dumped more veggies into the washed lettuce and began tossing them with large wooden spoons. "Of course, once I got my first job, I used that paycheck to get my own damn Hershey bar, and when Jane told Mom I wouldn't share, Mom told me anything bought with my own money was mine. Felt so good to finally taunt my sister with something she couldn't have."

Malia laughed. "You didn't share?"

His sigh was full of regret. "No, I did, and she was still mean to me." Palmer moved on to the dressing, and she watched with fascination as

135

he measured out olive oil, apple cider vinegar, garlic, and a bunch of herbs before shaking it up and drizzling it over the salad. The result was almost festive—the various colors popped from a mass of rich green. "Do you cook?"

"To survive. It's not my favorite thing," she admitted. "I'd rather work and grab takeout, which isn't so bad now that I can do Uber Eats. I can get a relatively healthy meal."

"True." He finished the sauce, muttering with satisfaction after tasting it, and began plating.

A hunk of toasted garlic bread came out of the oven. Malia tried not to focus on his rear as he bent over the stove, denim molding to all those hard muscled parts her fingers itched to touch.

Down, girl.

"We can eat right here if you're comfortable."

"Sounds good." She looked down at her bowl, which was artfully arranged, a perfect amount of freshly grated Parmesan sprinkled on top.

He sat down across from her, bowed his head, and said his prayer under his breath. She immediately dropped her fork and followed suit. When she lifted her head, he was smiling at her, and her heart squeezed with pleasure.

The first bite of pasta exploded with flavor. The creamy sauce with the crunch of bacon and al dente pasta made this her new favorite meal. She tried not to moan like an animal. "Palmer, this is incredible."

"I'm happy you like it. Just make sure you save room for dessert." They ate in silence for a bit, enjoying their food.

She dipped bread in the sauce and nibbled. "Before we get into the family charts and other nitty-gritty details, we should agree on the party line. I told my sister I was dating someone, but he may need to work."

"So you didn't have another date?"

She wanted to squirm, but his gaze was playful. "No. It was too embarrassing to tell you."

"You can tell me anything, Malia." His tone was serious, brows drawing down into a slight frown. "There's literally nothing you can't say to me. It's important you know that."

A longing to test his promise cut through her. She couldn't imagine a relationship based on such lovely intimacy and honesty. It was what she dreamed about but hadn't come close to yet. "I think that's easy to say for men but hard to follow through with," she said slowly.

"True. But I want that from you. For us."

Wariness made her stop eating and stare. "There is no us."

"Sorry, didn't mean to spook you. I meant *us* in whatever capacity you want. Business partners. Or friends."

She still didn't like the route he was going, but she couldn't announce she refused to be his friend. After all, she was in his beautiful house, eating a meal he'd prepared for her. The entire scene screamed of intimacy. Malia decided to let it go.

"What was your favorite and least favorite thing about growing up in a big family?" he asked.

"My favorite was the family dinners. No matter what sports, dates, or fights took place, our asses were in the chair for dinner together the majority of the week. We were told we could be mad at each other, but we still had to share a meal. Usually by the end of it, we'd forgotten who was feuding with who and moved on."

"I like that."

"Me, too. My least? Besides having my wardrobe raided all the time, exactly what I'm going through now with my sisters." Malia concentrated on her plate, not wanting to look him in the eye. "They act like the bosses of my life. Just because I want to make different choices doesn't mean I'm wrong. They're obsessed with me following a specific timeline, and the idea I'm not married yet drives them crazy." She let out a sad laugh. "Like it's their disappointment and not mine."

He lifted a brow. "Do you feel like a disappointment because you're not married yet?"

The question was too direct. But his earlier words stuck in her mind, and Malia wondered if she could test it and be honest about it all. "Yeah, I do. Which is terrible. I sound selfish and privileged, like I need some true love or man to complete me. I'm happy, don't get me wrong, and I appreciate everything I have. But there's a part of me that feels . . ." She trailed off. She didn't want to say it—not aloud.

But Palmer leaned in, and his voice was so gentle. "Feels what, Malia?"

Ah, hell. She swallowed hard. "Feels empty. Silly, right?"

"Not at all. Feelings are just feelings, and they're valid. Don't let anyone try to get you to rationalize them away."

His response startled her. She took another sip of wine and regarded him across the counter. "That was a good answer."

He shrugged. "Just being real."

"What about you? You said you don't believe in marriage or permanent relationships. Is your family worried about that?"

"I never sought out commitments before because I've never needed them. I enjoy being in a relationship when I am—I experienced two healthy ones the past few years. But when they ended, I never felt the need to chase or offer more. Maybe it's not part of my makeup." He swirled his wine around his glass as if deep in thought. "My family is like yours—they look at all these weddings surrounding me and see me lonely and unhappy. They don't believe I'm complete without someone in my life."

Malia wondered about the women who'd previously claimed him. "Why did you break up?"

His hesitation warned her she wouldn't like his answer. "They wanted to get married. I didn't."

Sadness overtook her for a few moments. Palmer would never be her future husband because they wanted opposite things. Why did the fact bother her? She didn't want anything to do with him, anyway.

Except sex. The man was hell on her rioting hormones, and the thought of one dirty, endless night was an itch deep under her skin. But it wasn't worth it. One night of sex could lead to bad things.

Like her wanting more.

Malia redirected the conversation into neutral waters. "Let's go back to the plan. I came up with a script for us that should work. We met at work and have been dating for three months. I think that's enough time to begin getting a bit serious but still new enough we don't know everything about each other."

"Agreed. You gave me a hard time in the boardroom and refused to be nice to me. You said no the first time I asked you out. My family will like that."

She smiled. "You sent me flowers to apologize for your boorish behavior, and I agreed to give you a chance."

"I took you for sushi, and we closed the restaurant because we couldn't stop talking."

"Our second date was lunch. We ate at Bryant Park Grill. You slid your hand across the table and our fingers met, and suddenly, we were holding hands." Her breath caught a bit as she spun the tale that was becoming their story. "On our third date, you invited me over."

"I cooked. We baked cookies together afterward, and I fed one to you. That was when we had our first kiss."

Her tummy slid to her toes. Her gaze fastened to his mouth, pressed in a firm line. The air came alive and crackled with latent electricity. "We didn't want to tell our families because we wanted time to see if this could be real."

His voice dropped. "And it is. So I invited you to the wedding to finally introduce you to my family."

Her blood roared. Her palms dampened, and it was torture not to slide her hands across the counter and touch him. "Yes."

They stared at one another for a long time. "Malia?"

"Yeah?"

"I want you to bake cookies with me tonight."

She fought her way out of the fog. The innocent request seemed to hold undertones of danger.

"I want you to taste one of my favorite recipes."

Why did it sound like he was seducing her? She was going out of her mind. "Oh, I'm not a great baker. Maybe I should sit this one out."

A tiny smile settled on his full lips. "When I tell my mother we made cookies together, I don't want to lie to her."

His words seared through her like a hot poker. This was the exact moment she needed to pull back and take control of the situation. Lines were getting blurry. Dessert took on a whole new level of meaning. "I'm not sure about this, Palmer."

"I am. Once you taste them, you'll thank me."

She shifted back and forth, sensing danger ahead. "I don't think—"

"The cookies are white chocolate with coconut and macadamia nuts."

"God, yes. Okay. Let's bake."

Palmer began to laugh, and she laughed with him, the tight tension wafting away like it had been only her imagination.

~

Palmer snuck a glance over at Malia. She was measuring the flour with total concentration. Her brow creased in a frown, and she checked the level twice, shaking the cup so clouds of flour burst in the air.

Malia had rolled up the sleeves of her yellow blouse and donned an apron to keep her white capris clean. Her braids were twisted into a loose knot, showing off her swanlike neck. The golden brown of her skin was kissed with a slight sheen of sweat and a touch of flour. He wanted to kiss her nose, then those gorgeous lips. He wanted to hold her close and make her laugh and then make her moan.

But that wasn't going to happen tonight.

"I'm done with all the dry ingredients. What's next?" she asked.

"We're going to combine it with the wet ingredients in the mixer. I've already chopped up the nuts and chocolate and measured the shredded coconut."

"You did all that while I was just in charge of this?"

He couldn't help but grin at her disappointment. "This is your first time, you're learning the steps. Next time I'll give you more duties." He tutored her in the fine art of mixing until the dough was perfect. "Now, do you want fun shapes or just round?"

"Shapes."

"I thought you'd say that." He whipped open the top drawer and took out a bunch of cookie cutters. "We got gingerbread men, flowers, Disney characters, and—"

"Disney!" She grabbed a Minnie Mouse in delight. "This is so cool!"

"Disney fan, huh?"

"Who isn't? Why do you have rocket ships and airplanes?"

He shot her a look. "'Cause I'm a guy. I like big things that can fly."

"Got it." They began creating their cookies and placed them on the greased cookie sheet. "Who taught you how to bake?"

"All my sisters had basic skills, so I learned different things depending on what they made. When I started getting good, they bought me more equipment and I became the official dessert supplier. Even Mom asked me to wrap up Christmas cookies for gifts at the hospital."

"That's cute."

He scowled. "Baking is highly skilled and takes precision. It's certainly not cute."

"Sorry." He watched her fight a smile, and pleasure buzzed in his veins. She was so easy to talk to. He hadn't enjoyed an evening at home like this in a long time.

Malia broke the brief silence. "Can I ask you a question?"

"You can ask me anything."

"Will your family have any concerns that I'm half Black?"

He paused and placed the cutter down. "No. Will yours worry that I'm white?"

"No. Davinia's husband is white, and they have two boys. What about your family? Will there be any other mixed couples at the wedding?"

"My brother-in-law, Lincoln, is Black—he's married to Georgia, and they have two girls. My cousin Jarod is married to Nina, who's from Nigeria. They'll be there."

Her shoulders visibly relaxed. "Okay, cool. I just didn't know, and every family is different."

"Did you have issues with that before? Dating out of your culture?"

She seemed to seriously consider the question. "It doesn't bother me if I'm into someone, but I also know because I'm mixed, a lot of guys think of me as more white. Especially since I'm light-skinned."

He studied her face. "I bet that could get a little weird."

She laughed. "Yeah, it does. My father's family is from the Bahamas, and Mom is Irish, Scottish, and French. Both of their parents were supportive, so I had close relationships with my grandparents. I love learning about each side, but it does get a bit confusing when you feel you have to choose sometimes."

He kept quiet, wanting to hear more.

She continued. "My public school was pretty diverse, but it was hard to decide what groups I wanted to belong to. It's difficult when people term you too white, or judge you because they think you're not dark enough to be really Black. My sisters and I all struggled with that when we were younger, but I've moved beyond being labeled or judged. My Black heritage is important to me and I love that part of myself."

Palmer loved her honesty and could only imagine growing up with that type of inner struggle. "You don't need to choose anymore?"

Her smile stole his breath. "I choose by love. I choose both. Chiara and Tessa became my best friends, and that was my choice. As I got older, I had more opportunities to work with Black women and other people of color, and I was glad we decided early on that Quench wasn't going to be a whitewashed company. Everyone agreed."

He loved her answer. "The world is a bit jacked up with race. I can't imagine the hard choices and stuff you had to go through. And I'm not going to tell you I don't see color, because I've never had to see it. I had opportunities too many people didn't."

She didn't argue with him or try to make him feel better. Just nodded. A thought hit him that he felt he should also address. "In the beginning, when I was trying so hard to get you to date me, was I too . . . pushy?"

"Yes."

He winced. "Another thing I never thought of. God, did I ever make you feel threatened? I'd never felt anything so intense; I never imagined how it might look. Here I was assuming you should trust me, when I hadn't proven anything to you yet. Malia, I'm sorry if—"

She cut him off, stepping closer. "No, it's okay. I never felt that from you. Yes, you were arrogant and pushy, but it never was a power thing. I knew it was different." She gave a tiny snort. "If not, Tessa would've taken you apart before I was able to. Trust me."

He relaxed, treasuring her honesty. "I'm glad. It's time I start seeing things more clearly. But I do want to say my family has always been open and loving to everyone."

"I'm sure they are. Hey, thanks for discussing this with me. It's important to know before I get there." She lifted her sticky hands. "Done."

"Okay, let's make some magic." They washed their hands, and he slid the pan in the oven, then set a timer. "Please tell me you don't like crispy cookies."

"The softer the better."

"I knew we'd be a perfect match." He caught her genuine smile before she seemed to catch herself and pull back. But the hours together had done their work. She was definitely more comfortable with him in his environment. Her muscles were relaxed, and her amber eyes held less shadow. He wished the evening would never end. "One last glass of wine? You don't have to drive."

She looked at it longingly. "Half a glass. I have a full day tomorrow."

He watched Malia sip the ruby liquid and the way her tongue swiped across her bottom lip to gather the lingering drop. His pants tightened, so he walked around the counter to gain some distance. "Any other questions before our big premiere?" he asked.

"Hmm. Georgia is the ELA teacher, Jane is the nurse, and Veronica is home with the three kids?"

"Yep. And Christine is the yoga teacher. Who are their husbands?"

She ticked them off on her fingers. "Raoul, Lincoln, Ryan, and Matthew?"

"Nice job. I don't think you're expected to know all the kids. What are my mother's pet peeves?"

"Sloppy eating and not asserting my opinion."

"Be careful if there's soup."

Malia rolled her eyes while he laughed. "I have impeccable manners."

"Then I think we're ready."

"I think we are."

Something about the tone in her voice created a longing to close the distance. Palmer cupped his glass with both hands so he'd keep them off her.

As if she sensed the same energy, she wandered around his place, taking in her surroundings. She stopped in front of his bookshelves. "Did you read all these, too?" she asked. This time, there was no challenge, just curiosity.

"Most of them. Some are keepsakes—signed copies from authors or limited editions. I try to keep them pristine, so a lot of times I'll pick up an older copy so I don't have to be careful."

"I break the spine and dog-ear the pages."

He shuddered. "I finally found your major flaw."

She laughed. "I call it true book love." Her fingers trailed along the straight spines, and he tried not to imagine what she'd feel like against his naked skin. "Poetry, too?"

"Guilty. You have no idea what an asset that's been for the wedding business."

"How involved do you get in the day-to-day planning now? I know you mentioned you were running your cousin's wedding, but are you more hands-off? Or are you calling the caterers and florists making sure everything's good?"

"No, I'm past that now. I have handpicked teams depending on the couple's personality and needs. I picture myself as the overseer, but I do work closely with all my teams—I'm on standby for any disasters or help. That's the backbone of my business, and I never want to lose sight of it." He thought of Pandora on her wedding day. He'd attended briefly because she was a high-profile client with television cameras lined up outside, so he wanted to make sure everything was tight. Once he caught the joy on her face, the feeling of satisfaction rivaled no other. Knowing he had a small part in helping her get there kept him motivated to run Endless Vows and be the best.

The timer rang. He donned oven mitts and slid the trays out of the oven, testing the cookies with a toothpick. *Perfect.* "Okay, now it's time for the best part. The tasting."

"It smells so good," Malia said, joining him.

Instead of warm cookies, the scent of her skin drifted to his nostrils—reminding him of ripe summer plums and rainfall. His arm brushed hers as he slid the spatula underneath and scooped one up.

"Aren't they supposed to cool?"

"Yep, but I never make it." She chuckled as he blew on the heated treat, trying not to burn his fingers. A piece broke off from the corner. "Here, taste this." He tried to hand it to her, but it was crumbling, so he automatically brought it to her mouth. Her lips parted and she received the morsel on her tongue.

A sexy moan broke from her lips. He imagined the tastes of white chocolate and coconut melting warm and gooey over her tongue. Her eyes half closed in ecstasy. "Oh God, it's so good. It's like a—" She halted the rest of her sentence, her gaze suddenly wide and locked on his.

A ravenous hunger tore at his gut, a primitive male cry to touch, taste, possess. "An orgasm," he whispered.

Palmer moved forward so they were barely touching. The air thickened and crackled with sexual energy. He studied the golden rim of her irises, the lush curve of her lips, and the sharp angle of her cheekbones. His hands shook with the need to reach out, but he kept still.

Slowly, as if in a dream, she rose up on her tiptoes and leaned in so their mouths were barely a whisper apart. He caught the flare of want in her eyes and shuddered, longing to step in, lower his mouth, and kiss her the way he'd been dreaming of this past year.

"Malia." His voice rasped into a half groan. "You're in charge."

She blinked, as if coming out of a fog. He wondered if she could hear his heart beating, sense his arousal pressing against his jeans. He locked down his muscles and waited for her decision, praying she'd pull his lips to hers so he finally knew her taste and texture and how it would feel to have her hands all over his needy body.

Malia backed up. "I . . . I can't."

He immediately brought his hands up and eased away. Freaking her out too early wasn't in the plan. Palmer wanted her to be one hundred percent eager to welcome him into her bed with no regrets. "It's okay, Malia." He let out a ragged breath, but his lips twisted in a half smile. "I think it was the cookies. They're like an aphrodisiac."

She relaxed, obviously eager to follow his lead. "You're probably right." She began to gather up her stuff. "I better go. I think we've got this covered."

"Wait a moment." He quickly packaged up a few cookies and handed her the bag. "For later."

"Thanks." She fumbled with her purse and flew to the door. "I'll see you next Saturday."

"Let me know if you need anything beforehand. My driver's waiting out front."

Palmer watched her go and stood for a while in the sudden silence. It was as if the room had become limp and airless. Malia's presence had brought a spark of life to the quiet he normally sought, a hint of what could be for him if she became a part of his world.

On Saturday, she'd meet his family. She thought he was using her to make a good impression on them so he'd be free of their expectations. But he intended to use their time together for a much bigger purpose.

To show her another part of himself—one he rarely invited a woman to view.

For the first time, Palmer craved sharing himself with another without surface niceties or bullshit. Malia Evergreen was real, and he wasn't afraid to knock down all her walls and show her all the ways he could make her happy. She deserved so much more than the long line of losers who couldn't appreciate the gift in front of them. She'd lost her confidence in herself and in relationships. In hope.

Palmer was going to give it all back to her.

He stood in the kitchen eating a cookie and thinking about the possibilities ahead.

Chapter Fifteen

Malia walked into the reception and caught her breath. She smoothed down the sleek black gown that clung to her hips and pooled to the floor in a shimmering wave. The material was beaded with silver so it sparkled when the light caught it, but the simple, dark material was classic for any wedding. A silver lariat chain emphasized the deep V neckline and perfectly tailored cut. Feeling confident in her appearance was important when she met new people.

It also hadn't hurt when Palmer's eyes popped the moment he saw her.

The ceremony was held at sunset at the Lighthouse in Chelsea Piers. Looking out across the water, she'd watched the couple recite their vows against the fiery backdrop of explosive colors, the sun an orange disk hovering in the sky. Boats gently rocked on the Hudson River, adding to the picture-perfect view.

Cocktail hour was outside and a complete blur. She'd held tight to Palmer's hand as she was maneuvered into endless groups and introduced, sipping wine and nibbling on appetizers while casually chatting. There had been no time to really dive deep into family dialogues, so Malia had used the hour to catch her breath and prepare for the reception.

That's where the real work would begin.

The decor was rich and elegant, with gorgeous wood floors and lantern lighting casting a shadowed glow. The colors were yellow and cream, depicted in the endless roses and peonies, and the tables were banquet seating cut up into smaller tables rather than the usual round. Floor-to-ceiling windows surrounded the space and offered the sight of night falling softly around them.

"This is stunning," she whispered as Palmer led her over to their assigned table. The wedding party was lining up, and guests were streaming in to grab another drink and claim their seats.

"It's a great venue and ticks a lot of boxes for my brides and grooms. We were worried about the weather and exact time of sunset, but my team timed it perfectly."

He'd introduced her to Lacey and Aidan, who seemed a bit nervous that their boss was in attendance. Palmer spent a few moments talking to them, going over every last detail of the schedule—from the cake to the assigned dances and the special dessert and cordial bar. Malia was amused at their eager effort to please him—and a bit of hero worship as they nodded and listened—but there was also an underlying respect that warmed her.

"You're not going to get all control freaky on me, are you?" she teased afterward, when she caught him frowning at one of the bartenders who said he was out of a certain chardonnay. Palmer had immediately retrieved a manager, and within minutes, a happy guest was drinking her favorite wine.

He grinned, his fingers warm and strong around hers. "Maybe. It's hard stepping back when this is your industry. I want everything to be perfect for them."

Her heart softened at the remark. "It already is. They look so happy."

"Yeah, Tom is a good guy, and Barbara was always my fave cousin. Ouch!" He whirled around from the slap to his head.

"You always said *I* was your fave cuz!" a feminine voice shrieked. The woman had a head full of explosive red curls, a slinky black dress, and heels that were easily five inches. Malia would have broken her neck wearing them, but damn, they were beautiful—bright yellow with gold spikes that were both funky and elegant. "Have you been lying all these years?"

He laughed and rubbed his head. "You still give a good wallop, Ella. I may have a concussion."

"Don't be a baby, whiner boy. Who's this?"

Malia smiled at the thrilling demand in Ella's voice. "I'm Malia. And I think if you take your shoes off to dance, they'll be coming home with me."

Pleasure shone in the woman's hazel eyes. "Oh, I like you. Finally, someone I can dish with. I'm Ella, and I'm Palmer's favorite cousin. I'm at table four, so come talk to me later. Better yet, grab me for a dance. He may be a hotshot moneybags around here, but he can't dance for shit." Ella threw her head back and cackled, then rushed off to the next person.

Palmer looked hurt. "I can dance."

"I'm sure you can."

"No, for real."

Malia pressed her lips together and took her seat. Palmer's family filed in and gathered at the table just as the lights dimmed and the announcement of the wedding party began. She was relieved for the delay in table chatter, even though she'd immediately liked Palmer's sisters and found them easy to engage with. His mom seemed nice, too, but there was something about meeting the matriarch of the family that made her nervous.

The introductions were accompanied by loud yelling, hand clapping, and booming music. The bridesmaids' canary-yellow dresses were bright and hopeful, and the wedding couple made their grand entrance dancing enthusiastically. Yeah, this was going to be a party wedding.

Her favorite type.

They watched the newlyweds' first dance, to John Legend's "All of Me," a classic favorite, and Malia found herself sneaking glances at her date.

He was hot.

He'd warned her he looked hot in a tux, but nothing prepared her for his James Bond–type entrance when he stepped out of the car. Classic, conservative black Armani had been tailored impeccably, emphasizing every lean, hard muscle. His Cartier rose-gold watch glittered in the light, along with diamond cuff links with his initials on them. His shoes were wing-tipped Italian leather. He smelled of spice and sin. Freshly shaved, thick gray hair tamed neatly back from his forehead, the man was devastating, carrying himself with an innate confidence that stole her breath. He was seduction in motion, and her body immediately perked to attention, ready to play.

It was going to be a long night. Especially with her rules solidly in play of no touching. Malia finally admitted she'd instituted them more for her, not him.

Suddenly, John Legend faded and morphed to "Despacito." On cue to the music change, Barbara spun out of her new husband's arms, faced the crowd, and ripped off the train of her dress. The guests screamed with delight as she began to boogie synchronized steps to roaring approval.

Palmer closed his eyes in a painful expression.

A giggle threatened. "I guess you got the dress tailored in time," she whispered.

"Yep. Though, at this moment, I'm regretting it."

The dance was short, and everyone began to settle. Palmer leaned over and whispered in her ear. "Get ready for the inquisition." Goose bumps broke out on her skin from the intimate rush of his breath.

"Malia! We're all so excited to meet you." Georgia clapped her hands together in zeal. All the husbands were crowded together at one end of the table, leaving the ladies on the other side. Seems the sisters wanted to dish privately, and something told Malia she was the main course. "Tell us everything. How did you meet?"

She glanced up at Palmer. "Work, actually. I was his advertising rep for Quench."

"She was in charge of making sure I paid buckets of money for ads."

"I was in charge of making Endless Vows more profitable," she retorted, gaining an approving look from his oldest sister, Veronica. "I didn't like him at first. Thought he was bossy and arrogant."

His mother, Dolly, gave a delighted grin. Her gray hair was styled in a sleek bob that curled under her chin, and she wore a sky-blue dress that flowed when she walked. Malia liked the quiet elegance that seemed a part of her. She had laugh lines by her mouth and eyes, and her pale green eyes matched her son's. "Palmer, you've finally met a woman who won't take your guff."

He gave a masculine snort. "You have no idea. She put me through my paces before she finally agreed to go out with me."

Jane sighed. "That's so romantic. How long have you been dating?"

"Three months?" Malia cocked her head in question. "Is that about right?"

"Three months, four days to be exact," he said.

Christine studied them intensely for a while. The youngest sister of the crew sported a willowy body with long limbs and reminded Malia of a ballerina. Her long blonde hair streamed down her back with no fancy styling. Her dress was a basic floral sheath, and she radiated an aura of serenity, even as her gaze sharpened on them and seemed to be sifting through each of their words, almost like she was looking for holes in their story. Malia briefly wondered what she'd do if Christine jumped from the table and accused them of lying. It was freaking her out.

"How did he change your mind?" Christine asked, nibbling on a piece of bread. "What did he do to convince you to give him a chance?"

"Gradually wore me down until I promised him one dinner, and if I still didn't like him, he'd leave me alone."

Dolly shot her son a chiding look. "I raised him to be more polite than that toward women."

"I was polite!" Palmer interjected. "You guys don't realize this woman is a shark in the boardroom."

Veronica waved her hand in the air. The light sparkled on her fancy rings and stack of bracelets. She looked like a fashion model, with impeccable makeup, a short red dress that showed off her ripe curves, and a fancy upsweep to her honey-brown hair. Malia knew that as a mom stuck at home with kids all day, she'd probably jumped at the opportunity to dress up and go out for an adult evening. It was exactly what Davinia was going through. "Tell us a little bit about your job, Malia. Is it all selling ads to companies for—Quench, right?"

"Yes, Quench. It's a media company for women that I founded with my best friends. I just switched roles, though. I'm in charge of our new not-for-profit arm called the Quench Foundation." She squeezed Palmer's arm in gratitude. The muscles clenched under her touch. "Palmer invested a large amount in the Children's Hunger Initiative."

"She's a good saleswoman," he murmured with a smile.

Christine pursed her lips, regarding them thoughtfully.

"That's so nice," Jane said. "He's always been generous with his profits, but I love that you two can do this together."

"It's been a real bonding experience," Malia said with a straight face.

Palmer cleared his throat and reached for his wine.

"It must be hard to make time for each other with your busy schedules," Christine said casually. "Where do you live, Malia?"

Oh yeah. Christine was going to be a challenge. Malia buckled down, her competitive spirit soaring. It was imperative she believe them by the time they left the wedding or Malia would feel like a failure. "Nyack, so it's perfect when Palmer stays at his house on the weekends. I love it there—the architecture is amazing and allows us some quiet time."

His sisters all agreed, obviously entranced by her answers.

Christine squinted with suspicion. "So what do you think about his hobby?"

For a moment, she panicked. She looked over to Palmer, who held her gaze steadily and gave a small nod in reminder. It came to her in a rush. "Oh, baking! Isn't that a wonderful hobby for a woman to take advantage of? I asked him where he learned, and he said from all of you. And then I kind of swooned, because it was obvious how much he cares about his family."

"That's so sweet," Georgia squealed. "I cannot handle this—it's been forever since I've seen Palmer so happy. Do you have any siblings, Malia?"

"I do. Three sisters, and I'm the youngest. We're very close."

Jane shook her head. "You both have so much in common."

Dolly radiated joy, glancing back and forth between them as if they were about to declare their engagement. "I knew you'd find it eventually," she whispered, reaching across the table and grabbing her son's hand. "This is what you always deserved."

Red rose in his cheeks. "Okay, Mom, please don't scare her off."

Everyone laughed except Christine. "Did he bake anything for you yet?" she asked.

"Actually, he did. The most amazing cookies—his favorite. White chocolate coconut macadamia."

"I see." She sipped at her champagne, falling eerily silent.

Malia was saved by the servers as they began with their first course of a seafood corn chowder and a mesclun salad with crisp green beans drizzled in a lemon-honey dressing. She bowed her head and said thanks along with Palmer and his family. The simple gesture made eating seem more thoughtful.

She made sure she used her best table manners for Dolly, relieved she knew which fork to use and not to put her elbows on the table. She finished her soup without making a sound and started in on her salad. Conversation flowed, and she easily batted out answers, most of what they'd studied up on. Palmer's sisters seemed impressed she knew a bit about each of them, and Malia began to warm up, sensing victory.

Until she carefully cut into one of her green beans.

The dressing made the fork slippery, and when the knife cut through, the bean exploded off her plate and bounced off Dolly's head.

Oh. My. God.

Malia stared, horrified, as the woman jerked back, her voice rising in shock. "What the—did someone throw a bean at me?"

Malia opened her mouth, humiliated to have to make such a confession when things had been going so well. She bit her lip and forced herself to speak up.

Suddenly, the sound of slurping filled the air. She turned to see Palmer's face buried in his soup, making loud noises as he sucked up the liquid in awful, wet slurps that made even Malia shudder.

"Palmer Sterling Matterson! What are you doing? You know I hate when you make sounds like a caveman rather than a civilized human being. Where are your manners?"

Dolly glared at him, the bean forgotten, and Palmer looked up guiltily. "Sorry, Mom."

"I should hope so. Malia and I shouldn't be subjected to such things."

Dolly shot her a look of comradery, and she jumped on board. "Babe, straighten up. You've upset your mom—I told you to breathe while you eat."

His eyes danced with mischief. "Of course, honey dove."

She gave him a warning look, but it was too late. Jane chortled with laughter. "That's so adorable—he calls her *honey dove!*"

Veronica shook her head. "What happened to my brother? Dude, that's embarrassing. Get ahold of yourself."

Malia kicked him under the table, and he shot her an innocent look. But she was grateful for him saving her, so her gesture held little heat.

The rest of the meal followed without incident. She got to chat with Georgia's husband at length, a tall, quiet man who seemed to balance his wife perfectly. He'd been to the Bahamas several times, and asked questions about her family. Before long, they were sharing funny stories and laughing about their childhoods with ease. The ceremonial cake cutting and parent dances took up some time until they were released from their seats and invited to the other room for dessert and cordials. The serious dancing picked up, and Palmer's sisters immediately pushed Malia out on the floor. She loved to dance and had no issue throwing herself into the music and joy of the occasion, laughing as she parodied some of the classics such as the Cha-Cha Slide and the famous conga line. Palmer scurried to his brothers-in-law, who sat to the side, sipping cordials and catching up.

Ella found her on the dance floor, and Malia pointed down at her bare feet, shouting in her ear, "Where are those shoes? You think I'm kidding?"

Ella laughed, and they began twerking together while Georgia and Jane joined in, shaking their butts while some good, clean rap busted through the speakers. By the time she was done, her legs hurt and she desperately needed water.

Palmer met her with a full glass, laughing as she guzzled it all in one gulp. "I love a woman who can keep up with them," he said, pointing out the trio still on the floor, now doing some dirty dancing with available guests.

"Your family is amazing, Palmer," she said seriously. "I know they asked a bunch of questions, but I think I was expecting it to be done with more hostility. It's obvious they want you to be happy."

"Yeah, they do." Something flickered in his eyes, then quickly disappeared. "I'm glad you're having a good time."

The music switched to a slow, sexy beat, and couples flooded the dance floor. As everyone paired up, Veronica motioned them out with a fierce frown. "Get out here," she mouthed.

Uh-oh.

Dolly appeared next to them. "Why aren't you dancing?"

Malia spoke up. "Palmer hates slow dancing. The few times we tried, he stepped all over my feet and said he felt embarrassed."

His body stiffened beside her. Oh yeah, he didn't like that. She tamped down a giggle.

Dolly frowned with confusion. "But he's always danced before! When did this happen, Palmer?"

He cleared his throat. "Recently. I'm trying to get over it, but maybe I'll skip this one."

Malia patted his shoulder. "It's okay, boo boo bear. I don't need to dance as long as I have you."

Oh yeah, his glare was so sharp it could shred her to pieces.

Dolly cocked her head. "Boo boo bear?"

Malia covered a snort. "Palmer just adores his pet names! Sorry, if you'll excuse me, I have to go to the restroom."

She disappeared before he could come up with a zinger, laughing as she did her business, washed her hands, and fussed a bit with her hair. She looked into the mirror and startled when she saw the image reflected back. Cheeks flushed. Sweat gleaming from her skin. Eyes filled with an excitement and zest for life she hadn't seen in a while. She was having a better time than she imagined being with Palmer in his world. She'd expected it to be more like work, but he was surprising her.

Again.

She opened her purse to apply some lip gloss when a woman joined her by the sink. She reminded her a bit of Tessa, with wild, dark corkscrew curls, gorgeous blue eyes, and endless ripe curves wrapped up in a classy scarlet dress. Their gazes met in the mirror. "I love your dress," the woman murmured.

"I was just admiring yours."

They both laughed. "I'm Alexa. Can I just tell you something that may seem a bit weird?"

She hoped the woman wasn't a whacko but nodded. "Of course."

"You look deliriously happy."

Malia smiled. "Oh! Thanks—weddings are nice, aren't they? I'm with one of Barbara's cousins. My name is Malia."

"Nice to meet you. I'm a friend of Barbara's. I own a bookshop in New Paltz. She's a regular customer, so we became good friends." Her blue eyes sparkled with mischief. "Sorry, I just had to comment when I saw your expression. It's that giddiness from love. I've been married to my husband, Nick, for a decade, but I still recognize the butterflies."

Malia blushed, but the woman seemed so genuine and charming, she couldn't help confiding a bit. "He's kind of hot. And really nice. It's been a long time since I had a decent date, let alone a connection."

Alexa beamed. "That's so nice! It's rough out there. My friends and I had to rely on a love spell to find our husbands."

Malia blinked. "A—love spell?"

Alexa waved her hand in the air. "Never mind, it's hard to explain. Much easier to deal with an app, maybe, but it worked back in my day." She grinned, checked her hair, and turned. "It was nice to meet you, Malia. If you're ever in the area, come see me at my store, BookCrazy. And good luck."

"Thanks, I will. Do you have the love-spell book in stock?" she joked, drying her hands with a paper towel.

Alexa sighed. "No, but I'm sure it's out there in the world wreaking havoc with someone."

The woman disappeared, and Malia shook her head. *How strange.* But she was lovely. If she'd known before about a good love-spell book, she would've definitely given it a try. She wondered why her sisters never tried to foist that on her.

Malia pushed the thought away and headed back into the main room, then stopped in the doorway, peering out with wide eyes as the sudden beam of a spotlight shone brightly on her.

What the hell?

A voice echoed through the room amid some laughter. "Malia! We waited for you—it's the bouquet toss!"

No. This wasn't happening.

Blinking in the bright light, she looked at the stage where the bride held her bouquet, and a small group of about seven females stood in the center on display. In one horrified realization, she saw most of them were under fifteen. One was an old lady with white hair, grinning with pride.

And they were waiting on her.

Forcing a smile, she walked over and tried to calm her wildly beating heart at her state of singleness being the focus of everyone's attention.

The old lady leaned over and winked. "I've got my eyes on a guy at the Senior Club, so I'll be a bit aggressive."

"Good luck," Malia said.

The music drummed up, they counted down from three, and the bride tossed the bouquet . . . straight to Malia like a gunshot to her chest. It was pretty much impossible not to catch it.

The white-haired lady uttered a curse. "I'm running out of opportunities here," she muttered. "Congratulations." Then she stalked off.

Malia forced a smile, hurrying back to the table where Palmer's sisters squealed and jumped up and down like she'd won the lottery. It was so awful, she began to laugh, and then her gaze swerved and met Palmer's.

Everything fell away. The sounds and music and chatter became a distant hum as she fell into those piercing eyes that filled with a shocking warmth and heat and something else—something bigger that made her stomach fall and her breath stutter. Something that she longed for so badly, it was almost painful. As if she'd been wandering around the world endlessly, looking for her person, and finally found him right in front of her.

Lips curved in a smile, he bent over. "Guess we're next."

"Just a superstition," she said, her voice raspy. "Plus, she aimed for me."

"Hell yes, she did. How bad did you feel taking it away from Greta, our resident spinster?"

"That's terrible." But she couldn't help grinning back as she stared into his face, just inches from hers. "You're enjoying this a bit too much."

"I know. Malia?"

"Yeah?"

"This was literally the best wedding I ever went to." He reached out to touch her cheek, but dropped his hand when the DJ cut in and called for the last dance and she was dragged away.

By the end of the night, Malia was hugging his family like they were long-lost friends while they chattered on about future get-togethers. She made sure to answer carefully, according to the plan she and Palmer had put together. "Unfortunately, I'm going on some trips back-to-back, so it will be a little while before I have a free night or weekend."

"Oh no, where are you going?" Jane asked.

"Boston," she said.

"I'll be heading out to see her regularly, so don't worry if you don't hear from me for a while," Palmer said.

"No worries, we'll leave you two alone," Georgia chirped. "Don't want Malia to think we're one of those families that like to suffocate."

Palmer's expression confirmed that was exactly the type of family he had. Malia understood it well.

Everyone began to leave except Christine. The youngest sister stood in front of them, face serious as she took her time before speaking. "You know that dinner conversation was bullshit, right?"

Malia froze.

Palmer seemed to recover faster and answered in a calm manner. "What do you mean, Chris?"

She laughed and shook her head. "It was so rehearsed I can't believe they all fell for it. Did you do a weird study session or something? I could tell by your energy you were repeating lines from memory."

Warning bells clanged in Malia's head. Her palms sweat. She was doing the worst thing when she panicked—losing her power of speech. Oh, how she despised this awful weakness, but it was like the words were a gob of peanut butter and nothing would emerge smoothly. She hoped Palmer had a good answer.

"I have no idea what you're talking about. Are you seriously questioning our relationship?"

A knowing smile transformed Christine's face, and then his sister was laughing with delight. "No, little brother, I'm not. Not anymore. I mean, I didn't buy that obvious Q and A at the table, but I watched you when she caught the bouquet. I've never seen you so happy. You're a true goner, Palmer. It got me a little sentimental." She reached out and gave Malia a warm hug. "Sorry if I freaked you out. I worry about him and the way he's so good at keeping women at bay. He locks up his heart like a vault, but you got through. I'm so happy to meet you, Malia. I know we'll be great friends." She kissed Palmer on the cheek and tugged at his hair playfully. "Be good to her, dude." With a jaunty wave, she joined her husband and strolled out.

An awkward silence fell over them. Malia shifted her weight, suddenly glad she still couldn't speak. She wouldn't know what to say.

Did he really look at her like that? Or had he been playing a part in case Christine was watching?

Did the answer even matter when she was set on not being involved with him?

Finally, he spoke, but she noticed he avoided her gaze. "Come on, I'll take you home."

They didn't speak during the long car ride. She was so exhausted from the evening, she took the opportunity to close her eyes and avoid any type of questions. Malia felt too vulnerable. If he made a move, she didn't feel strong enough to battle both him and her weakening body.

Palmer insisted on walking her to the door. "Thanks for a wonderful evening. You were . . . perfect."

Something lodged in her throat, so she just nodded and gave him a quick smile. "Thanks. Talk to you later."

Malia hurried in and shut the door without waiting for him to walk away. Then she leaned against it with a long sigh, wondering how one night could change everything.

Chapter Sixteen

"Tell me about the wedding."

Malia hesitated as she regarded Chiara from across the booth. An intense whirlpool of emotions washed through her. How could she possibly explain the evening in a few choice words? She took a sip of her seltzer and bought some extra time. "Why don't we wait for Tessa? Then I can tell you together."

Chiara blew out a breath. "Fine, but why is she late? She's the one who insisted we meet here for an early dinner. I mean, I adore spending time with you guys, but Sebastian and I don't have much time lately with the upcoming high school graduation and Veronica's nighttime party habits. I'm looking so forward to summer when he'll have some time off."

Chiara's husband was a high school guidance counselor and dedicated to all his students, always volunteering in whatever capacity was needed, including weekends at the Dream On Youth Center. "Oh, that's awful! I thought she was sleeping so well."

Chiara stirred her straw with a frown. "I know! All of a sudden she's up screaming at three a.m., and I'm walking her till five. I've got an appointment with the doctor—it may be gas or something simple."

Tessa finally came racing in and slid into the booth with a huge grin on her face. "Hey, ladies. What's up?"

"You're late," Chiara accused. "I was just complaining. I'm not getting enough sleep, and time is precious. Veronica wakes up every night screaming."

"She didn't see the tail end of *The Walking Dead*, did she?" Tessa asked.

Malia burst into laughter. "You would ask a question like that!"

Tessa shrugged. Her face was flushed, and her corkscrew curls sprang wildly around her shoulders. "Makes sense to me. Your hubby likes those horror shows. What if he was watching one with her around and she saw a zombie, and now she wakes up freaked out every night?"

Chiara began to look nervous, so Malia jumped in. "That is the most ridiculous thing I've ever heard. Ignore her, Chiara." Malia regarded Tessa with a scolding stare. "And why don't you tell us why we're here. You look like something big is going down."

"Oh, it is. Plus, I want to hear all about the wedding in person. Did you sleep with him?"

Malia choked on her next sip of seltzer the exact time Mike showed up. "Sleep with who?"

"No one!" Malia managed to squeak out. "Don't listen to her. Mike, can I get a chicken Caesar salad, please?"

"Same for me," Chiara said. "And a glass of wine since this woman who used to be my friend freaked me out. I'll pump and dump."

Tessa stuck out her tongue, then recited her order. "Grilled cheese with tomato on rye, please. I need comfort food."

Mike winked at them. "Got it."

Tessa watched him head to the kitchen with a bit of glee, then leaned in to whisper. "Emma will be here soon. And she's bringing a date!"

Ah, now Malia knew why her friend was excited. "Are we here to spy?" she asked in amusement.

"Of course. But I didn't tell you the even better news. I gave her a mini makeover."

Chiara perked up. "Wait—didn't she get her hair and nails done at the spa?"

"Yes, but then I finally convinced her to get new glasses, too. It's amazing how different she looks from those few changes." Tessa beamed with satisfaction. "It made me sad to know she never spoiled herself or indulged in these feminine rituals that make us feel good. Apparently, her parents were frugal and extremely religious, so they didn't believe in spending money on beauty stuff. They liked her to look conservative. I told her it was time to take control of what *she* wanted in life, and she agreed."

Chiara sighed. "This is why I can never be mad at you for long. You're a good person, Tessa Harper."

Tessa grinned. "I really didn't do much. I was happy to be a part of it—for her, not Mike. She helped me realize I'd done her a disservice. I was intent on helping her get noticed by Mike. Isn't that awful? I lost my way and the true meaning of Quench. I focused on the guy as the goal instead of her happiness."

Malia felt a surge of love for her friend. Tessa believed in the power of women being in charge of their lives, from looks to spirituality to who they chose to love. Tessa was a magician with figuring out what women needed to boost their confidence without compromising. Readers loved her sassy wit, straight talk, and willingness to tell the truth about how crappy women were with self-talk and what they thought they deserved. "You're such a softie," Malia said with affection.

Tessa waved off the compliment. "Not really."

Malia threw up her hands. "Stop being humble. Accept the damn compliment for once. You're amazing, and that's the end of it."

"Agreed," Chiara said.

She loved the sudden hint of color in her friend's cheeks. "Fine. I am pretty great." She preened, but Malia knew it was more for their benefit. "More importantly, Emma's meeting her date here for dinner."

Chiara laughed and shook her head. "Oh my Lord, you are so bad. You wanted to put her in a situation where Mike was forced to see she's moved on."

"No I didn't!" She paused, taking in their stares, and shrugged. "Okay, maybe. But it really doesn't matter how he reacts—this is for Emma to feel good about herself and know she has options."

Mike brought their salads and Chiara's wine. "Hey, about that sleeping comment. Are you talking about Palmer? 'Cause I liked him. He seems like a good guy, Mal."

Her cheeks got hot. "No, it wasn't, and I don't want to talk about him, Mike."

He shrugged. "Okay. Whatevs—as the kids around here say."

Tessa giggled as he walked away and dug into her salad. "Speaking of Mr. Hot Billionaire, how was the wedding? Give us the deets."

Malia shot a glare at the nickname her friends wouldn't stop using and kept it to the facts. "It went well. I think his family truly believed we were a legit couple. His sisters and mom were really nice. The whole evening surprised me—I had a good time." Perfect. There was nothing to pick apart with her statement.

"Did you sleep with him?" Tessa demanded.

"No! I told you I'm not interested in him. Not for a relationship." She tried not to squirm under their dual stares. "Now I need him to bail me out for Pam's wedding. Once that's over, we have no need to see each other except for business meetings."

"Oh, you're interested in him," Tessa retorted. "You should see your blush—it's so guilty you'd be jailed without a trial."

Chiara smothered a laugh. "Sorry, babe, I agree with Tessa. When you don't want us to know how you really feel, you get all factual and reserved. Why don't you just tell us the truth?"

Malia faced her best friends, took a breath, and gave up. "Fine. I thought I hated him, but I don't. I think about having sex with him constantly, and the more time we spend together, the more I realize he's actually funny, and smart, and, well . . ."

"Well?" Chiara prompted.

She uttered the word with a shudder. "Nice."

That made Tessa crack up, but Malia didn't take offense. God knows, if she didn't laugh she'd cry. "Priceless. The big bad billionaire is a sheep in wolf's clothing," Tessa said. "Do you have a new plan for moving forward?"

"No. Pam's wedding is this Saturday. I have a jam-packed week, so hopefully I can avoid him until then. Now that the paperwork is done and we have a solid plan, we can pull back on our regular meetings. I'm sure my feelings will go away once we stop seeing each other."

Chiara looked at her in sympathy. "Why are you doing this to yourself? I don't understand. If you like him, and he's wild about you, why not try things out? Have fun. Have great sex. See what happens."

"What are you really afraid of, Malia?" Tessa asked directly. "Why won't you give him a chance? I feel like we're missing something. You've spent the past year miserable, dating a bunch of guys who are beneath you. Here's one you actually like who has everything going on."

She tried to find the words to explain. Putting her emotions into words was tough, but it was important not only to share with her friends but face it herself. "We want different things. He's not interested in marriage. And the more I get to know him, the more I'm terrified of falling too hard and getting annihilated."

"Isn't that a risk with any guy you date?" Chiara asked.

"Maybe. But Palmer is bigger than life. He's got this mega empire to run and a huge, demanding family—he's not the type to be home for dinner every night or stay up walking babies with colic. I want someone who's more focused on home and family. I've always had this idea about the man I'm going to marry, and Palmer doesn't fit."

Tessa narrowed her gaze. "Not gonna lie. I'm disappointed in you. The whole thing feels like a cop-out because you're afraid of getting messy, and life just isn't about that. Look at the hell Chiara went through to get her happy ending. I think you need to figure out if being safe is worth the risk of missing out on something fated for you."

"Well, I'm sorry to be such a disappointment, but I've made up my mind," Malia said stiffly, recognizing the way she was reacting in defensiveness but not being able to help it. "After this wedding, I have my appointment to begin my shots, and I'm going to need all my focus on that. I hope you understand."

Tessa rolled her eyes. "Oh hell, girlfriend, I didn't mean to make you mad. We'll be there for you every step of the way—I know this is a big deal, and you've waited a long time."

She relaxed a bit at her friend's concession. "Thanks. I just don't need an intense affair right now. I want to focus on work, my fertility process, and deciding what I want next."

"Understood," Chiara said. "Oh, look, I think that's Emma." Her jaw dropped. "Wow."

Malia turned around and gasped. The first thing that struck her was that the woman wasn't wearing a hat.

The second? She looked younger.

Tessa was a genius.

Emma's hair curled softly around her face, the strands glossy without a hint of Aqua Net spray. The awful glasses had been replaced by updated tortoiseshell frames that accented the sharp curves of her face. She still wore a baggy pantsuit that swallowed her petite figure, and the same orange lipstick, but there seemed to be a new confidence within as she walked with her shoulders back instead of ducking her head.

She stopped in front of the booth, her smile almost shy. "Hi."

They all spoke at once, enthusiastic over her new look. "You look so good," Malia gushed. "I love the new glasses."

"Your hair is divine. How do you feel?" Chiara asked.

"I feel good." Her cheeks flushed, and her eyes sparkled. "I keep looking in the mirror not believing it's me." She nibbled worriedly at her lower lip. "Tessa said I shouldn't hide behind my hats, but I feel naked without them."

"Tessa was brilliant to advise you on that. We can see your face so much better, and you're not hiding your hair! It's still you."

All of a sudden, Emma brought her hand to her throat, and she blinked madly, as if holding back tears. "Thank you, girls. For being such good friends when I've never really had many."

That did it. They all got emotional and mushy and began professing how much they cared for one another.

It was Tessa, of course, who got things back on track. "Okay, now get your butt in that booth so we don't intimidate Arthur if he comes in and sees a bunch of silly women crying with his date."

Emma laughed and took a seat in the booth behind them. It wasn't long before Mike came out and stopped by her table. "Hi, Emma. What are you having? I know you liked the turkey the last time you came for lunch. How come you're not sitting with the girls?"

"Hello, Michael. Someone will be joining me, so I'd rather wait to order. Can I have water with lemon?"

Malia peeked between the wide spaces of the barrier. It was obvious Mike wasn't even looking at Emma, his attention on his notepad as if he wasn't finished writing something. "Sounds good. The special tonight is chili, but it's spicy, so you probably—hey, what did you do?"

Malia held her breath with her friends as they strained their ears to listen.

Emma's voice sounded like her usual prim and proper self. "Nothing much."

A pause. "Yes, you did. You look different. Where's your hat?"

"I decided to try a new look for a change."

Mike scratched his head. "Huh. You don't like hats anymore? You wear them every day."

Emma's tone sharpened with a hint of irritation. "Not anymore."

"Are those new glasses?"

Malia barely caught her impatient sigh. "Yes, they are."

"Did your vision change or something?"

"No. I just changed my frames."

More head scratching. "Seems like a lot of money to spend when you can still see with the old ones. My vision plan is terrible. You must have a better one."

Malia almost buried her face in her hands. This was so . . . bad. Why couldn't he say something, like she looked nice? What was so hard about that? But she didn't want to butt in and interrupt.

"Well, I think these look better on me," Emma said defensively.

Mike shrugged. "Okay, it's your dime. Want me to bring water for your girlfriend?"

Tessa's face turned into a scowl. Malia was surprised she hadn't already marched over there to start yelling at Mike.

"No. And I'm not meeting a female. Oh, here he is. Hello, Arthur."

Good for her. The woman sounded syrupy sweet, and now Mike was narrowing his gaze as Arthur walked in. And what a sight Arthur was.

He wore an old-fashioned blue suit with a white carnation in the lapel. A fedora perched at an angle on his bald head, and he snapped his cane with precision as he strode in with purpose, wrinkled face wreathed in a smile. "Emma, so nice to see you again. Thank you for inviting me."

"Of course. I was looking forward to it."

Mike couldn't seem to stop staring, struck mute as Arthur stepped neatly around him to kiss Emma's cheek and slide into the booth. They began to chat, ignoring Mike, until he muttered something under his breath and moved away.

"Classic," Tessa whispered. "I'm so proud of her."

"Mike doesn't seem happy," Chiara said. "I wonder why?"

Tessa kept her voice low. "Because he's never seen her in this capacity before. I suspected he was deliberately rejecting Emma so he didn't have to deal with his feelings. There's never been anyone since Rory's mom died."

Chiara nodded. "I think he feels guilty about wanting to move on. Sebastian and I might have another chat with him. Try to push him to take more chances. Veronica has definitely put the light back in his eyes. Now, he needs a companion to run with."

Mike came back out, practically stomping over. "Emma, do you want turkey again? It's fresh and thinly sliced the way you like it."

"No, thank you. Arthur and I are going to share some nachos."

Mike blinked. "Nachos? You've never eaten them before." Did he just give Arthur a glare, or was it a trick of the light? "Won't those beans give you gas?"

Oh no. He didn't.

Emma's quick indrawn breath was easily heard. "Michael, we will both share the nachos and have two of your margaritas. One with salt, one without."

He gaped at her. "But I was getting you tea!"

"Tonight, I'll have a margarita."

Mike shut up and left again.

Arthur laughed. "Strange waiter. You know him?"

"He's the owner and the father of one of my previous students," she muttered grudgingly. "Forget about him. I heard you won your last poker tournament."

"I did. Let me tell you about it."

Arthur began to try and dazzle her by going into all the ins and outs of his skill set, so they stopped listening. Mike managed to serve the nachos and drinks with just a bit of muttering under his breath. Arthur got points for paying the bill after they were done, and he began to walk Emma out.

"Will you be here for breakfast tomorrow?" Mike demanded right before Emma left.

Malia watched her pause, tilt her head, and pretend to consider. "No. I'll see you next week."

She left him sputtering at her back.

Mike didn't seem to notice they knew exactly what was going on. He stomped over and jabbed his finger at the door. "What is going on with Emma? She's acting weird. And who was that guy? He was rude—did you see what he tipped? Ten percent!"

Tessa rose to the occasion. "Why do you care?" she asked coolly. "You've never cared before what she wore or who she ate with."

"I don't care! She's your friend, is all, so I was concerned. I don't like to see women being taken advantage of, and that guy is trouble. He was trying to get her drunk."

"He looked nice to me," Malia offered. "Handsome, too. It's about time Emma got a man in her life."

Mike's face turned purple. "She's dating him? Oh, I get it. She had to get all fancy like because he's some kind of high-browed, degree-holding academic jerk. She wanted to impress him. I should've known."

Chiara gasped. "What are you talking about? Emma doesn't care about stuff like that."

Moody temper seemed to bite at him. His features were strained. "Sure she does. She looks down on anyone who didn't go to college. That time she came for Scrabble night, she was making fun of me. When I made a decent word, she'd pretend to be all nice and tell me good job."

Suddenly, the light bulb went off. Was that why Mike had been treating Emma so miserably? Had he believed he wasn't good enough for her? What a mess.

"Mike, you are so wrong," Tessa said with a sigh. "Emma's not like that at all. She's a bit socially awkward and sometimes doesn't say the most expected things. But that doesn't make her a snob."

Malia shook her head. "Shame on you for judging her. Your opinion not only insulted Emma but yourself. You're a self-made business owner who raised a beautiful family. A degree means nothing, and Emma knows that."

A few moments of silence descended. Mike shifted his weight with obvious discomfort. "Huh. I never thought about it like that."

Chiara's voice was gentle. "You've been very rude to her for no reason."

A deep frown creased his brow. He scratched his head. "I didn't mean it. Got mixed up. Maybe I'll talk to her." He disappeared into the kitchen.

Malia shared a glance with her friends. "That was eye opening," she finally said.

"I had no idea Mike believed that stuff," Tessa said.

"It just goes to show no one knows what someone believes about themselves," Chiara said. "We all have so many insecurities. Shame on us for not digging deeper."

"You said to stay out of it," Tessa reminded her.

Malia raised a brow. "You're blaming Chiara for this mess? You were the one who dragged us into this whole love triangle."

"Not exactly a triangle with only two people," Tessa muttered. "Listen, I gotta go. Chiara needs to get back to her hubby and my godchild, and you need to get out of your head and have sex with a hot billionaire." Tessa left in a whirlwind, sticking them with the check that Mike never let them pay anyway.

Chiara laughed and shook her head. "That one's going to kill the man meant for her."

Malia winced at the thought. "I feel sorry for him already. Come on, let's bounce."

They left, and the whole drive home, Malia couldn't stop thinking of Palmer. Of how good it was to spend the evening with him. Of how badly she'd wanted to touch him. Of how nice his family was, making her feel comfortable and included.

She had one more event to get through, and then she'd begin the demanding two weeks of shots to prep for her egg retrieval. This wasn't a good time to date or get bad ideas in her head about Palmer Matterson. He wasn't interested in the life she wanted. Playing too close to the fire would surely singe not only her fingers, but her heart.

Yet, Chiara's words kept playing in her mind. God knows, Malia had her own insecurities about love. Did Palmer? And if so, would that be something else they had in common? It seemed the deeper she dug, the more gold she found. And even though her mind was firm on her choices, other parts of her were beginning to take over.

She just didn't know what was going to happen next.

Chapter Seventeen

What is my shoe size?

I have no clue. Wait—no one's going to ask that!

Size 14. Big, right?

Impressive.

You know what they say about men with big feet?

Yes. They wear big shoes.

Palmer chuckled. Their work schedules had exploded this past week, so instead of meeting, Malia suggested texting each other fun facts and quizzes to prep for tomorrow night's wedding. He'd never had this much fun conversing digitally with a woman.

Emeril interrupted by charging through the door with his usual determined expression. "Quitting time. Everyone's meeting at the bar for a drink. Come hang out."

Palmer pocketed his phone. "Sorry, I have too much work to get through. Can't do happy hour."

Emeril ignored him, lifting up a four-pack of his favorite Juice Bomb IPA. "Figured you'd say that, so happy hour has come to you. You've been stuck in this office nonstop and need some human contact."

Palmer rubbed his hands over his face. "My problem is too much human contact. I had to convince Marissa Bruschetti I'm not giving her a refund because her father-in-law got drunk and fell into the fountain at the Met. How am I liable for that? I warned them not to let him have any cocktails until the reception began."

His assistant never missed a beat. He retrieved two frosted beer glasses from the wet bar, poured, and handed one over. Palmer took it gratefully, the foam head perfectly presented like a gift. "That's why you get the big bucks," Emeril drawled, dropping into the seat across from his desk. He sipped at his beer with his usual precision and gave a sigh. "This week wasn't a picnic for me, either. I made the new marketing assistant cry."

Palmer cocked a brow. "Why? What happened?"

"I noticed when I walked by her desk, she seemed to act weird and switch off her screen like she was hiding something. So of course, I had to find out what it was about. I snuck around the other corridor and surprised her."

"Please don't tell me it was porn."

"Online shopping. At Kruger. She was buying shoes for her niece's wedding."

Palmer winced. "From our main competitor? She didn't even want to check out our new inventory?"

Emeril smirked. "Guess not. I told her it wasn't appropriate, but she could shop wherever she wanted on her lunch hour. She burst into tears."

"You're a monster."

"She kept apologizing. Said her niece is on a budget, and Kruger was having a discount sale."

"I hope you fired her."

"I sent her to the Chelsea shop to pick out some stuff at half price, and now she's thanking me and giving me little gifts every time I pass her desk. I'm so uncomfortable, I can't visit the third floor anymore."

"Could be worse."

"Dan was caught with porn, though. He opened up some link, and it had a video that came on full blast. I got tech to fix it, but not before it made an impression on the sales team. Anyway, he's at happy hour if you want to hear the details."

"No, thanks. You always get involved in the weirdest crap."

The man gave an elegant shrug. "Everyone adores me and tells me things. I can't help my fabulousness. Speaking of which, now that we're off the clock, what's going on with you?"

Palmer's phone beeped and he immediately reached for it. He read the text and fought a smile, quickly tapping out his answer. "Hmm."

"Why are you looking all glowy and shit? Who is she?"

He looked up and gave the man a hard look. "Nobody. Also, not your business."

Emeril narrowed his gaze, studying him intently. Then his face cleared, and he began to laugh. "Oh my God, it's Malia! You're seeing her!"

"This is not gossip hour, Emeril."

He held up his beer glass. "It's precisely gossip hour, boss."

"Then why don't we talk about your last date, where you ended up treating three of her girlfriends to dinner because you got conned."

Emeril took another sip of beer. "I was not conned. I did it because I wanted to and I'm a gentleman. Now stop changing the subject. I know you're texting Malia right now. You have that same puppy-dog look you got in the conference room when you thought no one was looking."

"Get the hell out of my office."

"Not yet." Emeril settled in with delight. "Tell me everything."

"I really should've fired you when I had the chance," Palmer muttered as he hit the send button. "As you know, I'm working with her on Quench Foundation business. She also was my date at my cousin's wedding last weekend."

"You managed to keep that fact from me. Well done."

"Thanks. I think I've finally gotten her to like me, but things are moving slow. She's stubborn." And beautiful. Smart. Kind. Passionate. She had him tied up in knots, haunting his dreams, and glued to the phone in anticipation of her next text.

Emeril stared at him with surprise. "This is more serious than I thought. What's the plan?"

"We're going out tomorrow night to her cousin's wedding. I intend to charm her and finally get her to admit she wants to date me."

"Wait—another family wedding? That's commitment. What if she still doesn't want to date you, though? What if her family thinks you're stuck up and weird?"

Palmer gave a fierce glower. "They can't. I won't let them because there's no plan B. I guess I could send her endless flowers and love notes? It's our made-up courtship story, which may be a nice touch."

Emeril grunted. "You know how to bake, boss. Send her cake and cookies and pies. She'll eventually say yes."

He tapped his fingers against the desk. He felt as if there may have been a breakthrough during Barbara's wedding. They'd bonded and gotten closer. When she caught the bouquet, he'd been tossed into a tornado of emotion he'd never experienced before. He craved to hold her, and tease her, and fuck her, and make her happy. This woman had become his obsession, but he was afraid she didn't feel half of these things for him, which was . . . awful. "Malia is special."

"You deserve some happy. She'd be lucky to have you."

He blinked. "Thanks, Emeril. That was really nice."

The man gave a delicate burp. "Welcome. Can I use your contact to get a reservation at Cote? I'm craving a good steak, and it's my third date with Rachel."

Palmer rolled his eyes. "Go ahead, you need to call Brian. Take my driver, too. I'll be stuck here awhile."

"Thanks, boss."

"Thanks for the beer."

Emeril left, and the office fell back into silence. Usually he loved working late Friday nights, when everyone disappeared and it was just him in his office, overlooking the city like a conquering hero. It fulfilled him in a way nothing else did.

Except lately, since Malia, it hadn't felt the same. He was restless. And a bit empty.

The phone buzzed.

If you had to be a Disney princess, which one would you choose and why?

Palmer didn't hesitate. Belle. She's got a big-ass library to herself. Plus, the beast is cool. You?

Moana. She gets to go out on great adventures, lives on a beach, and is best friends with an outrageous chicken.

He leaned back in his chair and put his feet up on the desk. Took another sip of beer. God, he loved learning these details. Each was like discovering another piece of a puzzle he never wanted to finish putting together.

But the doubts kept creeping in, doubts he'd never experienced before. Each day, he was becoming more engaged in this budding relationship. Except . . . did she feel the same? Or was this just a distraction for her?

He had no control if she decided to take their relationship back to strictly business. For the first time, he was vulnerable, and he didn't know what he was going to do about it.

Take the leap and hope for the best?
Or begin to step back and go slower, protecting his heart?

~

What would your superpower be?

Malia sipped at her wine and cuddled into the mass of pillows propped up behind her. It felt so good to be home after a busy week. She'd worked late every night and couldn't wait to get into comfy sweats and go to bed early tonight. But then she got Palmer's text, and an hour had passed as she got caught up in their snappy dialogue.

She stared at the screen with a grin. They'd been texting on and off the past few days, beginning with serious questions to get him prepped for tomorrow's wedding, then morphing into the ridiculous. Each time her typewriter notification rang, her nerve endings zinged with pleasure. Once again, he'd surprised her. Palmer had a playful side he wasn't afraid to show.

She thought about the question for a bit before sending her answer. Time travel. I'd get to understand history better and how things connect in the world. I think it could help me be a better person.

Wow, that's deep. And noble of you.

What about you?

Flying. 'Cause it's cool.

My sisters would approve of your answer.

He sent a GIF of Snoopy cursing the Red Baron, and Malia laughed.

She'd never had this with a man before, just random conversations that embraced a lightness instead of the seriousness she seemed to always covet. Maybe she'd been too focused on completing a questionnaire for the men she dated—to make certain she wasn't wasting her time. It was a good plan, but allowing herself to be silly with Palmer gave her a glimpse of another part of herself she'd almost forgotten.

Where are you now?

Her fingers tapped rapidly over the keyboard. In bed drinking wine. You?

Still at office drinking a beer.

She tamped down a giggle and sent her impulsive response. What are you wearing?

The three dots gave her pause. Versace, dark gray suit. Silver tie. White dress shirt. Black socks. Size 14 Italian loafers. You?

Gray sweats. Pink hoodie. Socks with poodles on them.

That's hot.

Malia laughed out loud. Ready for the wedding?

Yes. I hope your family likes me.

She hesitated and read the words again. He shouldn't care. This was a ruse to keep them safe from their families' meddling—not a real date to fool anyone into thinking they were a couple. Except, lately, it felt like they were. Being a couple while pretending to be one.

Even worse? She was beginning to wish they were.

Malia stared at the screen. After the wedding, she'd go on her fertility treatments, and they wouldn't see each other. Sure, they'd work together on the foundation, but now that the initial setup was done, they wouldn't need to meet as much. Work could be completed over the phone or via email. There'd be no further reasons to text, or have lunch, or meet at Mike's for coffee. They'd go their separate ways. It was for the best, right? They wanted different things. Pretending they didn't would only lead to hurt and disaster.

Malia?

Her heart shrank a bit in her chest. Palmer's question hung in the space between them, meaning more than it should.

Gotta go. See you tomorrow. She threw the phone on the nightstand. He never texted back.

Chapter Eighteen

When Palmer picked her up, it took him a few moments to catch his breath.

She stood before him, radiant in an emerald-green dress that hugged her figure and stopped several inches above the knee. The endless stretch of smooth brown skin and muscled calves rocked him. She wore sexy stilettos that forced her hips to roll as she walked. She had loosened her braids, and her dark hair was swept to the side, allowing her big amber eyes to peek from the fringe in a seductive peekaboo. The scent of plum and musk wrapped around him and made him dizzy. She was Eve incarnate, a confident powerhouse of a woman who he itched to make his, even if only for a short while. He wondered if he'd survive a night with her—if she'd bring the same fierce passion to lovemaking as she did to her daily routines.

Palmer wanted to find out.

"You're staring," she finally said. Her face reflected a hint of vulnerability, as if she was afraid he'd say something to break the spell.

"You're stunning."

Pleasure shone on her face and made his heart sing. "Thank you. I keep thinking of you in Bond terms. Elegant, polished, and handsome."

"One of the highest compliments you can give a man. As long as it's not Timothy Dalton. He was my least fave."

She laughed, and he escorted her into the car.

The drive took them upstate, leaving the city far behind. He kept up a casual chatter in the car so she felt at ease. Her abrupt sign-off in her text last night warned him he'd gotten too close. Malia had thorns protecting the rose inside, and Palmer sensed it was a delicate dance to get her to slowly open up.

The ceremony was held at the Overlook Lodge, a small chapel down the road from the Bear Mountain Inn. The room burst with guests who cheered when the couple jumped the broom, a tradition Palmer always loved to watch. There was something about leaving the past behind and committing to a whole new future that moved him. He formally met most of Malia's family, but there was little time for conversation. Afterward, they made the short drive down to the main inn for the reception, just in time before the rain began.

Palmer took in the decor and rustic setting, his mind clicking madly as he made mental notes. He'd never attended a wedding here and was impressed with the sprawl of mountains set off by the large, wide windows. The lake glittered like black ice in the darkening shadows of twilight, and endless regal trees thicketed the property, leading to a private zoo and multiple trails to explore and hike. He needed to get this place on his hit list. He'd done Mohonk Mountain House many times, but he'd missed this gem, which would satisfy clients who wanted that Hudson Valley feel but at a less expensive price.

Malia waved at a few guests and led him into the main room. "Can I ask you a serious question?"

"You can ask me anything," he responded.

"Have you ever attended a wedding without judgment?" He quickly glanced down to make sure she wasn't upset, but mischief danced on her features. "It's like you're scribbling notes in your head and measuring if Endless Vows could have done better."

He laughed and relaxed. "We could have done better," he confirmed with casual arrogance. "But I love this venue and never booked it before, so your cousin got one on me. Or her planner. Did she have one?"

"No, she did the whole thing on her own."

"Next time someone in your family has a wedding, give out my card. I'll personally take care of them with a discount."

She shook her head. "Think I can tear them away from Sunshine Bridal in Cape May?"

He stopped in his tracks. "Yes, because I'm better than Gabe Garcia."

She laughed at his frown. "Aww, boo boo bear, you can't handle a little healthy competition?"

He tried not to shudder. "Can we start with a new slate at this wedding?" he asked. "No ridiculous nicknames for each other. I really do want to make a good impression with your family, and your father will never respect me with an endearment like that."

She squeezed his hand. Sparks shot through him at her touch. "It's a deal. Let's go."

They joined the table where her family had already gathered, sipping cocktails as they waited for the wedding couple's big entrance. He liked that they weren't doing a formal sit-down dinner for the reception, and instead, the four hours would be like a long cocktail hour. High and low tables were scattered around the space for guests to mix and wander, and food stations were set up against the wall. The band was already in place, and the lead singer had a nice deep voice, perfect to sing some wedding classics. The room was sparsely decorated, with bunches of wildflowers on the tables, allowing the lodge and its natural surroundings to be the main star.

Palmer stood next to Malia and her mother, Sasha, who reminded him so much of his own mother. She seemed like a true mama bear, heavily involved with her family, radiating warmth and laughter. Her golden dress shimmered and set off her auburn hair. He'd been able to exchange some polite chitchat with everyone, but as with Barbara's wedding, he figured the deep stuff would begin shortly.

For now, he turned to watch the familiar show play out. The bride looked perfect in a pearl-encrusted mermaid dress, but as the first dance got underway, his gaze kept straying back to his pretend lover.

A crack of lightning exploded in the air, competing with the moody ballad "The Way You Look Tonight." The rain pelted against the window like a bully with his fists. Palmer tucked Malia a little closer to his side, even though it was against the rules.

No unnecessary touching.

He hoped to break some rules tonight. It was his last chance to really form enough of a connection so that she'd want to see him on a personal basis. He couldn't keep using Quench Foundation business to feed his starving need for her presence.

The song ended, and they announced the guests could help themselves to food. By the time they'd filled their plates and resettled, he was surrounded by her three sisters and Sasha. Her father, Clinton, obviously realized the interrogation would begin and had situated himself with his sons-in-law for protection. Palmer didn't blame the man in the least. The same exact thing had happened at Barbara's wedding.

Davinia dove in without hesitation. "Palmer, why has my sister kept you a secret?" she demanded. "How long have you been dating?" The oldest sister seemed to be the leader of the crew, with a bossy, take-charge manner. She wore a sunshine-yellow dress with a bow and braids twisted on top of her head. Wide brown eyes held a spark of intensity that reminded him of Malia.

"About three months now," he said easily. "Both of us have been a bit leery about dating, so when we began, we decided not to tell our families. We wanted to wait. I'm sorry I had to delay so long to let Malia RSVP—I was afraid I needed to be on call for a big wedding, but I got coverage. I think she was afraid you'd all believe she made me up."

Malia stepped in. "I told him if I introduced him to my big, obnoxious family, I wanted to know he'd stick."

Davinia and Aliya laughed. Zinnia stuck out her tongue, and Sasha slapped her daughter on the wrist for the display. "Ouch! She called us obnoxious, Mom."

"We are sometimes," Sasha said. "But let's be on our best behavior tonight."

Sasha turned away, and Zinnia gave Malia a cross-eyed look and mouthed, *Loser*. Palmer couldn't help laughing—she was obviously the fiery one, with a snarky wit and tendency to ball-bust her sisters. Her face was narrow, with a sharp chin and high-cut cheekbones. She was the most petite of the sisters, but her scarlet-red strapless cocktail gown cut a bold presence.

"I wouldn't let Eric come to Sunday dinner for months," Aliya confided. "I knew once he did, Mom would expect regular attendance, Zinnia would force him to do the dishes, and Davinia would recruit him as an extra babysitter." Aliya was the third born, with an athletic body and a tiny basketball belly. Her hair was cut in a short bob that curved under her chin. She glowed, and Palmer could tell she was one of those women whose body embraced pregnancy. Her hands were constantly rubbing the mound and a small, secret smile rested on her lips. She was definitely the most chill of the group.

Davinia shrugged. "We don't like fainthearted men."

"I want to know how you met. Give me all the juicy details," Aliya said.

Palmer recited the story as if it were second nature, with Malia jumping in and out to finish his sentences. Sasha was grinning and staring at her daughter with such joy, it gave him a funny feeling in his gut. He'd expected her to be more pushy—demanding Malia follow her sisters' path of marriage and babies because of her own beliefs and traditions. But her look told a different story, as if she dreamed of Malia finding love not to just check a box but because Sasha believed it would bring her true happiness. Sasha probably didn't think anything else could live up to the power of love, no matter how satisfied her daughter was with the other parts of her life.

Exactly what his own mother always expressed.

Everyone sighed at the end. Zinnia popped a bite of crab cake in her mouth, chewed, and went straight for the gut. "Why are you still single?"

Malia groaned. "Really, dude?"

Another slap at her wrist. "Zinnia, that's rude!"

"Mom, stop hitting me. I'm just asking because I'm curious, that's all. He's obviously a fox—look at him."

He fought off the blush as Malia's sisters all stared at him, sizing him up. Damn, he refused to break this early. Palmer straightened up and grinned. "Thanks. I'm still single because I'm a bit of a workaholic. I'm also involved with my own family a lot—I have four sisters. Lots of nieces and nephews."

"Never been married, then?" Zinnia asked.

No one yelled at her this time. Sasha even leaned forward to catch his answer.

"No."

"Kids?"

He shook his head. "Nope."

They shared a knowing look. Malia looked like she was trapped in her suffering, unable to help. He reached out and squeezed her hand in reassurance. Her family would have to do more than that to scare him off.

"Do you babysit?" Davinia asked.

He started to laugh. Davinia's comment was exactly what Veronica would say. If he ever introduced those two, they could rule the world.

Suddenly, Malia's father appeared at the table, giving him a hard stare. "Palmer."

He stopped laughing immediately. "Yes?"

"Why don't you join me at the bar for a few moments."

Sasha glanced at them both with surprise. His heart pounded in his chest, but Palmer forced a smile. "Of course."

Malia's sisters tittered.

"Daddy, why don't I come with you," Malia offered in a high-pitched voice.

Her father patted her shoulder with affection. "I'm sure your date will be fine without you. Just want to have a man-to-man chat."

Her face paled, but she nodded. "Sure. Have fun!" Her gaze pleaded with Palmer to make sure he didn't screw up.

They went to the bar, where Clinton ordered two glasses of expensive whiskey. The man was smartly dressed in a classic black suit and paisley tie. He was average height but held himself with a confidence that was matched by the steady gaze of his dark eyes. Silver glinted in his hair and trimmed mustache. His voice held a rich, velvety tone that reminded Palmer of Malia.

"Enjoying the wedding?" he asked.

"Yes. It's always fun to attend as a guest rather than an employee," Palmer said with a smile. "It's also nice to meet Malia's family. She speaks very highly of all of you."

Clinton inclined his head and sipped the amber liquid. "I'm sure she mentioned a few other things about us. Like her sisters' nosiness. Her mother's pushiness. My tendency to judge my daughters' boyfriends harshly."

He hesitated, not sure how to respond. Was the man warning him about something? Hell, he hadn't dealt with a woman's father testing him in . . . forever. He stuck with safety. "Nope, didn't mention any of that."

A gleam of amusement sparked in Clinton's eyes. "Smart. Wanna know why I really pulled you aside? Are you ready for the truth?"

Ah, shit. No. "Yes, of course," he said, managing to sound like he wasn't scared the man was about to pounce and accuse him of fake-dating his daughter. Or worse.

For one horrible moment, Clinton regarded him with a narrowed gaze, lips tight, seriousness etched into his elegant features. Then he laughed. Tipped his head back and gave a good old-fashioned belly laugh that immediately relaxed all of Palmer's tense muscles. "I'm just messing around," Clinton said with a grin. "Sorry, couldn't resist. Wanted to save you from the inquisition out there and give you some breathing room. Though you looked like you were holding your own."

Palmer grinned back, immediately liking this man. "You got me good."

"Were you nervous?"

"Not at all. Just a tiny bit terrified."

Clinton slapped him on the back, and they finished their whiskey, chatting casually about the wedding business.

On cue, Malia suddenly appeared by her father's side with a fake smile plastered over her face. "Hi!" she chirped. "I was just getting myself a drink and figured I'd check on you."

"We're done here." Clinton got up, gave Palmer a side wink, and stalked off.

Damn, he loved a guy with a sense of humor. He bet Clinton needed one to live with five females. Palmer certainly did.

"Oh my God, how bad was it? Did he suspect anything? Did he interrogate you? I tried to get here as fast as possible, but—"

He cut her off by taking her hand, happy the gesture was allowed by her rules. He lingered, liking the feel of her fingers within his. "It's okay, Malia. We had a very nice chat. He didn't suspect a thing."

"Are you sure? I've never seen my dad pull anyone aside before."

"I promise, there's nothing to worry about."

She gave a relieved sigh and ordered champagne as the band switched to a slow song and the floor filled up with couples. "I got nervous, especially after my sisters' endless questions."

"I can handle them fine, you know," he said, tipping the bartender and handing her the flute.

"Not worried about you. It's me."

"Why?" He studied her face, which looked a bit flushed. "I'm answering okay, right?"

"Yes. Too much, I think." A frown crinkled her brow. Palmer snapped down on the urge to trace the delicate line, then cup her cheek. "I'm starting to wonder if this was a good idea. I should've had you be your old arrogant self to piss them all off. Now Mom will start inviting you to Sunday dinners."

Malia looked so depressed he couldn't help but grin. "Do you know how many Sunday weddings there are? I'll have plenty of excuses to give. Are you sure it's not something else?"

"What?"

He leaned in. "Maybe you're starting to like me. Maybe you want me to come to Sunday dinners and that's freaking you out."

She jerked back, but the flare of truth in her eyes startled him just as much. Somehow, they'd begun to stop playacting. Unfortunately, Malia didn't know how to handle it. "Not at all."

"Lie."

She pressed her lips together and he watched her greedily, fantasizing over those deep red lips and having her mark him all over. Branding him as hers. He grew hard and shifted his weight. "I'm not," she denied weakly.

"Then dance with me and prove it."

She shook her head. "Against the rules."

He angled his body so he could speak directly in her ear. "Some are made to be broken."

She shuddered. "Palmer, I—"

Lightning flashed. Something crackled, and with a giant crash from the sky, the room was plunged into darkness.

Ah, shit.

Palmer immediately grabbed Malia's hand as the lights turned off, intending to keep her close. Voices rang out in concern as people began to move around. He allowed his eyes to adjust to the dark while his brain fired nonstop, going through the wedding guide of surviving and thriving in disasters—one he'd personally written for Endless Vows employees.

"I can't believe this—Pam must be freaking out! Do you think they have a generator?" Malia asked.

"Definitely, but it may not power everything. Maybe the lights will come back, but that noise sounded pretty bad. I'm going to bring you back to your sisters' table, okay? Stay tight to me."

She obeyed, and he retraced their path from memory, moving amid clusters while various discussions rose to his ears on what to do next. He hoped the venue was smart enough to calm the guests, because many people often panicked in the dark.

"Malia! Oh my God, this is awful—I can't see anything," Sasha said, voice filled with worry. "Girls, everyone stay with me. I don't want anyone wandering away until someone in charge lets us know what to do."

"Everyone stay calm," an assured voice rang out. "We're getting the generator up, so it shouldn't be long."

"Oh, good, the manager is on top of it," Davinia said with relief.

Palmer knew the staff was going to be tested. Thank God there weren't any other weddings at the venue, but the full-service restaurant upstairs and the main lobby bar held enough people to strain the focus from Pam's wedding. If the lights didn't come up and the generator didn't fire on all circuits, this was going to be the wedding reception from hell.

"Malia, I'm going to talk to the manager. Please don't move from this spot."

"What are you going to do?" she asked.

"Help them out so your cousin has a shot at making this a good memory rather than a bad one."

"But you don't know this place or the staff or anything!" Zinnia burst out.

"I'll be right back if they don't need me."

He waited for Malia's response, not wanting to abandon her if she got upset or wanted him to stay.

"Go," Malia said, her voice strong. "Don't worry about us."

Satisfaction stirred. There was a confidence within her command that told him she believed in him. It was silly, but she suddenly made him feel like Superman, and God knew how badly he wanted to be a superhero for her, just for a little while.

He donned his cape and left.

Chapter Nineteen

"Malia, this is outrageous. What does he think he can do?" Davinia asked.

She nibbled on her lower lip and hoped something happened soon. It had been a full twenty minutes, and things were starting to get messy. She heard Pam crying as people tried to console her. The band guy kept yelling out announcements and telling jokes, but no one was listening. Not even a flicker of light flashed again, and the storm seemed to grow worse, banging at the windows and rocketing everyone's stress levels.

At least they'd gotten to eat first.

"He's probably seeing if he can help in any way because he's versed on these things," she said to her family. "I'm sure we'll hear something any moment."

"We didn't even get to do the money dance yet, and that's my favorite," Zinnia said glumly.

Suddenly, there was a flurry of activity. Now that her gaze had adjusted, Malia watched as a group wheeled in a table filled with candles and lanterns that blazed with light. Some applauded as they began to disperse the lights to different tables, and then Palmer was bringing a large box over to the singer. Their heads ducked in conversation.

"Oh, good, at least we can see!" her mom said.

A tall, thin man in a suit stepped onstage and clapped his hands. "Attention, everyone! I'm the manager here at Bear Mountain, and I'm extremely sorry you've all had such an experience. Unfortunately, we are having issues with our generator, so there's still no power. But that's not going to stop us from continuing the wedding."

There was a burst of sound, and then the band leader was talking into another microphone, probably on a battery. "We're here to celebrate Pam and Elias's love story, and a little storm isn't going to stop us—is it?"

A loud murmur rose from the crowd. Then the wedding cake was carried in, lit up with dozens of candles, while everyone oohed and ahhed. Soon, the entire space was bursting with soft light from various-size candles and lanterns, creating a romantic atmosphere that gave Malia the chills.

The singer began to croon a cappella, and his voice was beautiful, rich, and husky. The band joined him in harmony, humming or chanting the chorus, and within minutes, the entire vibe changed. Couples began to dance. Pam and her husband clung to each other while he wiped her cheeks and whispered in her ear. The rain belted drops of water and the wind roared, but inside, all was safe and filled with love.

Palmer moved beside Malia, taking her hand again with a possessiveness that gave her a thrill. "Better?" he asked.

Her chest tightened. Longing flowed hot in her bloodstream. Her sisters thanked him, and they joined their husbands on the dance floor as song morphed into song. "Thank you," she said, resting her other hand on his chest.

He stiffened, and then his gaze captured hers, those pale green eyes simmering with hunger. "Dance with me, Malia."

She shuddered. Opened her mouth to say no. But as he slowly guided her toward the group of tightly swaying bodies, she didn't protest. She wanted to hold him like this for a little while. Just this once.

They danced under candlelight while Roberta Flack's "The Closer I Get to You" spilled into the air. He gathered her in his arms as if she'd always belonged there. Thigh brushed thigh. Her hands loped around his neck and entangled in the long strands of hair that brushed his collar. His breath whispered over her cheek. Her breasts pressed against his hard chest. She melted into his body heat as he moved in tight circles, his hands resting against her lower back. The shadows cloaked them from prying eyes. No words were needed, because there was nothing to say.

The rest of the evening unfolded in a dream. They ate cake. Chatted with various family members and hugged a glowing Pam, who confided that her wedding would be the one everyone remembered. The rain faded to a lazy drizzle. Guests left.

Davinia hugged Malia goodbye. "He's like a romance hero," she said with a grin. "You finally did it. You found someone who's perfect for you, and now you don't have to worry about doing that ridiculous thing with your eggs. I told you love would come naturally! You just needed to be patient." She gloated with pride.

Malia stared at her sister as her heart shriveled. They would never understand, and by getting them to love Palmer, she realized she hadn't freed herself at all.

Now, she was trapped within the ruse. She'd only wanted to buy herself some breathing space, but she had made her situation worse. Somehow, she'd need to eventually tell them the truth rather than spin some sort of ridiculous breakup story. She'd have to tell them Palmer wasn't right for her, either—because he didn't see the future that she dreamed of.

Somehow, Malia was never enough.

She watched as her sisters gushed around him. Even her dad thanked him for his help and gave him a half man-type hug.

They climbed into the car, and she closed up on herself, craving to be home. She needed silence and comfort. She needed to get away from this man who was stealing her heart and not meant for her. She needed to be safe again.

Malia felt his gaze on her, assessing, but she remained quiet and pleaded a slight headache to keep from talking. He didn't take her hand again. After Barbara's wedding, the trip was silent but throbbed with awareness and possibility. Tonight, it stunk of her failure.

The driver pulled up to her place and she stumbled out. Malia knew Palmer would insist on walking her to the door, so she got her key ready, hoping he'd allow her a quick exit. Her fingers fumbled, but she finally got it open and turned halfway. "Thank you. They loved you. I'll call you later this week."

His hand shot out and blocked her entry. "I want to talk to you, Malia."

Oh God.

She forced herself to sound casual. "Can we do it another time? My headache's getting worse, and I really need to sleep."

"Then I'll get you an aspirin and some water, and we'll talk while the meds work."

She bristled and snapped. "Why do you always have to be so damn pushy? Can't you give me space?"

"Not tonight." He pushed the door open, stepped aside, and gazed at her while he waited.

She studied his implacable expression and muttered a curse under her breath. She wasn't going to get rid of him until he had his say, whatever it was. Palmer didn't scare her physically. No, this was all emotional—a frikkin' minefield she desperately wanted to avoid.

Better to get it over with or he'd stand outside her door all night, waiting.

"Fine. But make it quick, please."

"I will."

He hadn't been in her place yet, and she noticed he took in the surroundings with an interest that bothered her. Why did he care so much? She'd had plenty of men in her home who'd prowled around a bit but never seemed eager to get to know how her visual surroundings told its own story. Other than her bedroom.

Palmer seemed to sense it immediately. "Where's your bathroom?" he asked as she slipped off her heels, wincing at the ache in her arches. She pointed toward the hallway, and he stalked in like he had every right to be there. He exited with two Advil, went to the kitchen to fetch water, and handed them to her. "Now, sit. You're exhausted."

"Which is why I wanted you to leave," she muttered, popping the pills.

He gave a small grin. "I know, but if I let you escape tonight, I'm sure I'd get a polite text first, then be ghosted."

She hated he saw through her so easily. "I wouldn't do that."

"Lie." He removed his jacket with slow motions, twisting his neck back and forth. "These things are sometimes as restraining as your shoes."

She snorted. "You'll get no pity from me. Men get away with murder. They age beautifully, can be comfortable most of the time, and are respected when they fight back. We get the crap."

He quirked a brow. "Hmm. Mind if I grab a cocktail?"

Malia sighed. "Liquor cabinet is over there."

He took his time grabbing a snifter, filling it with ice, and pouring some bourbon over it. He swirled the amber liquid, smelled it, then took a sip. Malia hated how sexy his every movement was. He prowled like a caged panther, stopping at various points around the room, picking up a knickknack and studying her book collection while he sipped his drink.

Her place was simple yet sophisticated. Her books were worn with tattered covers, and the latest Alyssa Cole novel lay on her coffee table. Stacks of fashion, business, and architectural magazines were scattered on the high glass tabletops. Mosaics and artwork accented the burnt-orange walls. A series of African sculptures were displayed in her living room, along with neutral furnishings that allowed her tastes rather than the actual furniture to become the decor. It was a place where she felt most herself, and she suddenly wanted to share it with him, which made her even crankier. "Are you going to get to the point, or are you still doing the self-guided tour?"

Palmer flashed her a grin, that crooked front tooth confirming he'd never had braces. "I like you feisty. Unfortunately, there's something else going on, and I want to know what."

"Just a girl who's tired and wants the party to end," she said.

"Your sister said something before we left, and your whole mood changed. Before that, when I held you in my arms, I felt what was happening between us. But now, that damn barrier is back up and I want to know why."

Malia stiffened at his outrageous arrogance. He had no right to demand anything from her. The depression that had settled turned on its edge. Temper lit up her nerve endings, and the tide of frustrated emotions broke free. "It's none of your business," she snarled, jumping up from the couch. "Big deal—we danced a little. My family liked you. We convinced them we were a real couple. Now it's over and we go back to normal."

"We were never normal," he said through gritted teeth. "And stop trying to downplay what's going on between us. Why can't you just own it?"

"Own what? That my body wants you? You're an attractive man, so it's not rocket science that I'm tempted. I'm just not going to blow up my life to scratch a quick itch. We made the rules and helped each other out. It's time to move on."

Palmer shook his head and carefully placed his glass on the table. "You want to push my buttons tonight? Go ahead and try and hurt me. I'm glad you finally admitted we practically ignite when we touch each other. But we both know this is so much bigger than sex. Why won't you admit it? We're good together, and I'm asking for a chance. Why are you so afraid?"

"I'm not!"

"What did your sister say to you?"

"She told me I'd finally found Mr. Right! That now I can give up the silly idea of freezing my eggs because I managed to get my husband and baby daddy naturally. The right way. God, she's probably planning our damn wedding! How does that make you feel, Palmer? Do you feel the noose ready to choke you? The desperate single woman who craves all the things we're taught we shouldn't need anymore? Everything you said you never wanted?" She broke off, raw and vulnerable, trying to turn away. "I can't do this anymore."

He closed the distance and blocked her retreat. "Now we're getting somewhere. Malia, I can't promise anything for the future right now, and neither can you. Next week, you'll begin the shots because that's what you need to do, and I support you. I don't want you to change a thing."

"Then what do you want?"

The pain that flickered over his face made her grow still, surprised by the naked emotion he allowed her to see. His soft voice racked her with a shudder. "Maybe I just want you to let me make you happy. No hidden agendas or intentions. No bigger plan to reveal." His jaw clenched as if it was painful to utter the words. "I want to be allowed to show you in every way possible the way you should be treasured."

Oh no. Not this. This was too big to fight off or respond with a clever, cutting comment. Her insides disintegrated to mush, and all that was left was her throbbing, needing heart, vulnerable to him. All those endless complaints of dates that never turned into success slapped her in the face, and Malia realized the terrible truth about herself.

She was a liar.

She'd never intended to give her entire heart and soul to any man. After so many failures and rejections, she'd locked her real self up and thrown away the key. She preached about being open and dedicated to finding love, but she'd been fooling herself the whole time.

She was afraid of real love and all its messy, terrifying complications.

She was afraid she'd never be worthy of everything her sisters and Chiara had.

She was afraid it wasn't meant to be for her.

Her voice sounded weak to her own ears. "I don't know if I can."

Palmer reached out to cup her chin and tilt her face upward. The gentleness in his grip didn't reflect in his gaze. No, those pale green eyes demanded, burned, commanded she surrender and give him this one precious win. "Yes, you do. Ask me, Malia. Ask me now, before I walk out that damn door."

He'd promised never to kiss or touch her intimately unless she asked. Alarm bells rang in her head, but her body had already decided. Automatically leaning into his seething warmth, she savored the spicy male scent of him, the lust in his eyes as he stared at her, the wet throbbing between her thighs. With no way to deny him or herself any longer, Malia stopped fighting and stepped into her full power.

Reaching up on her tiptoes, she tangled her arms around his broad shoulders, holding tight. "Put your hands on me, Palmer. Put them everywhere."

His head lowered and his mouth roughly claimed hers.

The kiss held no gentleness or getting to know one another. It held no politeness or apologies. It was a primitive, dirty explosion of lips and teeth and tongue, clinging desperately to each other as the hunger broke in rough waves between them. He ravaged her; devouring, sucking on her lower lip, his tongue pushing deep, tangling with hers. He kissed her like she was his last meal and reason for living. She kissed him back like he was the answer to all the questions she'd sought.

Never breaking contact, Palmer backed up step by slow step into the bedroom. It was a sexy seduction that had her gasping for breath and craving more. "I want to make you scream," he whispered roughly into her mouth, his hands already unzipping her dress and tugging it down to reveal her bare breasts. "I want to make you beg. I want to make you come so hard you'll never forget you've always belonged to me."

The possessive words caused a rush of wetness between her legs. Her skin itched and her legs shook as he stripped her bare, dragging down her lacy underwear until she was naked before him. Malia was comfortable with her body, but the way he ate her up with his gaze made her feel like a goddess.

Desperate to feel his skin, she tore at his shirt with clumsy motions while his hands touched her all over. Sliding down her back to cup her ass, caressing her trembling belly, and moving up to play with her breasts, tugging on her hard nipples, then bending down to take them into the hot, wet cave of his mouth and suck. She arched and grabbed at his hair, a little wild and on an edge she'd never surfed before.

Her lovemaking usually consisted of slow, careful foreplay. Checking in with the other to see what felt good and what didn't. A satisfying experience, even orgasms, which put a smile on her face and eased the tension inside her.

But with Palmer, it was on a whole other level. She wanted it rough and real. She wanted to finally fall over the cliff and see what was at the bottom, to see if she could experience the type of sex her friends had talked about and she quietly fantasized of.

Malia wrestled his shirt off, drinking in endless lean muscles, crisp dark hair, and hot, silky skin. The scent of spice and musk rose to her nostrils, and she sank her teeth into his shoulder, licking him, then biting.

His fingers clenched in the curves of her ass. "Fuck, you're a queen," he muttered, spinning her around and pressing her onto the bed. He stared down at her, and a thrill caught her unawares. He was still half-dressed in his fancy suit, thick hair mussed, eyes glittering with lust. "You're *my* queen."

"Then be my king," she drawled, tugging him close, devouring his mouth while she stroked her hands down his roped arms and taut stomach.

He groaned, his erection jumping under her hungry fingers, until he quickly shed the rest of his clothes and pressed her fully against him. His head lowered and he palmed her breasts, rubbing his lips over a tight nipple, then bringing it deep into his mouth. "You taste so sweet. Need more of you."

He slid down her body, nipping, nibbling, and pushed her thighs apart, his broad shoulders holding her open. Malia shook under the intensity, the sheer toe-curling pleasure as his hot tongue licked over her pussy, making hungry moans under his breath. She jerked underneath him, almost pulling away from the overwhelming sensation, but he held her tight as his mouth turned teasing and languid, keeping her at the razor edge of release.

She chanted his name and was rewarded when he gently kissed her clit over and over, his fingers stroking and holding her open. Finally, his fingers sank deep inside her wet channel, moving back and forth with complete demand. She arched, digging her heels into the bed, and with one swift movement, he wrapped his lips around her throbbing clit and sucked hard.

She exploded, twisting side to side at the brutal pleasure that rocked her with delight. He kissed her inner thighs and worked his way back up. Her weakened arms barely managed to wrap around his neck. "Oh my," she whispered, pressing her lips to his.

He gave her a lopsided, satisfied grin. "Let's do that all night long."

A laugh escaped. "Yes, let's. But first, why don't you finish what you started?"

"Bossy as hell. This what you want?" He slid his cock over her wet, sensitive folds, and her eyes rolled into the back of her head. "Yeah, I think it is."

"You're just as arrogant in bed as you are out of it."

"I have a lot to be arrogant about."

She dug her nails into his back as he teased her some more. Her head spun at the way he brought both humor and heat into bed, and what all her previous encounters had been missing. Who would've known she liked to play?

Malia reared up and grasped his erection with both hands, squeezing lightly. "Maybe, but you're too slow. And you're talking too much."

He sucked in a breath as she punished him with her fingers, cupping and sliding a tight vise around his girth. She relished the silky steel in her grip, the way his head tipped back in masculine pleasure, the power she held over him in this perfect moment.

"Condom."

He quickly sheathed himself while she helped. Then he reached out and grabbed under her knees, sliding her down the mattress and pushing her thighs apart. She watched under hooded eyes as he held her gaze and slowly pushed inside, filling her up slow and wide and deep. Her body clenched around the invasion, but she was wet and ready enough that he slid right home.

He gritted his teeth. "You feel like heaven. Never gonna leave."

"Don't. But first, move. God, yes, like that."

The tempo built to a savage pace, and she embraced every dominating thrust, clutching at his shoulders and rolling her hips to meet his. He whispered dirty commands in her ear that edged her closer to climax, and then he did this amazing twist and hit her G-spot, where everything shimmered bright and vivid and beautiful.

He growled with satisfaction. "Right there, baby. Give it to me. Come."

She cried out and let go, her body shuddering helplessly underneath his damp, muscled skin. He cursed like a prayer and followed her, jerking his hips with a long groan.

They collapsed together in a tangle of limbs, breathing hard, and she glanced at his face. Malia waited for the panic; waited for her mind to trip and settle into high gear, listing all the reasons this had been the wrong thing to do. Instead, she smiled, and he smiled back. They entwined their fingers while their breathing slowly settled back to normal, the sweat cooling on their naked bodies.

"How's your headache?" he finally asked.

She began to laugh, and he laughed with her, rolling her close.

And Malia knew she'd remember this night for the rest of her life.

Chapter Twenty

"You want to talk?"

Malia glanced up at his question and studied his face. They were lying in bed, lazing around. They'd ditched their phones and shut the curtains on all windows so barely any light leaked in. She was propped against Palmer's chest with his arms wrapped around her. They'd slept till noon, darted to the kitchen for coffee and eggs, then went straight back to the bedroom.

His jaw held rough stubble that created a pattern of scratches sprinkled over her cheeks, her breasts, and her inner thighs. Malia noticed his eyes held swirls of jade that reminded her of plunging into calm island water. His hair stuck up in odd angles, thick and unruly. He was gloriously naked, and she'd learned every part of his body. The jagged scar on his chest where Georgia had lost her temper and thrown a rock. The uneven patch of eyebrow after falling off his bike. His long-tapered fingers and rock-solid calves, and that one foot was slightly bigger than the other. He was ticklish on his left side by his stomach and burst out laughing when she trailed her fingers lightly over that spot.

"Not really," she said. She nibbled on his index finger and felt his erection press against her buttocks. "Do you?"

"Each time I try, I get distracted by sex."

She smiled and kissed his palm. "Don't blame me. You're the one trying to break a world record."

He laughed and shifted her. "I had a lot of fantasies over the past year I needed to try out. If I ask you something, will you tell me the truth?"

"Yes."

"Are you going to break up with me tomorrow?"

Malia stiffened, then slowly relaxed. She bit his palm, then soothed with her tongue. "I think so."

He groaned. "I knew it. Forget queen—you're pure witch. I'm too incapacitated to have the brainpower to fight you."

She reached down and stroked his erection. "You are definitely not incapacitated. Plus, I'm doing exactly what you've been asking. I'm grabbing on to this moment to be with you. You have all of me until tomorrow."

"Then what happens?" he demanded.

"I begin fertility treatments later this week."

"Third day of your period, right?"

She blinked. "I keep forgetting you know a lot about this. Yes, everything is scheduled to the hilt. No sex. Daily shots and appointments. Fluctuating hormones and emotions. I know what I've got ahead, and I need to focus on me. Last night was my gift to myself."

"And this morning." Palmer arched his hips, then flipped her over to press her deep into the mattress. "I got a gift for you now."

She stabbed her fingers into his hair, caught between a laugh and a sob. It was worse than she'd imagined. He'd hypnotized her with his perfect body and sweet words and sharp humor. He made her laugh and sigh and come harder than she'd ever had. He held back nothing from her, not afraid to whisper in her ear what she meant to him, what she'd done to him, and how he never wanted to recover. He was a man she could fall madly in love with.

And though every single one of her arguments from last night still made sense, Malia didn't care any longer. She was grabbing the moment and sucking the marrow from the bones of life. She was brave and bold, and finally let her body go free and take what it wanted.

Him. All of him. She couldn't get enough.

Malia reached out one hand, flailing around the nightstand, then found the condom. In moments, he was sheathed and deep inside her, rocking slow and steady so her clit scraped against his erection. He sucked on her nipples, refusing to go faster even when she begged and writhed and dug her heels into his ass. Again and again, he rubbed against her sensitive tissues, alternating between deep shocking strokes and shallow teasing ones, and then the waves crashed over her and through her and she let go with his name on her lips.

With a muttered curse, Palmer flipped her around to all fours, pulled her hips back, and slammed back in. She lost her breath and her words, only able to moan.

"That's it—give me more, baby. You're so damn sexy."

He cupped her breasts as he rode her hard, and when the next orgasm came, she threw back her head and screamed.

Afterward, he disposed of the condom, cleaned them both up with gentle, loving strokes, and climbed back into bed. Tucking her against him, he pressed kisses across her forehead, and Malia had never felt so completely treasured in her life.

"I'll be there every step of the way," he finally said. "I'm simply asking you to let me."

Tears stung her eyes. "I can't promise anything, Palmer. We still want different things."

"Right now, all I want is you." He kissed her swollen lips. "Now, sleep."

She did.

~

Malia took a deep breath as the nurse showed her again exactly how to prep each shot and self-inject them. Her palms dampened with sweat. The idea of sticking a needle in her belly made her want to pass out, but damned if she wasn't going to do this.

"Don't worry, it's always scary the first time." The nurse, a wonderful woman named Jo, gave her a smile and patted her arm. "You want to grab right around here where there's some extra flesh. You're doing great so far." Jo repeated the actions and began schooling her on which shot needed to be refrigerated and the various combinations of mixtures for each.

"Do you mind if I record you?" Malia asked. "I'm afraid I'm going to get all messed up and forget what you said."

"Of course! Go right ahead, I wore my fancy uniform today."

She took out her phone and filmed Jo going over all the basics, even though she had an information sheet and had already spoken with the doctor. Malia had imagined the shots would be prepped and ready, but she had to go through something like shot school, where she learned how to remove the needle, prep the mixture, and inject herself. Finding out she had to do three shots per day had been a little overwhelming, especially since each one needed to be administered at a specific time and couldn't be missed. Once again, she was glad she'd delayed the process until she felt more settled into her new job. Unfortunately, her work schedule was still busy, but if she'd waited for a break, she knew she'd be waiting forever. As overwhelmed as she was, she was grateful she'd just picked the day and finally committed.

The sacred FedEx package would be coming the next day with all the supplies. She felt a mixture of relief, excitement, and a sliver of sadness. She'd been warned by Dr. Davies that if her body didn't respond to the shots, she might need to increase the doses or the time frame. She was also told not to worry. As with any medical process, mental status was critical, and Malia believed in the theory. She swore she wouldn't pass the time obsessing in a negative manner. She needed to trust her body would do what it was supposed to so she could have some viable eggs for her future child.

Malia left the appointment with her head spinning. She had so much to accomplish this week with the Children's Hunger Initiative and working up proposals for two clients Palmer had referred. But she wasn't feeling very boss-like today. Already the appointment had left her feeling a bit open and vulnerable, and she couldn't stop thinking about Palmer.

The endless hours they'd spent together this past weekend had ultimately changed her forever. Besides experiencing the best sex she'd ever had, a door had flung open inside, and she liked who she'd become in his arms. Too much of her past had been spent chasing the ideals of a good man, and too many had left her with the bitter taste of disappointment. Palmer not only allowed her to lean into her sexuality, he challenged her in so many other ways. She loved talking with him, discussing a broad range of topics always peppered with his sharp sense of humor.

Even better? He listened.

The way he stared at her, attention focused completely, made her feel seen for the first time. He seemed to sift not only through her words but the emotional tone hidden underneath, where too many didn't bother to seek out. Malia didn't blame them. She was a private person who opened up slowly, and men seemed to find her distance off-putting. Palmer just charged through like the arrogant man he was, but his fierce interest made it completely forgivable.

The elevator doors swished open, and Malia walked into the clinic lobby, still thinking of her lover and what would unfold between them in the next few weeks. The only choice was to walk away. She couldn't give any effort to a relationship that might not even be good for her. As perfect as Palmer was in so many ways, he still didn't see his future the way she did. He had no intention of getting married or having kids.

Her heart gave a hard pang, and she ducked her head as she pushed through the double doors.

"Hey, girl! You walked right past us!"

Malia stopped short at the familiar voice and turned. Chiara and Tessa jogged up behind her, both dressed smartly for work. "I'm so sorry, I was caught up in my thoughts and—wait, what are you doing here?"

Tessa rolled her eyes. "You think we were going to miss your first appointment? We're here to take you for coffee."

Chiara gave her a quick hug. "We said we had your back, and we do."

"Plus, we need to know how the wedding went and why you wouldn't answer our texts all day Sunday," Tessa added.

Malia laughed, a bit weepy, and hugged her friends. "You guys are the best pains in the ass ever."

"Um, thanks? Come on, let's go. I need a latte like I need a roll in the hay with Chris Evans," Tessa said.

"That's pretty bad," Chiara said with a laugh. "He didn't make my laminated list, though. Hemsworth did."

Malia snorted. "I'm so over superheroes. Give me some Michael B. Jordan goodness—shirtless as Creed."

"Not even some hot Aquaman?" Tessa asked.

"Oh, I'd take that any day."

Tessa giggled. "Actually, methinks you're a Kinney-in-a-suit girl."

The image of Palmer whispering dirty commands in her ear while he thrust deep inside seared through Malia's brain. Her face heated and the girls hooted in approval.

"You totally slept with him," Chiara said in wonder, staring at her with googly eyes. "It's all over your face."

"I need caffeine," Malia muttered, stomping into the coffee shop. She was about to order her coffee when she remembered she was supposed to stay away from caffeine while she was on the shots. Another big change—she was kind of addicted. She went with a hot decaf chai instead and squeezed into a corner table where there was relative privacy. "No coffee, no sex, no alcohol," she said a bit glumly, taking a sip of her tea. It was good at least, with a nice spicy flavor.

"Think of the cleanse you're giving yourself!" Chiara said, obviously trying to be upbeat.

Tessa didn't bother. "That sucks. How bad are the shots?"

"It was awful. Not to be a whiner, but sticking multiple needles in my poor stomach freaks me out. Plus, the instructions felt like I was studying to be a mad scientist. I have to do all the mixing and stuff."

Chiara winced. "Can you call the doctor if you forget?"

"Yeah, and I took a video today. I think there's just going to be a learning curve at first. I have to make sure I set all these alarms so I don't forget—the timing is strict."

"We can do it, too, and text you, just for backup," Tessa said.

Her heart melted. She was so lucky to have them. "You guys are amazing—thanks. I'm a wreck, but then another part of me is really proud of myself for going through with it. I just wish my family supported me. Davinia made an awful comment at the wedding that spiraled me out." Malia told them what she'd said.

Chiara sighed. "I'm sorry, Mal. I know family can be a challenge, and I'm sure she didn't mean to upset you. But I also wanted to ask if you'd be willing to share your journey? I've been thinking about it, and though we've done a few things with fertility before for Quench, we've never had a full account of each step a woman goes through when she decides to freeze her eggs. I think our readership would get so much from it, and your personal story may help shed light on the process for other women. Like your sister."

Malia thought over the possibilities and agreed with her friend. It was exactly what they were trying to do with Quench. "I think it's a good idea," she said slowly. "I just need to wrap my head around sharing so much personal information with the public. I've kept it from my family, and by doing this, it would all be out there."

"We can always use a pseudonym for you, and I'd get your full approval on everything I wrote. Think about it."

Malia nodded. "Okay. I'll seriously think about it."

"How was the wedding? More importantly, how was it with Palmer?" Tessa asked, changing the subject.

Malia dragged in a lungful of air and faced her friends. "Things got complicated."

Tessa gave a snort. "All the good things eventually do. Tell us everything."

She did. She went over the wedding and their passionate night together. She admitted all the things stuck deep in her heart about Palmer and how she needed to focus on her fertility journey now.

"How did Palmer react to that?" Chiara asked, sipping her hot, frothy brew.

A reluctant smile tugged at her lips. "With his usual manner. Said he wanted to just be there for me on my terms."

Tessa raised a brow. "That's hot. He keeps surprising me."

"Me, too. But it's too much right now, guys. I'm going to be a wreck for a while. It was only the first appointment, and I already feel emotional, which is not like me at all."

Chiara reached out and squeezed her arm. "This is a big deal. I'd think something was wrong if you weren't emotional. I think you made a good decision. Focus on you and just go with the flow. We're here anytime you want to talk or cry."

"Or watch sappy love movies I hate, like *The Notebook*," Tessa said a bit grumpily. "I'll do it for you."

Malia laughed. "Thanks, I know that's a sacrifice. I think work may be good for me. I have some new referrals from Palmer, and Deanna already said she could take over whatever I can't get to these next few weeks."

"I have another great distraction," Tessa said. "I'm having a big Memorial Day party at my place. I'm inviting everyone at Quench and some of my interns so they can get to know one another in a social environment. We're going barbeque chic."

"You're grilling?" Malia asked in surprise. Tessa was more the five-star catering type.

"No, of course not. I'm hiring a chef to grill for us," she said proudly.

Chiara laughed. "Guess we're not bringing hot dogs and hamburgers."

Tessa gave a mock shudder. "Things will be a bit more gourmet than that. Think mushroom blue cheese burgers and falafel sliders and bratwurst with spices."

"Sounds awesome," Malia said. "I'll be there."

"Can Ford come?" Chiara asked.

Tessa's face clouded. "Does he have to?"

Chiara shook her head. "Really? He's Veronica's godfather and Sebastian's best friend. I don't know why the two of you fight so damn much, but I think it would be nice if he was included."

"Ugh, fine. Invite him."

"Thanks."

Malia looked down as her phone buzzed with demand and quickly read the text.

Thinking of you. How did your appointment go?

Warmth shot through her veins. Palmer had been checking up on her and obviously cared. Even though she was focused on doing this alone, knowing he was there if she needed him comforted her. She quickly texted back.

Good. Having coffee with Chiara and Tessa now. Thanks for checking in.

"Do you want to invite Palmer to the party?" Tessa asked.

She looked up from her phone. "I don't think so. That would allow him to get more deeply involved in my life. It's best I keep him at a distance."

Chiara and Tessa shared a look. Chiara seemed to pick her words carefully. "I think it may be a bit too late for that, babe. Sex changes everything. And he seems pretty serious about committing to you. Are you sure you don't want to give him a real chance? He may change his mind about things."

"I don't want to be one of those women who falls for a man and believes he'll change. That's dangerous."

Tessa nodded. "True. But it's also wrong to cut off any possibilities when you feel such a deep connection with someone. That type of certainty can be a gift."

Malia stared at her. "Did you just say something really deep about love?"

Tessa shrugged. "Maybe. I have my moments. I'd be open to finding my person one day, but he'd need to be quite extraordinary to handle all this."

They burst into laughter, finished their drinks, and headed to work.

Chapter Twenty-One

He'd waited three days after she started her shots. He couldn't wait any longer.

Palmer rang the bell and ignored the pitch in his gut. He hadn't called or texted a warning. He'd checked in with her regularly but knew the shots were probably getting a bit intense. He remembered visiting Jane that first week for a quick check-in and found she'd spiraled a bit. Not that he could understand without having a female body, but it was as if the whole process had begun to hit full force, throwing her into a free fall of doubts and emotions. He'd sat with his sister, let her cry, and listened. Later on, she confessed his visit had made a difference. He considered it one of the best things he'd done in his life.

Palmer didn't know if Malia would reach out if that happened to her. He doubted it. His queen was fierce and probably believed she could do this on her own. Yes, Chiara and Tessa were like her sisters who had her back, but he needed to know she was okay. He wanted to be a part of her life—both the ups and downs—and the only way to prove it was to show up.

Malia opened the door and stared at him in shock. He shifted his feet like he was her date for prom and had to meet her father. Dammit, he was a grown-ass man who wanted to check on the woman he'd been deep inside for hours. Was that wrong?

What if she didn't want to see him? What if she was angry and felt crowded? What if she regretted their weekend together?

He swallowed past the lump in his throat and held up the bouquet of multicolored roses. "I brought you flowers," he said stupidly.

Slowly, her face transformed and brightened. A big smile curved her lips. "Come on in, boo boo bear."

He laughed, relief pouring through his veins, and stepped through the door. Immediately, he was hit by the need to back her up against the wall and kiss her until her mouth opened for his tongue and her body melted against his and she chanted his name like a prayer. Palmer clamped down on the possessive rush and spike of testosterone, reminding himself it wasn't what she needed right now.

Instead, he took in her adorably rumbled sweats and T-shirt, Princess Leia braids artfully secured on her head, and red painted toenails. He stepped forward, lowered his head, and gave her a full kiss on that gorgeous mouth. Then handed over the bouquet. "You look ravishing."

Palmer loved the flush on her cheeks and the way she ducked her head. "I look like a total mess and should kick your ass out for not texting first."

"I brought you dinner."

She gasped with delight and bent over to peer in the bags. "You did? What'd you get?"

"I went with some traditional comfort food. Lasagna and a nice healthy salad. I also brought cake."

Was it possible he caught a tear in her eye or just a flicker of light? Her voice sounded breathy and full of wonder. "I love cake."

He grinned. "Yeah, I know. You had two pieces at both weddings, which made me think you'd like my strawberry cake with whipped cream. Strawberries are in season, so I had to do something with them."

"You made a cake for me?"

He squinted at her with suspicion. "Of course. I'm not going to buy one that could be stale or crappy when I can make it fresh. How do you feel?"

"Better, now that I have lasagna and cake and flowers." Malia stared at him with those wide golden-brown eyes full of gratitude, and his heart shattered right then and there. All he wanted was to have her look at him like that for the rest of his life.

The thought stunned him. He felt like tiny birds were flying around his head from the realization.

Palmer cleared his throat and headed to the kitchen so he didn't maul her. She needed friendship right now, not hot sex. "Let me set it up and we'll eat. How are the shots going?"

"I have one more in forty-five minutes. So far, it's not that bad other than feeling like a pincushion and being really tired. No extreme highs or lows yet."

"Good. I know everyone reacts differently. I just don't want you to feel like you have to sail through this because you need to succeed. There's no trophy for not complaining."

Her laugh warmed his ears. "How do you know me so well? Tessa said the same exact thing."

"You're competitive and hard on yourself. Most successful people are. That's why you need cake."

He moved around her kitchen comfortably while she sat at the granite countertop, relaxed, allowing him to take control. He set the table, pulling out the food and finding the plates and serving ware. The time spent in her home had given him a sense of where things were and allowed him to ease into the role of caregiver. He found a vase, cut the stems, and put the flowers in water. He liked the way she kept looking at them with such happiness. She deserved more simple gestures to remind her she was special.

He called her over to the table and they dug in. "How's it been at work?" she asked, moaning with delight as she tasted her first bite.

Palmer hardened immediately and tried to focus on his plate rather than her sexy sounds. "Endless Vows participated in a worldwide expo, and our new wedding sneakers seemed to be a big hit. I'm filming a commercial for them, and our retailers have reported decent sales. I'm hopeful eventually we'll get them to be a standard in the market rather than a quirky luxury."

"You booked the Quench website advertising for fall, right?"

"You're not in charge of my account anymore, are you?" he teased.

She tossed him a grumpy look that made him want to tweak one of her braids. "I just don't want you to back off on something that's been successful for you."

"And for Quench. Don't worry, I intend to use my credit well."

She stuck out her tongue at him and he laughed.

"Your mama would slap your wrist right now."

Malia finished her lasagna and started on the salad. "You're right, she would. Speaking of which, have you heard back from your family about the wedding yet?"

"They all texted me about how much they loved you with tons of heart emojis. That's it."

She tilted her head with curiosity. "Mine, too. So it's been a full week for both of us, and all's quiet on the home front. Usually, after a wedding, my sisters go full steam on me."

"Seems our plan was a total success."

Their gazes locked. The air crackled between them, full of heat and electricity and a lustful hunger that punched at his lungs and left him breathless. His fingers clenched around his glass as he fought to stay in his seat and not reach out and touch her. A shudder seemed to rack her body, and he gulped down his ice water to hopefully cool off. "Malia?"

"Yeah?"

"It's really hard right now to be platonic."

She gave a half laugh and shifted in her seat. "Yeah, I know. I'm starting to feel those hormones."

An alarm rang out and she slowly got up. "Shot time."

"Need some help?"

She wrinkled her nose. "No, I've got it."

"I'll cut the cake." Palmer cleaned up the table, put the leftovers in some containers, and served up two slices. He waited awhile for her to return, and when she sat back in the chair, her legs seemed to shake. "You okay?"

"Sure. I'm fine."

He stared at her, then spoke softly. "Malia, you can tell me the truth."

She made a face. "I hate giving myself these shots. I never knew I'd be such a whiner."

This time, he didn't hesitate. He walked over, tugged her upward, and wrapped his arms gently around her. She stiffened only a moment before softening against him, her limbs entangling with his, her head tucked against his shoulder. A sense of rightness overcame him, as if this was the exact place he'd been searching for without knowing it. "My mom said I used to be so scared of shots I'd run and hide when she announced it was time to go to the doctor."

Her laugh was muffled by his chest. "Did not."

"Truth. And I was scared of the dentist for so many years, my teeth had begun to get so bad. I needed some major work done."

"You have beautiful teeth. I love the crooked front one."

"I'm the last kid, and we ran out of money for braces."

She held him tighter, her sigh of satisfaction as sweet as a symphony. "What else are you afraid of?"

He dropped a kiss on the top of her head. "My mom getting sick. My family staying safe. My company failing and becoming obsolete. Dying before I discover the meaning of life."

"Are you getting any closer with the last one?" she whispered.

Raw need shook him to the core, but he kept his voice light. "Yes. I think I'm getting closer every day."

Malia pulled back and tilted her chin up. He cupped her cheek and looked at her face for a long time, studying every graceful slope and curve, staring into her eyes to catch all the hidden secrets he longed to find. "I'd like some cake now."

Palmer smiled to hide his disappointment and slowly released her. "Prepare to have your sense of taste blown."

They ate. He was happy with the density and texture—a dry cake put him in a bad mood. The cream was light with a touch of vanilla flavor, and the strawberries were firm but sweet. He watched her eat with gusto and felt as if his talent finally had a bigger purpose. To make Malia happy.

"You should have become a wedding cake chef," she muttered, stabbing a strawberry with her fork. "Combine both talents into one."

Palmer laughed. "Hmm, I never considered baking wedding desserts exclusively. I try not to get involved with the cakes too much. Emeril said I'm too bossy. One time I got so passionate about having cream cheese frosting with carrot cake instead of chocolate, I almost lost a client."

"Yuck! I don't blame you—allowing that combination is criminal." She tilted her head and regarded him curiously. "What's one of the biggest wedding disasters you had to deal with?"

He lifted a brow. "You want me to pick *one*?"

"The first one that comes to mind."

He pondered the question before shaking his head. "Oh, I know. The bride had insisted on a horse-and-buggy carriage from her home to the church. The wedding's theme was Cinderella, so she wanted everything decked out like the movie. My team called me in a panic because the horse showed up and looked as if he was going to drop dead of old age."

Her face dropped. "Oh no! I always wondered about those horses that pulled the buggies."

"The bride was a huge rescue animal advocate and began crying when she saw this sad, old white horse, decked out with feathers and ribbons, pulling this magical carriage, and said she refused to leave until we fixed the situation."

"You're kidding."

"Not. I headed straight over there. The horse was definitely old, and slow as dirt, but didn't look hurt or abused. Still, I'm an animal lover, too, and I didn't like the look of it. So I called my friend Owen Salt—he's a lawyer for animal advocates and is married to Senator Jonathan Lake's daughter. They both work locally at Animal Advocacy and know all the ins and outs of the horse-and-carriage program."

"What did he do?"

"Owen promised he'd get the horse out of the program and into a horse rescue farm in the Hudson Valley—part of the Robin's Nest Inn. I agreed to pay for it and swore a vow to the bride that her ride would be the last one the horse ever did."

Her eyes widened. "Were you able to promise such a thing?"

"I had enough money and connections to back it up, so yes, I did. She calmed down and got in the carriage to go to the church. The rest was pulled off without a hitch, even though she was an hour late. The poor groom thought she'd ditched him."

Malia laughed. "Okay, that was a disaster, but you still saved the wedding. Not bad if that's one of your worst failures."

He thought over his past and grew serious. "That's all surface. The places I've really failed are when I was too selfish to hear another's opinion or hurt people in my quest to get what I wanted. I've worked my ass off, but I've taken my power and money for granted too many times, forgetting that others are less privileged. Those are my worst failures, Malia. They're just hidden."

Palmer knew this wasn't the way to convince her to drag him back into her bed or prove he was good enough to love her. But in a strange way, he felt lighter telling his dark truths. Too many had seen the glossy image he presented and didn't know the bad stuff. It was a relief to expose himself, even if it meant shattering her ideals. He wanted Malia to see all of it. He just didn't know if it would help cement her views that they shouldn't be together in a romantic relationship.

He took a breath and looked into those golden-brown eyes that squeezed him tight. And within those depths, he saw only a deep understanding and appreciation that allowed him to relax the tension in his muscles.

"Palmer?"

"Yeah?"

"Tessa is having a party this weekend for Quench and some other friends. Would you like to go?"

A big-ass grin broke from him. "You asking me out on a date?"

"No. Because we're not together right now, remember?"

He scratched his head. "I guess. Seems like kind of a date, though."

He loved the snap of her glare. "Do you want to argue about distinctions or go to the party?"

"I'll choose the party."

"I'll email you the address."

"Can I pick you up?"

A half laugh escaped her lips. "You're so bossy. Fine. Two p.m."

Giddiness swept through him. "It's a date." He held up his hands as she opened her mouth to yell. "I mean, an afternoon with a friend. And now, I better get home and let you rest."

Palmer cleaned up the table, put the leftovers in some containers, pressed a kiss to her forehead, and headed to the door.

He savored the disappointed expression on her face when he didn't push for a more intimate embrace. There was one thing he'd learned that was key in winning any big battle.

Always leave them wanting more.

He'd gotten Malia to ask him out. Maybe it had been the strawberry shortcake or maybe it had been his truth. It didn't matter. He just hoped he was one step closer to winning her heart.

Chapter Twenty-Two

When they arrived at Tessa's barbeque party, Malia's senses exploded with the sights and sounds around her. She had forgotten how her friend liked the element of surprise and shock. Once again, she'd used it well.

Tessa's yard had been transformed into a glamping-type experience. Three separate grill stations were attended by chefs with high white hats, serving up sizzling hibachi, seafood samplers, and classics resembling burgers and hot dogs. A sweet potato, baked potato, and fry bar offered endless toppings. The in-ground pool had just been opened for the year, offering blow-up unicorns and flamingo floats, and a tiki bar flanked the deep end, creating a self-serve cocktail station. Colored umbrellas were scattered about, shading sunbathers as they sat or lounged on cushioned sectionals. Malia saw several people involved in multiple yard games like volleyball, boccie ball, and cornhole. Eighties music played on the surround speakers.

Malia took in the banquet-size timber-carved table that held red, white, and blue place settings with bunches of flowers and American flags proudly displayed. Tessa's uncle was a veteran and her friend was passionate about such celebrations. She caught Palmer's surprised expression. "Tessa is the ultimate party planner," she said with a grin.

"Forget Quench. I'm hiring her as my partner at Endless Vows. She'll be my secret weapon." Malia laughed, but he gave her a concerned look, his hand touching her cheek. "Are you sure you're feeling better?"

She made a face. "Yeah, the mints helped. Who would've thought I'd experience the joys of morning sickness?"

"I'll get you a ginger ale. Be right back."

She watched as he confidently made his way through the crowd to the full-size sliding-door cooler on the patio displaying a bunch of soft drinks and juices. God, he was sexy. She loved a man who wasn't intimidated by strangers and was able to assimilate in a crowd. There had been many bad dates with men clinging to her side, citing they didn't know anyone. She was a bit too independent, and clinginess turned her off. She'd never have to worry about that with Palmer. He was able to handle himself with ease.

Malia headed toward the back deck where she spotted the hostess. Tessa squealed and bounced over to her. "Yay, you're here! What do you think? Isn't it fun?"

"You never fail to impress me, babe," she said, giving her a hug. "And what is happening with this outfit? It's insanely cool."

"Right?" Tessa posed, throwing her curls back and sticking her hand on her hip. The white ensemble was very Rachel Zoe, with a flowy cotton camisole stitched with flowers and matching shorts that flared out and emphasized her curvy hips. The stacked platform shoes were really sneakers with a subtle designer label that only Tessa could have snatched with her contacts. "I think it screams barbeque."

Malia laughed. "I think it was made for a summer day on a yacht, but who cares? It slays. Where's Chiara?"

"I hired a baby-friendly clown to amuse the littles," she said, pointing toward the pigtailed woman dressed in bright colors with a red nose. Chiara and her husband were bouncing Veronica in their arms while the clown made funny faces. Mike was with them, clapping his hands with grandfatherly enthusiasm.

"You think of everything."

"I try. Everyone is here. Where's Palmer?"

"At your service," he said, coming up behind Tessa with a grin. He handed Malia a ginger ale. "If you ever get bored of running your self-care company, you can take over for me at Endless Vows. This party is amazing."

Tessa beamed. "Thanks, I'm so glad you were able to come. I can't wait till you meet Ryder, Chiara's hubby."

He frowned. "I thought his name was Sebastian."

"Oh, it's both. Sebastian Ryder is his full name, but we all call him Ryder, except for Chiara," Malia said.

Palmer nodded.

"There's plenty of IPAs in the coolers, and Ford brought a keg with something like Coors Light." Tessa rolled her eyes slightly, and Malia bit her lip. "Mal, I have plenty of mocktails for later. Are you nauseous again?" she asked, motioning toward the ginger ale.

"A little, but I'll be fine."

Someone shouted Tessa's name. "Oops, be right back. Make yourselves at home!" She bounced off as fast as she'd arrived.

Malia took in the crowd and tried to rally. She knew the party would be fun, but her mood had plummeted over the past two days, and she was fighting a bit of depression. Her last doctor's appointment hadn't been as positive as she'd hoped. Her body was producing hormones a bit too slowly, so they'd added an additional shot to her daily doses. Making fun small talk when her belly felt bruised and swollen might have been a bit of a strain, but she forced a smile on her face and threw back her shoulders. Maybe being here with friends would get her out of her funk. "Let's get something to eat and I'll introduce you around."

Palmer's hand rested lightly on the small of her back. "Or we can go home, eat ice cream, then pretend to watch Netflix while we make out?"

She began to laugh, her spirits already lightening. How did he always know how to read her? The sun was hot on her skin, but it was the warmth inside that lit her up when she looked into his face.

He'd brought her flowers and dinner. He'd made her an entire cake. He'd shown her a vulnerability she hadn't suspected. He called every night like clockwork and sent her links on the internet about women going through the egg-freezing process so she wouldn't feel so alone. He made her laugh.

The emotions bubbled up inside, overtaking her, but she couldn't handle it right now. It was too much. Instead, she jerked her head toward the burgers. "I want to check out the designer burgers," she said. "I just hope she has classic mac salad. I hate the fancy Dijon mustard they try to elevate it with. Hellmann's is all you need."

Palmer gave her a shocked look. "Agreed! You never mess with perfection."

It was at that exact moment she fell a little bit in love with Palmer Matterson. The realization was too much to deal with, so she shut it down, locked it in a box, and concentrated on the party.

The time passed as they chatted with Kelsey, who'd brought her girlfriend and looked adorably in love, barely able to break away from each other. She introduced Palmer to Magda, the photographer. Magda was wearing a long black dress, even though it was humid, and the woman seemed not to have sweat glands. She fell into a deep discussion with Palmer on how wedding art should be elevated to a higher level, explaining a vivid vision that included a bride in a wedding dress with a naked man standing beside her. He seemed to love it and made arrangements to book her for some work at Endless Vows.

Ryder and Chiara finally joined them with Veronica in tow. "So good to meet you," Ryder said, shaking Palmer's hand. "I know everyone's grateful for your support of the foundation."

Palmer smiled at the baby, who looked back at him with wide eyes. "I like the way it gives me an opportunity to be more personally involved. I heard you do a lot of work with the Dream On Youth Center. How are the kids there?"

"Great. I'll introduce you to Maria, who's doing an internship with Quench. She's here today. As for the others, they're like all kids, looking for someone to listen and give a crap."

"Sebastian! Little ears," Chiara reminded, giving her husband the look. Veronica looked at her mother and began to gurgle, smashing her fist against her drooling mouth.

"Sorry. Give a, um, darn."

"Nothing wrong with a bit of color in her vocab, right, sweetie?" a masculine voice boomed from behind. Veronica turned and saw Ford, who easily scooped her up and began tickling her under the chin. The baby's giggles made everyone laugh. "Your godfather will show you exactly what to say when someone tries to mess with you."

Malia thought Ford was one of the most down-to-earth men, who too many women underrated. He had a rich, deep voice and a scruffy goatee on the edge of a full beard. He also volunteered at the youth center and spent his spare time working with underprivileged kids.

Tessa's face soured when she laid her gaze on the man. Malia watched her curiously, wondering why the two of them seemed to rub each other the wrong way. They could barely be in the same room together without some ridiculous fight breaking out.

Tessa's voice was stiff when she spoke. "Hi, Ford. Glad you could come."

"Thanks for inviting me. Even though you did some false advertising. Claimed it was a barbeque, so I wore my lucky shirt." He puffed out proudly at his tropical orange T-shirt that had a picture of a chicken pointing at a box of nuggets. BRO, IS THAT YOU? was scrolled across the front.

Malia guessed Tessa didn't share the same type of humor Ford did, since his shirt made her roll her eyes. "I don't know what you're talking about. This is obviously a barbeque."

Ford kept bouncing Veronica. "Back me up, guys. This is a fancy schmancy bougie party—not a barbeque. Did you see those burgers? They're stuffed with weird things, and there's not even hot dogs! Instead, one of those dudes gave me some Italian sausage thing and stuck it on a bun with veggies." He gave a mock shudder. "Where's the Cheetos and chips and dip? The corn dogs and baked beans? I bet you don't even have s'mores."

Uh-oh. Malia winced as she watched her friend's face turn red.

Tessa curled up and hissed like a pissed-off snake. "Are you kidding me? Those burgers are prime rib! And those are bratwurst, but of course, you're probably the type to think Ball Park Franks are high cuisine."

Ford shrugged. "Nah, but I like Nathan's. No need to lose your temper, T. It's a very nice party, just not a barbeque."

"Don't call me T! It's Tessa."

Chiara cleared her throat. "Um, Ford, maybe you should stop bouncing the baby. She just ate and has a bit of a gas problem."

"She looks fine to me," he said, rocking Veronica back and forth as she continued making delighted noises. "Your godfather knows what babies like, doesn't he?"

Palmer spoke up. "Excuse me, but you sound familiar. Do I know you?"

Malia rushed in. "I'm sorry, I forgot to introduce you. Palmer, this is Ford Maddox. He's a close friend of Ryder's and Veronica's godfather."

"Sorry, man, not sure we've met before. But it's nice to meet you now," Ford said with a grin.

"Weird, it's your voice, not your face." Suddenly, Palmer snapped his fingers. "Are you on the radio?"

"Oh, yeah! KTUZ Sports Radio. I do the *Sports Connector* segment and the morning talk show."

Palmer nodded, his face filled with excitement. "I love that show! I swear, no one can report a game like you, man. Not only do you know your stats but you see things too many announcers miss. You were the first to call out Adam Wainwright's Tommy John surgery when his pitches began to go downhill. Everyone else called it a slump."

"Too many young pitchers are getting overplayed and running out of options other than surgery. Pisses me off. And yeah, I get this instinct when an athlete is facing bad juju. It's a talent, I guess."

Tessa snorted. "Great, so you're some type of athletic doom psychic."

"Yep. And you do makeovers, right?"

Veronica made a weird noise, and Tessa grunted something under her breath. Malia was sure it was a curse word. "What kind of godfather are you? Stop shaking her; you can tell she doesn't like it!" Tessa grabbed Veronica, tossing Ford a disgusted look. "It's okay, sweetie, hang with your aunt Tessa."

Veronica looked trustingly at her aunt. Opened her cute, drooly mouth.

And spit up all over Tessa's pristine white outfit.

Chiara jumped into action. "Oh, I'm sorry, Tessa. Here, let me take her." She cooed and grabbed the rag hanging over her shoulder, wiping up the mess on Veronica's onesie. "Let's go inside and change. Is this your third outfit we're on now?"

"I'll go with you. Sorry, Tess," Ryder said.

Obviously feeling better, the baby began to happily babble as they walked away. Malia stared at Tessa, who was frozen in place with a look of horror. An awful yellow substance dripped over her chest and down the front of her outfit. Even worse? It smelled.

Everyone remained silent for a bit.

Finally, Ford spoke. "You should never wear white to a barbeque."

Malia bit her lip.

Tessa gave him an astonished stare, eyes wide, steam rising from her very aura. Then, with a murderous look, she stomped off and disappeared inside the house.

Ford shrugged. "She's so uptight. I'm gonna see if they have any ribs. See you later."

He headed off, and Malia and Palmer shared a glance. "Do you think she despises Ford as much as you despised me?" he asked thoughtfully.

"We had a sexual chemistry going on, so it was different. Hate sex is very powerful. I think Tessa would honestly murder him if they were stuck together for too long."

"Interesting." He seemed to be deep in his thoughts as he considered the pair. "You never know."

"Do you think it's almost time to bring out the cupcakes?" she asked hopefully.

He gave a smug grin. "You want 'em bad, don't you."

She laughed. "Yeah, I do. One was red velvet, right?"

"There's red velvet, carrot, and s'mores."

"Don't tell Ford—he'll eat them all. Let's get them out of the refrigerator before the other desserts come out."

He regarded her in shock. "Malia Evergreen, you are a bad, bad girl."

She fluttered her eyelashes. "Only with your cupcakes, boo boo bear."

Malia relished his deep-chested, full laugh. He grabbed her hand and they headed for their sugar fix.

She couldn't stop smiling.

~

Palmer looked around at the group Malia called friends and sipped his beer. He liked the people she surrounded herself with—besides being funny, they were kind and supportive of one another. Ryder seemed to look after Chiara, Malia, and Tessa, as if they were his responsibility. Palmer respected the guy and bet they could get to be friends, if he had the chance. After a brief discussion with Ford about his job, he felt a bit starstruck and imagined them all going out one night.

The various employees at Quench were quirky, enthusiastic, and sharp. The interns seemed a bit overwhelmed when he spoke to them, but now he noticed they were fused in with other groups and were playing pool volleyball. He wondered if the intern program could be beneficial at Endless Vows. Most high school or college students didn't even realize careers in the wedding field were so vast. Maybe he'd talk to Malia about it, or Tessa.

He turned his head and studied the woman at his side. Once again, just her presence sparked and soothed him in one twist. Her long legs were stretched out in front of her, mostly bare in snug denim shorts that had a cute fringe at the edge. The top was more of a halter that tied in the back and cut into a deep V. The sunny yellow color showed off her smooth brown skin and brought out the golden amber flecks in her eyes. Her lips were slicked with a sparkly gold gloss that he'd been having a damn hard time not staring at all day.

He knew her week had been hard with the injections. She was scheduled for the procedure next Wednesday if things went according to plan, but Palmer knew it could change quickly depending on how her body was responding. He'd sworn not to push her on anything until she had time to adjust. Instead, he'd tried to show her by his steady presence that he cared and was in this for the long run. By inviting him today, Malia had taken a critical step forward. It was an admittance that he meant more to her than she said. Palmer felt like they were on track to get more serious once she'd frozen her eggs and secured that doubt about having children.

Tessa's face lit up, and she jumped from her seat. "Emma's here!" she announced, walking over to hug the older woman. "I'm so glad you could make it."

Palmer stood to greet her and blinked in surprise. She looked . . . different. No more hat or clunky glasses. The modern tortoiseshell frames accented her delicate features. Her hair didn't look like a helmet anymore, and she seemed younger. "Hi, Emma. You look great."

She beamed with pleasure. "Thank you! The girls took me to the spa and Tessa did a bit of her own magic, and I've been getting compliments all the time. I miss some of my hats, though."

Tessa laughed. "I told you to wear them, just don't use them to hide anymore."

The women crowded together to chat, and Palmer moved over toward the guys. "How'd you get into planning weddings?" Ford asked curiously.

"I have four sisters."

Ryder laughed. "Damn, that's a lot of female energy to deal with."

"Tell me about it. I was the ring bearer and a front-seat witness to wedding and engagement chaos. I started to realize how many mistakes are made, and the idea of solving them to make my sisters happy and calm became a passion of mine." He shrugged. "I guess I kind of fell into the industry."

Ford tipped back his beer. "Do you like it?"

"Yeah, I really do. There's a lot of creativity, and I've been lucky to create my own business so I don't have to work under anyone else. We just began delving into products such as wedding sneakers. I'm never bored."

Ryder shared a glance with Ford. "I know you're in Manhattan, but I'm off this summer, and Ford does a lot of work in the city. Want to meet one night for a beer?"

Satisfaction surged. "Definitely. I'll give you my number to text." He felt a bit giddy that they wanted to include him. For someone in the business and public spotlight, he was a bit of a loner. Lately, work was his main companion, along with his family. Other than Emeril, he didn't have too many male buddies he felt comfortable hanging out with. It would be nice to be a part of Malia's inner crew.

Mike walked over, eating a s'mores cupcake. "Palmer, I heard you brought these. Where'd you buy them?"

"I made them."

The older man jerked back. "Are you kidding? Do you know how much I could sell these for? Can I buy any for the diner?"

Palmer laughed. "I don't really have time to bake in big batches, but I promise to drop off or give Malia any I do make. No charge."

Mike gave Ryder and Ford a judging look. "Why don't either of you ever try to cook? Look at this guy—he runs a big company *and* bakes!"

Ryder jumped in. "We cook, Mike. Just not so good, but that's mostly your fault. Why try when you do such a good job for all of us?"

Palmer hid a grin when Mike puffed up with pride. "Yeah, I guess you're right. Is that Emma?"

Palmer wondered why Ryder stiffened as if scenting danger. Mike's interest sharpened when Ryder nodded.

"Did I tell you about that guy she brought into my diner? All fancy schmancy, and now look at her. She's changing the way she looks and acts just to impress him."

"She said the girls took her to the spa," Palmer said.

Mike snorted. "Seems like more than that. Why are women always trying to change themselves to make some guy happy? She used to eat at my place all the time, clocked to a routine from where she sat to what she ordered. Now she hardly comes in anymore. And when she does, she ignores me. I think I should say something."

"Oh, I don't," Ryder said quickly. "Best to stay out of it, Mike. Hey, Veronica needs changing—want to help me?"

"Nah, I really want to talk to Emma." He stepped forward and Palmer caught the panic in Ryder's face. Something was going on with those two he had no clue about, but a storm brewed in Mike's eyes, and it was about to be let loose. Mike stomped over. Palmer, Ryder, and Ford drifted closer to eavesdrop.

The man interrupted the women's conversation. "Hi, Emma."

The older woman looked wary. "Michael."

"It's Mike. How are you?"

The group seemed to hold their breath as they waited for Emma to answer. Palmer found himself doing the same. "I'm fine, thank you."

"Did you bring that guy with you?"

Emma narrowed her gaze dangerously. "No. Why?"

"I just wanted to talk to you about a few things. Things I've noticed and heard."

Tessa cleared her throat. "Um, Mike? Maybe you two should chat later. In private. That way—"

Emma cut her off, head tilted to the side as she regarded him. "No, go ahead, Michael. I'd like to hear what you have to say."

Mike seemed a little put off by her firm tone, as if he was used to a meeker Emma. The woman had definitely been through a bit of a change since Palmer last met her. She didn't duck her head at all, just met Mike's gaze with a steely stare behind her now-chic glasses.

"Well, I see you decided to do this big change with yourself, and I wondered why. I know Tessa helped, but I noticed it revolved around this cane guy."

Her brow shot up. "Cane guy?" she repeated.

"Yeah, that dude with the cane that was with you at the diner. All of a sudden, you're fixing your hair all fancy and getting expensive new glasses. You even dumped the hats that you like. I wanted to say you don't need to change for any man, because if he didn't like you before, he's not worth it."

Palmer felt like he was watching a professional car race where the car was about to explode in a fiery crash but there was nothing anyone could do to stop it. Mike seemed smug with his speech, as if his advice had helped her.

Lord, the man didn't have a clue.

This time, Malia stepped in. "Well, that was interesting, but how about we move it inside? The bugs are biting me. Anyone else?"

Emma reared up in full feminine temper, closed the distance between her and Mike, and stabbed one finger at his chest. "How dare you say those things to me! Who I date and what I wear and how I look are none of your business."

Mike's jaw dropped. "I'm trying to help you! I'm giving you a compliment here, saying you're perfect just the way you are."

Palmer wanted to close his eyes to avoid this cringeworthy scene, but he now understood exactly what watching *The Real Housewives* was like. No wonder it was addicting.

"A compliment? You're paying me a compliment?" Her laugh was completely mocking. "No more. This time I'm going to talk and you're going to listen. I cannot believe all these years, the highlight of my day was to eat breakfast at your place and get to say hello to you."

Mike's eyes seemed to bug out. Malia stood with her friends in shocked silence as Emma transformed into a woman of fury.

"But I was a silly, stupid woman to think you were a nice man. A man worthy of my affection and respect. All this time, I believed you were special, because you were a wonderful father to Rory, and a fixture in this town, and a mentor to these beautiful girls I've come to love." Her fists clenched as she spit out the words she must've been holding back for so long. "Rory was an extraordinary woman. She took my breath away, and when she died, some of my faith was broken forever. I saw your pain and wanted to help, but I knew it wasn't time. So I came into your stupid café every morning and believed one day, you'd say a real hello to me. One day, you'd look into my eyes and I'd be brave enough to say something. To have a real conversation with you."

Mike opened his mouth, but her glare made him shut up immediately.

"I never was, though. I tried so hard, but I'm awkward. I know I don't fit in. After your endless insults, belittling comments, and rudeness, I knew you'd never like me. So I did these changes to feel good about myself and find other people who may like me. I even thought you might think I was a little pretty. But of course, you didn't, and that's okay now because I don't care."

"Emma, I—"

"I don't need you anymore, Michael. I don't need your pancakes or your pity or your approval. Because after all this time, I finally know the truth." She delivered her final words with a furious growl. "You're not worthy enough for me."

Emma stepped back and patted her hair. In seconds, the fury and hurt were gone, tucked neatly back behind her facade.

Mike took a step toward her. "Please, listen to me, Emma."

"No. Don't follow me." She marched away, head held high, and disappeared into the crowd.

"Dayum," Ford said. "All of this was over a stupid makeover? What did you do, Tessa?"

Tessa gave him a drop-dead glare and took off after Emma. Chiara and Malia slapped Mike awkwardly on the shoulder and followed. Mike remained silent, staring after her, his face stunned.

Ryder stepped up. "Mike? Hey, you okay?"

Mike shook his head, eyes filled with shock. "Did she say she liked me?"

"Yeah, she definitely liked you. Maybe give this some time to blow over. Women like space when they're pissed off."

He still seemed stuck in a trance, unable to move. "I never knew. Never figured it out."

"Us men can be a bit dense sometimes about that stuff," Ryder said.

"I like her, too, Ryder. A lot."

Palmer scratched his head. "Um, Mike? Maybe that's not a good thing to tell her right now."

"You don't think so?"

Ford groaned. "Hell no."

"She said I was a good father to Rory."

Ryder half hugged him, face filled with sympathy. "Because you were. And you're a great father to all of us. You're just not that great with women."

"Guess not. Rory's mom used to tell me that a lot."

"Bet she did. Hey, how about we get a drink? Let the girls calm her down a bit," Ford suggested.

"She said I was special. But I think I screwed up."

Ford thumped him on the back and led him to the bar area. "Yep. Let's talk about it." They walked off and left Ryder and Palmer.

Veronica began to shift and wail in Ryder's arms. "I have to change her."

"Want some help?" Palmer asked.

"Always. Come on."

Ryder led him inside Tessa's house, which was a palace of gorgeous design and sweeping curves. Rich textiles mixed with funky wall paint to create a bit of an artist's delight. She'd paired it with elegant accents like gilded mirrors, crystal chandeliers, and European custom furniture. Admiring her choices, he followed Ryder upstairs to one of the spare bedrooms, where a changing table was set up and a diaper bag sat on the bureau.

"Wow, I didn't know Tessa had a child," Palmer commented, taking in the rocking chair, pink elephant wallpaper, and crib.

Ryder laughed and laid Veronica down. "She doesn't. She created this room after Veronica was born for when she babysits."

Palmer shook his head. "She's a firecracker, isn't she."

"Yeah. God help the man who's tamed by her. Once she loves, it's forever."

Palmer grabbed a diaper and the cream, handing it over. Ryder cleaned and changed his daughter with expert motions, dressed her, and kissed her tummy as the baby gurgled in happiness.

"She's a cutie," Palmer said.

"Thanks. I gotta feed her. Can you hold her while I grab the bottle?"

"Sure." Palmer scooped up the infant and began talking softly to her, rocking back and forth while pointing out different things in the room. He'd spent many sleepless nights trying to help his sisters with their kids. He actually adored babies and the way they seemed to notice more in the world each day. The innocence and joy they allowed others to see was a gift, and he treasured his nieces and nephews for showing him a different perspective.

He'd just never wanted a baby for himself. Never felt a need to procreate or hold his own child. Never yearned for a wife and family. He figured he wasn't born with the nesting gene and needed to accept that was his natural path.

Ryder came back with the bottle.

"I can feed her," Palmer said.

"You sure?"

"Yeah. It's been a while, so I miss it. I took a lot of the night shifts when my sister Jane's husband was deployed for six months. She had two little ones and nearly had a breakdown, so I kind of became her nanny."

"I'm impressed, man. Go for it."

He handed him the bottle, and Palmer settled himself in the rocking chair, supporting Veronica up on one elbow. She greedily latched on and sucked hard, eyes already half-closed with pleasure.

"So what's the deal with you and Malia?"

Palmer had to give the guy credit. Ryder knew exactly when to strike to get the right answers. He gave a slow grin. "Nice surprise attack."

The man grinned back. "We all care about Malia. She's been complaining about you for forever, and suddenly, you guys are going to weddings and she's inviting you to parties. What happened?"

Palmer didn't mind the intrusion. He actually liked that Ryder was looking out for Malia. It was something he'd do with his own friends and sisters. "I screwed up. I was kind of like Mike with Emma at first. Gave her a hard time and played a role because I couldn't understand why she was getting under my skin."

"Pulling her pigtails, huh?"

He chuckled at the familiar line, looking back down at Veronica. "Yeah. Then she announced she was leaving as my account rep, and I knew I needed to be honest. Tell her I was interested. Of course, she didn't take that too well."

"Figured not."

"I began working with her for the Quench Foundation and asked her to give me a chance. When she wouldn't, I asked her to accompany me to my cousin's wedding so my family would stop trying to match-make me. Hoped for a way to convince her we'd be good together."

"Exactly like one of those Hallmark movies."

"Hope not. Those suck." Ryder gave him a judgy look, and Palmer backed off. "I mean, only a few. Some are good."

Ryder relaxed. "What do you think of her going through the fertility treatments?"

"I support her one hundred percent. I admire her for taking control of her future."

Ryder lifted a brow. "Hmm. Perfect answers."

"I mean it."

Silence settled between them, broken only by Veronica's tiny gasps and gulps. Palmer eased the bottle away and hitched her on his shoulder for burping. Ryder tossed him a diaper cloth, which he stuck under the baby's chin. With slow motions, he rubbed her back and began to pat.

"Want kids?" Ryder asked.

He hesitated, sensing deep undertones in the question. "Never wanted them. Never wanted to get married, either."

Ryder nodded. "Veronica was a surprise. Chiara and I never planned to even be together, let alone have a baby. Yet, I look at both of them now and can't imagine a different life."

"That's nice it worked out for you."

A burp sounded in the room. Satisfied, Palmer eased her back to the original position and replaced the bottle.

"Sometimes, things work out in a way we never expected," Ryder said.

"Definitely."

"Come on, dude, what do you really want? What's your endgame? Sleep with her? A short affair? Long-term relationship? Or did you give up and just want to be friends?"

Palmer's eyes widened at the sudden jab, and his temper stirred. "Just because it doesn't end with a ring and pregnancy doesn't mean it's not real."

"Agreed. But you're dating someone who's going through fertility treatments because she wants a baby. Playing with her head isn't a good idea, man."

He kept his voice low due to the baby in his arms, but his heart began ramming against his chest. "I'd never play games with Malia. Not anymore. Why do we need to figure out our entire future right now? I'm still struggling to get her to accept a real date!"

"You don't need to figure everything out now, but there should be some type of goal here. Because Malia may pretend not to feel anything, but I saw her face when she looked at you."

"How did she look at me?" he demanded.

"Like you're more than a fake escort. Like you're the real thing."

His lungs collapsed. He stared at Ryder as a wild craving clawed from his gut, a need to believe she was feeling half the things he did. "I want that," he finally managed to say.

Ryder studied him for a long while, then muttered something under his breath. "How do you really feel about her? No bullshit."

A hundred answers whirled through his mind, some witty, some profound, and some dodgy. But when he opened his mouth, only one sentence fell out. "I'm falling in love with her."

Ryder jerked back. Surprise flickered across his face, and then he slowly nodded. "Fair enough." The baby finished with her bottle, and

Ryder reached for her, propping her up with a big grin. "Come on, sweetheart, I need one more burp before we get back to Mommy."

"That's it? I tell you this big revelation and that's all you have to say?"

Ryder chuckled. "I don't know what I'm doing either, man. You two seem good together. I'd just advise being honest about what you both want. Like I said, things can change." He beamed down at his daughter and left the room.

Palmer settled back in the rocking chair, unable to stand on shaky legs. He was falling in love with Malia. Sure, he'd known it in a foggy sort of way, but actually saying the words was a whole other level.

The imprint of the baby in his arms still held. He thought of what Ryder said and how loving someone can change everything.

He had a lot to think about. Good thing he had some time as Malia was finishing up her fertility process. Because when she was done, they both needed to face some hard truths.

Chapter Twenty-Three

Malia was quiet as they drove to the clinic. Chiara and Tessa didn't try to make her talk, and she was grateful.

Finally, she was getting the surgery to retrieve her eggs. It had been an intense week of so many ups and downs, sometimes she didn't know if she was going to make it. Her belly looked pregnant and was covered with bruises. Yesterday, she'd burst into tears because Kelsey told her they'd run out of lemon-flavored seltzer. And when she'd caught sight of a mom walking into a candle shop with two cute toddlers on Main Street, she'd been hit with a longing so bad, she'd almost dropped to her knees.

The trigger shots hadn't helped. The strict schedule had continued up to the surgery date, and she was required to get one shot twenty-four hours before the procedure and another twelve hours before. She'd had to set her alarms and head back and forth between the clinic and home, having a mini heart attack worrying she'd hit traffic and be too late.

Malia had gotten no sleep last night, and when she looked in the mirror, she got scared. Who was this bloated, puffy-eyed, haunted woman looking back at her? Since Tessa's party, she'd been a mess, pushing Palmer away with excuses of not feeling well or too much work. She sensed his growing frustration, especially since they'd been getting even closer. But he didn't know the conversation she'd overheard. And Malia wasn't strong enough to tell him the truth.

Not yet.

The emptiness was too much to bear, so she pushed it all away, refusing to focus on anything else but her eggs and the hope of her future babies.

Chiara pulled up to the clinic and cut the engine. "Ready?"

Malia forced a smile and nodded. "Let's do this."

They accompanied her inside, and she was brought back to change into a gown and get prepped. Knowing her friends were in the waiting room, ready to hold her hand and support her when she woke up, soothed her nerves.

Dr. Davies came in with a warm smile. "Morning, Malia. Everything looks good, and we're ready for the retrieval. Now, we already went over the process, but did you have any other questions?"

She twisted her hands together. "No, I'm good."

"Then think positive and get ready to take a relaxing nap. I'm sure you need it."

In a short amount of time, she was helped into the stirrups and the IV drip began. Malia slowly closed her eyes and drifted to sleep, thinking of the beauty of endless possibilities.

~

When she saw Tessa and Chiara waiting for her, Malia gave them a thumbs-up sign.

"How did it go? How do you feel?" Tessa demanded.

"Good. Dr. Davies was able to retrieve sixteen eggs, which is great. But they'll call me tomorrow to let me know how many were viable. Some don't make it through the freezing process."

"Those are great odds," Chiara said. "Are you sore?"

"No, I just feel weird. Like I'm in a fog. I think I need to go home and rest."

"We got you covered. I'll stop by later with groceries and wine when it's safe to drink again. We can celebrate," Tessa said.

A wave of affection washed over her. "I love you both so much," she croaked out.

"No crying, please! Quick, Chiara, insult her."

Chiara rolled her eyes. "That's your job, babe. Come on."

They drove back to Malia's house, and she turned to face them. "I'm going to take a nap, so you both can get back to the office."

"No, we're staying with you," Chiara said stubbornly.

Malia laughed. "There's no need to babysit me, nothing is happening. I'm fine, and we won't know anything until tomorrow. Honestly, I'd feel much better knowing you were taking care of Quench. And Chiara, I've been working on my journal for that article. I want you to write it. I think it's important, and I want to do it."

Her friends exchanged a glance. "You sure?" Tessa asked. "You're not trying to be all martyr-like, are you?"

"I'm sure. Now go make us some money." She gave them quick hugs and let herself into her home.

The silence surrounded her. She changed her clothes, brewed some strong coffee, added cream, and sat in her comfy living room chair, sipping the hot brew and thinking. No matter what happened with the retrieval process, something had changed inside her. She felt different. By facing her deepest fears of never being a mother, she'd managed to make peace with one of her demons. But it had also unsettled her. She had to deal with the realization that she wanted a relationship with a man who didn't match the future she dreamed of.

The memory of Palmer's conversation with Ryder haunted her. After they'd calmed down Emma, Malia had made her way inside and gone upstairs to use Tessa's bathroom. The two men's voices tempted her to eavesdrop, so she'd eased over to listen.

"Want kids?" Ryder had asked.

"Never wanted them. Never wanted to get married, either."

She'd decided to freeze her eggs so she had more time. Time to decide when being a mother was the right move. Time to find the man who was her soul mate and wanted all the same things she did. But spending this precious time with Palmer would eventually lead to heartbreak. He wasn't going to change.

And neither was she.

An aching loss throbbed in her very soul. Loneliness overtook her, and she bowed her head, overcome with emotions.

The doorbell startled her. No one knew about the procedure except Tessa and Chiara. Needing the space, she'd told Palmer she still wasn't sure when the retrieval would be.

Muttering under her breath, she went to the door and her heart dropped when she saw him. Malia grasped the knob with trembling fingers. She was so tired—could she really deal with this confrontation right now?

Taking a deep breath, she opened the door and faced him. "What are you doing here?"

Palmer's face was serious as he studied her, his gaze sweeping over her figure as if concerned something had happened. "Why didn't you tell me, Malia? I was worried when you didn't answer your texts."

"I wanted to do this on my own," she finally said.

He stepped over the threshold. "I called Chiara and she told me. I'm glad they went with you, but I wanted to be a part of it, too. For you."

Her eyes stung and she shook her head hard. She felt as if she was on the edge of breaking apart. How could she want two different things so badly? How could she force herself to decide between the man she was falling in love with and the future she'd always dreamed of? "I can't do this right now, Palmer. We can talk later."

Her knees buckled, and he moved, sweeping her up into his arms. With steady strides, he brought her into the bedroom and laid her down. Tucking her under the covers, he adjusted the pillow and smoothed her hair back from her forehead. "You can yell at me all you want later. You can build your defenses back up and take on the world with your usual spitfire ways. But right now, sweetheart, all you have to do is sleep."

Hot tears stung her eyes. The sheer tenderness in his gaze seared through her, and suddenly, she was sobbing. She cried while he comforted her, respecting the sacred space, not trying to stop her or rationalize her feelings.

When she'd emptied all her tears, Palmer got her a tissue, placed a glass of water on the nightstand, and kissed the top of her head.

Her defenses broke open and left her heart raw. "Stay with me," she whispered.

The bed creaked as he lay down beside her. He pulled her in, and she relaxed against his muscled body, his arms wrapped tight around her. His delicious scent surrounded her, and everything inside finally took a deep breath and let go.

~

When she woke, he had soup ready for her and she joined him in the kitchen. Malia ran a hand over her hair self-consciously, but Palmer's appreciative gaze on her casual sweats and T-shirt reassured her. "I'm not sick, you know," she said with a half grin. But she began ladling the soup into her mouth.

"Soup is comfort," he said. "But my mother would be wincing right now."

She stopped slurping and patted her mouth. "Sorry. Guess I'm hungrier than I thought."

"The last week is the worst. Jane barely got through it."

"I'm assuming it worked out well for her?" she commented, focusing on her bowl. "She has two kids."

"Yep. Her boyfriend at the time didn't know if he wanted kids. They were seriously in love but decided to break up, and that's when she made the decision to freeze her eggs. She said she was tired of having her future kidnapped because she was worried she'd never be a mother."

"When did she finally meet her husband? How many years after?"

"Two years later. But it ended up being her ex-boyfriend. They were meant to be together the whole time. They just needed time."

She blinked in surprise. "Wow. They got their happily ever after. What changed his mind?"

"I'm not sure. Maybe losing her."

Malia dropped the spoon. The shattering silence between them throbbed with things unsaid and emotions too fierce to tame. "I figured out a few things myself recently."

Palmer stiffened, but his tone was mild. "I'd like to hear them."

Malia pushed back from her chair and regarded him with resolution. It was time to face the truth for both of them. She gathered her strength and committed to the only road left. "I was wrong. All this time, I tricked myself into believing all I wanted was a happy ending. But now I know the truth."

"What truth?" he asked.

Her lower lip trembled. "I believe in beginnings. It's the endings I try to avoid."

His body seemed to explode with tension. He stood and began pacing back and forth in the kitchen like a caged panther. "What are you saying, Malia? Something happened after the party, and you've been pushing me away ever since. What are you so afraid of?"

"I overheard your conversation with Ryder. I went upstairs and heard you talking and couldn't help listening in. You told him your truth—that you don't want kids or marriage."

He sucked in his breath. Those green eyes glittered with intensity. "You heard me say that, but you never confronted me? Asked me in what context I said it?"

She frowned. "Why should I? You haven't changed your position."

"Did you hear the rest?"

Malia shook her head. "I left after that. I didn't need to hear any more."

"So you didn't hear me tell him I was falling in love with you?"

She jerked back as if slapped. The trembling began deep inside and shook through her. "Wh-what?"

He towered over her, all strength and muscle and solidness. "Malia, I've been trying to take this slow and steady. I didn't want to overwhelm you or seem like some irrational man who declares his love in such a short time, but I'm tired of pretending. You're my damn person."

The words were like hot water, scorching her skin and beyond. Malia got up and stumbled back, desperately needing the space. "Stop. You don't even know me."

"Yes, I do. I've seen the true part of you. The part you hide from the world under those designer clothes and sharp wit and queenly attitude." He stared her down, hands on hips, gaze narrowed with ferocity. "You prefer beginnings because you can control them. But you can't control what's happening between us, and it scares the hell out of you."

She looked away. Her heart beat painfully in her chest, but her voice came out weak. "Please stop. I can't do this here. I can't do this now."

He got quiet, and when Malia dared to glance at him again, he seemed torn by her request. Still, he continued, as if demons were pushing him hard to get to a resolution. "I understand what you're saying, but I'm not like the other assholes you dated who'd never be worthy of you."

"Oh, but you are?"

"Damn right."

She gasped at his arrogant declaration, hating how much she wanted to believe him. Like a cornered animal, she fought with all her power, desperate to run away. "This has been a game to you from the beginning. I was an interesting challenge, but now we've been to bed together, and the shininess will begin to wear off. When that happens, you'll be like every other man who walks away because . . ." She trailed off. Malia didn't want to say the words.

Palmer grasped her shoulders and leaned in. "Because . . . ? Finish it, Malia."

Fury took hold, clean and sweet and pure, and she latched on to it. Her body shook with it, and he seemed to watch with fascination, as if unable to move or interrupt her blistering tirade. "Because I'm never enough!" Shame filled her at the admission, but it was like spitting out poison, freeing her body and soul with the awful truth.

He let out a vicious curse. "Yes, you are, you foolish woman. Don't you understand what's happening here? I was pulled to you because it was like holding up a mirror to my soul. I didn't think I knew what loneliness was until you stormed into my life—because now, when I'm with you, it's like I'm complete. And when I'm not, I feel like I'm missing a part of me, which really pisses me off, but it's the damn truth!"

"Stop!"

"No. Not until you stop running away from this and accept that I love you!"

His breath was hot on her lips, and with a cry, she moved forward and his mouth was on hers, kissing her with a brutal power that stripped the skin from her bones and left her naked and wrecked.

Her nails dug into his arms with punishment as he ravaged her, and Malia rose to each demand with one of her own, as teeth and tongue and lips battled in a seductive game. She held nothing back, finally letting the flood rip open and drown them both. His tongue plunged deep, her lips became bruised, and still the kiss went on and on, until nothing lingered but the truth.

She finally stumbled away and pressed her palm to her trembling lips. His breath came in ragged pants, his eyes wild with hunger.

Her voice shattered the pulsing silence. "I can't do this with you, Palmer. I want so much more of you than you can give, and neither of us are wrong. You changed my life. You stole my heart. But you aren't the one I'm supposed to be with. I need to be a wife and mom with the man I love."

He shook his head, agony flaring from his face. "You haven't given us enough time! Who knows where we'll end up together? How can you walk away from something we may never find again?"

"I'm going to be thirty-two years old, and I want to settle in to a life together. Buy a house. Try for a baby. Blend our lives in all ways. And though I know you think you can get there, I can't take that chance. I can't waste years of my life waiting for you to accept you don't want the same things I do. Don't you understand? I have to let you go, for both of us."

Palmer's hand trembled as he pushed his hair back from his fore-head. She watched him as she broke apart, inch by slow inch, cell by cell, and realized she'd done exactly what she'd been trying to avoid. She was destroying herself because she'd fallen in love with a man not meant for her.

His plea was raw and heartfelt. "Don't do this. You can't put con-ditions and contracts on love. You have to leap with me and take a chance. Please."

"I'm sorry," she whispered.

Palmer turned away and bent his head. The silence stretched between them. Finally, he lifted his head and strode to the door, his final words searing into her brain forever. "So it goes."

He left.

Malia sank to her knees and wept.

Chapter Twenty-Four

Palmer walked into his nephews' room to check on them. They slept as hard as they played. Limbs were entangled in a twist of Batman covers, arms splayed out, faces smushed into pillows. He smiled as he tucked them in neater, picked up a few toys that could trip them if they got up to go to the bathroom, and eased the door shut.

He'd been dreading the babysitting, not because he didn't want to see the boys but because he was afraid Veronica would grill him about Malia. Fortunately, she was in such a rush to get out the door, there'd been no time for conversation. Hopefully, when they got back, Palmer would be able to slip out with a quick excuse and buy more time.

His heart squeezed painfully at the thought of Malia. One endless week had passed since she'd sent him away, and it wasn't getting any easier. They'd been in contact via email, but it revolved strictly around Quench Foundation business. He was scheduled to visit the Children's Hunger Initiative to see how some of the new programs were being implemented, and Malia would be there. It was important he show her their relationship wouldn't affect his commitment, but the thought of seeing her made his gut twist in agony. If this was true love, he was damn grateful he'd never dealt with it before. The highs and lows were too much for him.

Maybe he was meant to be alone after all.

The front door opened and he shook off his thoughts. Veronica came in with Raoul, laughing and beaming with an intimate glow that hinted date night had been a rousing success. Once again, his chest tightened with longing. He wanted that feeling again. That feeling of belonging to another person who seemed to get you. Palmer had experienced only a flicker of it and now realized it was like a drug. Once taken, you craved more.

"How was dinner?" he asked.

His brother-in-law gave his wife a lusty kiss on the cheek and smacked her ass. "Heavenly."

"Stop!" Veronica admonished, but she was grinning. "*Dinner* was perfect. We ate outside on the water and even ordered dessert. How were the boys?"

"Terrible, as always. I tied them up and locked them in the closet to teach them some manners."

"Oh, good, I knew you'd be a great father one day," she said, dropping her purse on the table. Her statement sent a zing of pain right through him, but he kept his face rigid.

"Dude, gotta head up. Thanks for watching the rug rats," Raoul said, giving him a half-bump man hug.

"Welcome. I gotta go anyway." His brother-in-law disappeared upstairs, and Palmer walked toward the door. "Glad you had a good time. Call me earlier next time before you implode on the poor guy."

Veronica rolled her eyes. "Oh, puh-leese, he totally deserved my freak-out. It was the anniversary of the first time we met, and he completely forgot!"

"Guys don't remember that stuff. Next time, just tell him you expect dinner out and he'll happily give it to you. We don't do code well."

"Whatever. Guys always stick together. Hey, why are you running out so fast?"

He kept his tone light. "Figured you'd wanna finish up your date night."

Veronica laughed. "Definitely later. How's Malia?"

"Good, good. She's, uh, still in Boston, but we're talking a lot."

"When does she come back again?"

"A few months. At least a month. Whenever her business is over." His sister sharpened her gaze. Yeah, he had to bail. "Love you, bye."

"Palmer." His name was a command that he automatically obeyed. "You're lying to me. Oh no, what happened? And don't give me any of your bullshit—tell me the truth."

He turned and faced her. Forced a smile and tried to offer a smooth excuse, anything to keep from ripping open the wounds that hadn't healed, and instead, he found himself spilling his guts. "We're not together anymore. She left me, Veronica. And she's not in Boston."

His sister blew out a breath. "Come sit down. I want to hear everything."

He followed her into the kitchen. She poured two glasses of wine, pushed one toward him, and propped her elbows on the table. She listened while he told her the truth from the beginning, leaving nothing out. When he was done, he already felt lighter.

"So basically the main reason you broke up is because you don't want kids and she does. And she's afraid to invest all this time with you, and you'll never change your mind."

"That's about it."

"When did you tell her about your ideas on marriage and children?"

He took a healthy slug of wine. "I don't know. I never tried to hide it."

"Hmm, very ethical of you."

He frowned. "Are you mocking me?"

She regarded him thoughtfully as she tapped her finger against the counter. "A little. I think this actually got more complicated between you for no reason."

"I know! I told her she needs to give it some time for us to grow together. To see if that's something I could get on board with. She's not giving us a chance."

"Palmer, she just went through an emotional process of freezing her eggs. Motherhood isn't some foggy idea for the future—she's taking it seriously, now. Why wouldn't she be afraid to open her heart to a man who told her he's not interested in having kids?"

He cursed and tunneled his fingers through his hair. "I know. But it's different with her. I've never had these feelings for another woman. I want things I never expected."

Veronica smiled and shook her head. "For someone so damn smart, you can be dumb as a brick. That's what love is, dude. You've convinced yourself marriage isn't for you, but you never found a woman you actually wanted it with before. As for children? I watch you with all your nieces and nephews—you're a natural. I see the love and magic in your eyes when you look at them. There's no way a man like you isn't going to want to build on that love for Malia and want everything with her."

He stared at his sister, her words sifting in his head, pulling at old ideas he'd had because he was stubborn and it seemed to work. His other relationships had ended because he wasn't interested in forever. But that was all before Malia.

Malia, who he saw a future with as big and bright and bold as he'd ever imagined.

Malia, who showed him he'd been just as lonely as her, and together, they filled something empty inside.

Malia, who, like him, had a perfect life in all aspects except for sharing it with a soul mate.

He was in love with Malia Evergreen, but it was bigger than that.

Palmer had been happy accepting his limitations but had never dug deep enough to ask why. That would have required questions he had no intention of asking. It wasn't until Malia began bumping up against all those unexamined ideas that he began to realize maybe life wasn't about a checklist of things wanted and not wanted. Maybe there were endless shades of gray—compromises of old ideals that no longer worked for a future he suddenly wanted.

"I never thought of it like that," he said slowly. His mind seemed to shatter with revelations. "I just know I love her in a way I didn't think was possible."

"That's how love works. You need to talk to her, Palmer. You probably should have waited until after her hormones calmed down. The poor thing wasn't up for making another life-altering decision. Remember how hard it was for Jane?"

He winced. "I know. I never had the best timing."

Veronica laughed and squeezed his hand. "Get yourself together and tell her the truth."

He gave her a hug. "Can you do me one last favor?"

"What?"

"Don't tell Mom. Or Christine. Or any of them. They're gonna be pissed off I tried to bring another fake date."

A slow, victorious smile curved her lips. "No problem. How does next Thursday work for you?"

It took him a moment to recognize the blackmail. He sighed and surrendered. "Sure. I'll babysit."

"Thanks, little brother. You're the best."

Palmer left his oldest sister's house a little wiser, and a lot busier, but it was worth it.

He needed to speak with Malia.

~

Malia twirled her straw around in her seltzer while the ice clinked merrily in her glass. She was waiting at the diner for Chiara and Tessa, but she just craved home. Sweats and Netflix seemed to be the only things she wanted lately.

"Here you go." A giant chocolate milkshake with whipped cream and a cherry was slapped on the table in front of her. She looked up as Mike slid in the seat opposite her, features set with a weary depression she recognized well. "Figured you needed this."

She forgot about the calories and grabbed it gratefully. "How did you know?"

"You got heartbreak written all over your face, kiddo. Palmer?"

She nodded. "We broke up."

"Didn't realize you were officially together."

"We weren't, but then we kind of were, and now we're not."

"Got it. Should I kick his ass if I see him?"

Malia sighed. The whipped cream got stuck in the straw, and she had to use all her force to suck it through. "No, it's not his fault. We're just on two different paths."

"I think that's even worse." He looked around at the sparse crowd. "Maybe I'll close up early and go home."

Her jaw dropped. "You never close early. Is it Emma?"

Mike blew out a breath and stared past her shoulder. "Maybe. I didn't mean to hurt her. She thought I was special, but I treated her like crap, and now she doesn't even come in for pancakes anymore."

Her heart ached for the man. "Did you try and talk to her?"

"Not yet. She was really mad at Tessa's party. Figured I'd give her time to calm down."

Malia picked out the cherry and ate it. "Maybe we both just need some space and time to think about things."

"Hell no. That's the last thing you both need right now!"

They turned. Tessa stared at them, arms crossed in front of her chest, shaking her head.

Mike slid out of the booth and patted her shoulder. "What can I get you girls?"

Tessa pointed to the milkshake. "Two of those, please." Chiara protested but settled in after Tessa's hard stare. "You need it, too, babe. It's been a hell of a long day, and we're eating dessert for dinner."

They joined her, and Malia regarded them warily. She figured they'd listen sympathetically while she moped, and then she'd go home and mope some more. Breaking up with Palmer had taken more out of her than she ever imagined. She constantly ached to hear his voice or touch his hand or see his eyes crinkle when he laughed. She missed their conversations and business meetings and the way he'd text her every night.

How many times had she reached for her phone to text him she'd made a mistake? That life offered no guarantees, and to push him away seemed against her very heart and soul? How had he wrangled his way so deep into her life and emotions within a matter of weeks?

But she had done the only thing possible, and now she had to get to the other side.

"First off, how are you feeling?" Chiara asked. "Are you happy with the results from the freezing?"

"Yes, having twelve healthy eggs that withstood the process is good. I'm grateful I was able to do it. It's so damn expensive, and too many women don't have the options I do."

"True," Tessa said. "Fertility treatment costs are sky-high and not really covered under insurance."

"Speaking of which, I have the first draft of the article. It's really good, Malia. I think it's going to be huge for Quench readers."

She gave a wobbly smile. "I'm glad. I think it's important other women know about the process."

Chiara regarded her thoughtfully. "It wasn't so much the technical aspects that will make a difference. It's the way you opened up and let people really see you."

She shrugged. "Well, I tried, but you both already know me that way."

Chiara glanced at Tessa. "Not really."

Malia squinted and stared at them. "What are you talking about? I tell you my feelings all the time."

Tessa shook her head. "No, you don't."

"Babe, the way you described your loneliness made me cry because I recognized it in me," Chiara said. "Before Sebastian came into my life, I was happy, but not in that soul-deep, raw way it is when you allow yourself to love someone. And how you began to question your own worth? I felt the same exact way, but no one ever talks about it. For the first time, it was like I was really seeing you, Mal. The way you spoke about motherhood and being able to love someone like that?" She sighed. "It was beautiful."

Malia blinked, trying to process what her friends were saying. Was it true? Had she held back and glossed over her loneliness with humor and wit? Did she ever open up and really talk about the things she was afraid of? Even with Palmer, had she ever confessed her true feelings? Had she ever actually said out loud she loved him?

"I . . . I didn't know you both felt that way. I thought I told you everything."

"This isn't a criticism," Chiara said gently. "Just an observation. I loved seeing more of you, that's all. You're always so put together and fabulous and cope well in all situations, I appreciated hearing about your fears. About loneliness and wanting to be a mom and the other things you still want in your life. That's the stuff we built Quench on, babe. The real stuff."

The words suddenly made sense. She thought it over as Mike brought out two milkshakes and her friends dove in, hollowing their cheeks to suck out all the sugary goodness.

"Has Palmer tried to contact you?" Tessa asked after taking a break.

"No. I'm seeing him this week, though, at the Hunger Initiative. We're in the beginning stages of the backpack program, and I need to be there." Misery etched through her. "I have to make arrangements for him to deal with Deanna from now on. It's too . . . painful."

"Maybe you should talk to him again. See if you can make it work," Tessa suggested.

Malia gave her a shocked look. "There's nothing left to discuss. We want different things, and talking won't change that."

"But have you both really sat down and had a heart-to-heart? Mal, you were flying high from the procedure that morning. You weren't in a state where you could have a serious conversation about children. You were too raw. And Palmer shouldn't have pushed. I would've never told him if I thought he'd show up so soon," Chiara muttered.

"He's not looking for a ring on his finger and a car seat in his limo!" Malia burst out. "I tried to keep my guard up, but somehow, he snuck under. *Bastard.*"

"What if he showed up at your door and said he wanted to get married and have kids with you right away?" Tessa asked. "What if he was all in?"

"I think he'd be lying to himself."

"How do you know?"

She blew out a breath in frustration. "Why are you guys challenging me? I'm trying to save both of us from disaster. Nothing is worse than two people who want completely separate things. I clearly heard him tell Ryder he never wanted kids or marriage."

Chiara leaned forward, gaze intense. "Sebastian took that conversation completely different than you. He said it was obvious Palmer hadn't wanted marriage or kids *before*."

"Before what?"

"Before you. He's in love with you, Malia. Yes, you have to respect a person's wants and needs, but I think you're so focused on him *not* changing, you're refusing to allow him room for growth. I didn't want a baby. I never even thought about marriage, but when Sebastian blew those plans to shreds, I realized sometimes you can't see what's right in front of you. Personally, I think you're scared."

Temper hit. "Are you kidding me? You're trying to pull out the fear card just because I'm being real?"

Tessa sighed. "You dropped an ultimatum on the guy without even giving him time to adjust. You both went from pretend weddings to sleeping together to you freezing your eggs. You had no time for middle ground or to talk like couples do. Yeah, I think you're scared. But I think you're more scared of being in love, rather than if he'll be a father to your kids. It's easier to focus on a distant future thing rather than see the raw truth. You're afraid of getting hurt. You're afraid of love."

"Wow. Thanks, guys, I thought you were on my side," she said stiffly, hurt stabbing through her. "Haven't I been the one searching so hard? The one who wanted it the worst out of all of us? And now you're questioning my intentions?"

Her friends seemed torn, glancing at each other as if afraid to speak. Chiara's voice was soft. "Yes, you wanted it badly. But I think you wanted it in a perfectly wrapped-up package, and life isn't like that. It's messy and comes with compromises and hard decisions. Tessa and I don't want you to lose something just because it's not what you expected."

Tessa chimed in. "Fate has a funny way of throwing out our best-laid plans, but maybe that's because she's smarter than we are."

Malia jerked back. The words tore at her, ripping off the neat surface and revealing the rawness underneath. For the first time, she acknowledged her friends might be right.

She just didn't know what she was going to do about it.

Mike trudged over and glanced down at all of them. "I want to date Emma," he announced. "How do I do it?"

Her mind spinning, Malia met her friends' gazes and began to laugh. They were all screwed up, but this was her tribe, and damned if she didn't love them all.

Tessa groaned and buried her face in her hands. "Mike, you're killing me. It's going to take a lot for you to get her to listen. You pushed her hard."

"I know," he said miserably. "But I'd like to try."

"Let me think of a plan," Tessa said. "You have to be willing to put yourself out there, though. I know that makes you uncomfortable."

He shifted his weight and scratched his head. "I think I can do it."

"Good. Then I'll help you."

He nodded and grinned. "How were the milkshakes?"

Malia noticed they were all empty and everyone seemed a bit more relaxed. As usual, Mike always came through.

"Perfect," they all said together.

Mike turned and patted Malia's shoulder. "Love is scary as hell, but looking back at my life lately, I'm realizing the risk is worth it." Emotion glinted in his eyes. "Maybe together we can both try again."

Malia leaned in and gave him a hug. Then made her decision.

Chapter Twenty-Five

Palmer was chatting with Xander and Laura when she walked in.

He knew instantly by the prickling at the back of his neck. The juicy scent of plums and musk seemed to dance in his nostrils as Malia moved near, and he had to use all his business training not to turn around and beg.

Beg her to touch him. Beg her to give him a chance. Beg her to love him.

She greeted Xander and Laura with brief hugs, then almost shyly met his stare. "Hello, Palmer."

"Hi, Malia." They stared at one another for a few precious moments. He cleared his throat. "Was just getting a rundown on how the backpack program will work in August."

"We have more volunteers who want to meet you," Laura said. "We call you our angel investor."

Palmer laughed. "Believe me, I'm no angel. There's a lot of work to do, and this is the beginning. I'm grateful to the Quench Foundation for allowing me to get more personal."

"We didn't get to show you the garden last time. Come with us," Xander said, leading them to the back of the building. He was taken aback by the massive garden that held various vegetables, fruits, and herbs. "This is our mainstay, but it takes constant tending to keep up with our demands."

"This must be a ton of work to keep up," he murmured, studying the rows of tomatoes, peppers, and squash. "Who takes care of it?"

"We rotate a few volunteers who are members of the local gardening club. We've had guests do some community service here, too, but were hoping we could do more."

"Can we hire a horticulturist?" Palmer asked. "Add it to the budget?"

Malia gave him a surprised look. "We can look into it. Having someone part-time could be a big help. We'd just need to raise a bit more—"

"I can add the funds to cover that," he said.

Laura lit up. "Really? That's another bucket-list item for us."

"Then let's get it done. The baseline is healthy food, and you're trying to grow it right here. I think this could be big if we put in the time and money."

They delved into a deep discussion, and Malia made notes. He met more volunteers, who greeted him with genuine warmth, and after a few hours, Palmer felt like he belonged. He wasn't treated with kid gloves or looked upon as an interloper. He felt like a part of an organization that was going to help kids.

When he'd spoken to Christine about his commitment, she'd cried. He couldn't wait to bring his other sisters and mother over to help out. It was something they could all do together.

It was another gift Malia had given him. An opportunity to do something with his money he was proud of, to open himself up to something bigger than his own company. Emotion choked his throat, so he spun around to take a moment by himself.

A beautiful woman with silvery blonde hair and blue eyes approached him. A pit bull was behind her, but he noticed the dog's back legs were hooked to a scooter-type wheelchair. He ran beside her, tongue lolling out, his front legs doing all the work. "Palmer, it's nice to meet you. I'm Kate, and this is my dog, Robert. I've heard about you from my friend Arilyn, who teaches yoga with your sister Christine. She told us you were going to be involved in the program."

He snapped his fingers. "Yes, she speaks about Arilyn often! Nice to meet you. Hey, buddy," he said, leaning down to let the dog catch his scent. Robert gave him a wet nudge of his nose, and he laughed, scratching behind his ears. "You're a scary one, huh?"

Kate laughed. "He's been coming here with me for a while. Adores the kids, and they light up when they see him. Malia, it's so good to see you again. We met a few months ago."

"Yes, I remember." Malia made a face. "Actually, I remembered Robert first."

Amusement danced in her voice. "That tends to happen around him. Robert steals the show."

Kate chatted with them while Palmer gave the dog his full attention. There was something about the pit bull that made his heart soften, something in his gentle brown eyes that said he'd seen the ups and downs of life but hadn't lost his trust.

"Kate works in Verily at Kinnections Matchmaking," Laura said as she walked up. "So if anyone wants to get hooked up, I'm sure she'll give you her card."

Kate waved her hand in the air. "Stop scaring them, Laura. Nothing is more terrifying than a matchmaker."

As Xander and Laura moved away to talk to another volunteer, Palmer stood up and glanced at Malia. She was right beside him, her hip inches from his thigh. For a moment, their gazes locked, and everything else melted away. People chatted in the background—something about calling Kate to find a decent date—but all Palmer could see was the woman he loved, physically close yet emotionally light-years away.

"No problem. There's nothing I love more than finding someone their soul mate," Kate said, turning. Her hands reached out to both Palmer and Malia. "Good to see both of you, and thanks for—oh!" She jolted as if burned, then stumbled back a few steps. Shock radiated from her face as she stared at them, blue eyes wide.

"Are you okay? Did you trip?" Palmer asked, moving forward.

"Oh, stay back!" she said, slamming her arms in front of her. She kept glancing at them, back and forth, then her face seemed to clear. "How fascinating. I never would've thought."

Malia cocked her head. "Kate, what are you talking about? Do you need some water?"

Robert sat at his mistress's side, not worried at all, as if Kate's behavior was normal. Suddenly, Kate began to laugh. "No, sorry about that. Even after all these years, I never get used to it. How long have you two been together?"

Palmer's brow shot up. "Um, us? We're not, well, we were. Wait—I don't understand."

Malia's cheeks heated. "We're not together. Well, not now."

Kate tapped her pink nail thoughtfully against her lips. "Huh. That's too bad. Let's just say I can see energy fields, and yours are extremely, well, entwined."

"Things got complicated," Palmer finally said.

Kate nodded. "It always does. It's none of my business, but I want to say something. Some things are worth complications and messiness because underneath it's pure. And that doesn't come along as often as we think." She gave a loving glance toward Robert, her face seemingly caught up in a memory. "It's nice to find your person in life."

Palmer froze, thunderstruck by her words, as if she saw something so much bigger than they could in this moment.

Malia sucked in her breath, and their pinkies brushed together.

"Okay, I gotta go. Good luck, guys." Kate took off, her silver hair swinging, with Robert trotting by her side, the wheels of his scooter whirling.

Malia turned an inch toward him. "What just happened?" she asked in a half whisper.

"Something important." He dragged in a lungful of air. "I need to talk to you, Malia. Please." He waited while his heart pounded frantically.

She nodded. "Tonight."

"Yes. I'll come to you."

She nodded again, and then Xander called him over to ask a question, and he was pulled back into work mode.

But he began counting down the minutes until he could see her alone.

~

Malia opened the door and stared at him. He was dressed in the same outfit, hair mussed, eyes shadowed. Stubble clung to his jaw, and weariness stuck to his aura. Pale green eyes glittered with a broken ferocity that immediately called to her because she was experiencing the same thing.

He was quiet as he stood in the doorway. "Wine?" she asked.

Palmer nodded. "Yes, please."

He followed her into the kitchen, where she poured two glasses and handed one over. Malia tried to rally in the crushing stillness. "I think everything went well today. The backpack program will start on time, and it was really amazing of you to add funds for help with the garden."

His jaw clenched. "I'm not here to talk about work." He took a sip of the burgundy red, regarding her with intent.

Something inside her shifted and rose to the raw hunger reflected on his face, the sharpness of his words. He was right. There should be no politeness tonight. Her body wept with the need to touch him. "I pushed you away for a reason. You can't expect me to give up my dreams of being a mother. You can't expect I'm going to sleep with you for the next few years with no promise of a future. You can't expect me to do all the compromising."

His hand shook around his glass. "I spoke with my sister, and she reminded me I have terrible timing. You overheard me saying things to Ryder that scared you, and I pressed too hard. I stayed away because I wanted to respect your wishes, not because I agreed with you."

She nodded slowly. Examined the garnet liquid sloshing in her glass. "I want to tell each other the truth, even if it's scary. Even if the ending isn't what we want."

"I'm ready." He waited with a calm, predatory presence.

Nerves jumped in her belly, but she thought of her conversation with Tessa and Chiara and realized she'd been hiding from herself a long time. There was nothing left to lose anymore. "Looking back, I see how I liked to control things. There was a certain type of man I'd decided was for me, and if he didn't fit the bill, I locked him out. When I think about my dating history, it seems like a long line of disappointments, but at the same time, I was safe. No one ever got in. I was caught between two worlds—one where I desperately wanted to connect with someone, and the other where I could be in control and not get hurt. As the years went on, I turned inward and constantly wondered if I was lacking in something that made me lovable. It became like a festering wound and constant voice in my head. Maybe I wasn't enough."

She swallowed the lump in her throat. God, the words seemed to tear at her insides. The humiliation of admitting you were less and unworthy while pretending to be fabulous. But she was all in, and she wasn't backing down now.

"You snuck in when I wasn't looking. I thought I could handle the sexual chemistry, but when we started to spend time together, I began having feelings for you. You . . . surprised me."

He remained still, gaze locked on hers.

Malia dragged in a breath and took a hasty sip of wine. "It was easy to put you in a box because you couldn't be mine. Even your pursuit was easy to categorize as just a physical want. I thought I'd indulge once before I shut you out for good—allow my body to experience bliss but keep everything else sanely rational." A humorless laugh escaped her lips. "Until you were in my bed. Then I knew it was so much more than orgasms. I felt you in my soul, Palmer. Do you know how damn terrifying that is—to meet a man who makes you feel these things and worry it's only temporary?"

His eyes gentled. She waited for him to close the distance between them, but he didn't. His voice sounded like gravel wrapped in velvet. "Now I do. I know exactly what it's like to have your heart ripped out and given to someone else to care for. No wonder you were scared, baby."

She shuddered at the endearment and forced herself to finish. "I felt as if you were asking me to choose between you and a future I've planned and sacrificed for. I don't want you to wake up one day and think you made a mistake, while I try to pick up the pieces. I wanted to be prepared and make good choices. But since you left, I'm beginning to wonder if losing you won't be worse than giving up my dream." Tears stung her eyes. "Because I love you, Palmer. All those empty parts inside disappear when I'm with you. I made a mistake sending you away. You're the man I want to be with, no matter what happens next, because you're worth the risk."

Malia let her confession lie between them like broken rubble. Raw and vulnerable, she met his stare, waiting for his own truth. Whatever happened, she could at least say she didn't hold back. It was the first time in her life there were no safety walls to hide behind.

Palmer let out a long breath he'd obviously been holding. "Thank you, Malia. For your truth. For being brave. For being you." He set his wineglass carefully down on the counter. "My turn."

He took a step forward. Nerves jumped in her belly, and she realized how important his next words were. Maybe he needed time to think. Maybe he'd decided she was too much and wanted to step away from this whole relationship. Maybe . . .

"I told the truth to Ryder when he asked if I'd ever wanted kids or a wife. I never did. I didn't think it was for me, and having my entire family consistently pushing me in that direction had the opposite effect. I looked at them and wondered why. Oh, I was happy for them, and my parents only exhibited what a solid, loving marriage could be. But I never craved more from my previous relationships. I was able to easily walk away from all of them without regret. Until you. That's when I knew love wasn't what I'd imagined."

He eased closer, and Malia began to tremble.

"I see things now I never did before. A life with you that's full of surprises and comfort and passion—a life I can't give up. Now I see it all, Malia, as long as you're by my side. I'm not afraid of it anymore, because you're the one I've been waiting for." He reached out and snagged her around the waist, pulling her close. "You're my person." He cupped her cheeks, and she fell into those shimmering green depths. "I'm not here to promise a timeline or say I'm proposing this moment. I'm here to begin our lives together, and I need you to make that leap with me. Will you?"

Her body sighed in release, and the last of her defenses fell away. "Yes."

His mouth covered hers. She stabbed her fingers into his hair and met every silky thrust of his tongue, holding on tight. There was no time for play; for teasing; for slow, gentle kisses. This was a primitive claiming in the most uncivilized way, but Malia relished it, needing her mind to shut off and allow the very center of her soul to open up, to trust him, to finally surrender the last of her walls under the demands of his body.

He walked her backward into the bedroom, stripping off their clothes, and fell naked on the bed. She was ravenous to touch and taste every part of him, fingers sliding over sleek muscles, her mouth opening over tight abs and lower, taking him fully in her mouth to suck and pleasure, loving his curses and the desperate arc of his hips.

She fumbled with the condom, finally sheathing him, then climbed up his body and took him inside her with one fierce, hungry plunge.

Malia uttered his name like a chant, throwing her head back as she rode him with a wildness that unleashed from her very core. He palmed her breasts, pinched her nipples, and drove her forward. Her sensitive clit slid over his erection with every hard thrust, inching her closer, until he grasped her hips and took control, forcing her up and down with masculine demand.

"Come," he commanded, lust glittering in his gaze, and with one last, desperate arch of her hips, she shattered, absorbing the orgasm into every cell and muscle, shaking under the brutal waves of pleasure.

He flipped her over, pressing her body deep into the mattress, and slid back down while his hot mouth covered her, licking and sucking until she writhed underneath him. This time, when he entered her, his movements were slow and lazy, his body tight with control as he eased her back up, claiming every inch of her. This time, when she exploded, he was right with her, his hands in her hair and his gaze on hers.

This time, when they both collapsed together in a tangle of limbs, he whispered in her ear, "I love you, my queen."

"I love you, too, my arrogant king," she said, holding him close, feeling like after all the twisting, empty roads traveled, she was finally home.

Epilogue

"I'm not happy with the new ads," Palmer said, a frown creasing his brow. "I'm paying for prime location, and Endless Vows was squeezed out by our competitor. If this continues, I'm going to have to think about cutting back with Quench."

Malia held back a sigh as she kept lighting candles. "I told you, babe, that's not my department anymore. Did you talk to Hana?"

"Yeah, but she can't handle negotiations like you. Last time I threatened to walk, she started to tear up."

Malia turned on her heels and glared. "You made her cry?"

"Not exactly. More like blink a lot, like she was going to. Emeril nearly had a heart attack. I need someone stronger, Mal. It's no fun anymore."

"You promised to lay off and let Emeril and Andrea handle it. At this point, you'll have no one left wanting to work with you. Plus, you practically poached Magda from us and you're complaining?"

He puffed out. "She's been amazing. Definitely worth the faulty ad space."

Malia shoved a lighter in his hand and pointed to the balcony. "Go light the rest of those candles, please. They'll be here any minute. I promise I'll talk to Hana, okay?"

"Okay." He disappeared outside and Malia shook her head, tamping down a smile. The man was incorrigible, but he had a point. They needed a shark to deal with many of her old ad accounts, and Hana had been disappointing her lately. Too bad Tessa was so busy—she wouldn't take anyone's crap.

The doorbell rang, and Malia smoothed down her skirt. Excitement fluttered in her belly. This was the first official party they were hosting at Palmer's home, and the beginning of a new chapter. She'd just moved in with him, and their families were joining them, along with their friends.

He came back from the balcony and reached out, squeezing her hand. "Ready for this?"

She smiled up at him and adjusted his tie. "Always."

They opened the door and a stream of guests arrived. For the next few hours, Malia and Palmer played the perfect hosts, served chocolate milk and cocktails, and watched the crowd nibble on coconut shrimp, filet mignon tips, and chicken fingers. The kids played together, and Malia caught Davinia and Veronica in the corner, chatting up a storm. She laughed at the idea of them teaming up.

Chiara and Tessa came up behind her. "I love this place," Chiara said with a squeal. "The view is spectacular, and it's still close enough to Quench. Good choice."

"It's so good to see you happy," Tessa said, beaming.

"I really am," she said, joy bubbling through her veins.

The past few months had fallen into place with ease. They both volunteered at the Hunger Initiative. The Quench Foundation had begun garnering national attention, and now they had a roster with a list of charities that were booming due to specialized sponsors. Their families had officially met, and Malia had even shared with them her fertility journey. She'd shown her family the article Chiara had written for Quench and been stunned by her mother's support and apologies for making her feel unworthy. For the first time, she wasn't hiding who she was anymore.

She didn't have to. Palmer loved her exactly as she was.

She caught his gaze across the room, and the familiar electricity sizzled like an exposed current. They shared a look of blistering intent, and suddenly, Malia couldn't wait to get rid of their guests.

"Damn, girlfriend, you're looking at him like he's a rich chocolate truffle and you're PMSing. I'm starting to get jealous of you two. I'm the only one left," Tessa grumbled.

Malia tilted her head. "I didn't think you wanted anything serious."

"Seriously good sex would be nice. Things have been flat lately." She wrinkled her nose. "I think I need someone different. A challenge. The men I've been dating have been so predictable. Maybe I'll change things up."

Ford appeared by her side with a smirk. "Maybe you need to dump the pretty boys and find a real man," he drawled.

Tessa whirled on him, eyes blazing. "I date gentlemen with manners. Men well read, culturally aware, and career focused. Men who don't think a ball game, a beer, and a recliner is the meaning of life."

"Poor suckers. They're really missing out," Ford said with a big grin. "And girls like sports. How come you have nothing like that at Quench?"

Tessa threw him a withering look. "Because sports isn't one of our focuses."

Ford scratched his chin. "That seems kind of reverse feministic. There are tons of females who've made sports their career. Thought you covered women from every walk of life."

Malia didn't know whether to laugh or cry as her friend's head looked about to explode. "We do, and I'm not discussing Quench with you. Did you bring a date?"

Ford puffed up. "Yep. She's hot, too. I was just looking for her."

Uh-oh. Tessa seemed to lick her lips with anticipation. This wasn't good. "Is she the brunette with the Kim Kardashian body?"

"Yeah, did you meet?"

"No, but it looks like Roberto did. Is that his hand on her ass?"

Ford looked across the room and his face dropped. His date was definitely canoodling with Endless Vows' charismatic wedding planner. Malia had met him a few times, and he was smooth, with an easy charm and seductive smile created for handling temperamental brides and grooms.

"Son of a bitch," he muttered. "I'll be right back." He marched over, but Malia had a feeling it was already a done deal. Poor Ford didn't seem to have much luck with women. She wondered if she should give him Kate's business card to use her matchmaking services.

"That was mean," Malia said.

Tessa clapped her hand over her mouth to stifle her giggles. "I know. I'm sorry, but he just aggravates the hell out of me. Sports at Quench! What kind of idea is that?"

"Not a bad one," Chiara said thoughtfully. "I need to think about that."

"I don't think—uh-oh. We have trouble heading this way," Tessa said.

Malia turned her head. Mike had arrived and was making his way through the crowd, straight toward Emma and Arthur. He held a giant bouquet of flowers.

"Did you tell him to do this?" Malia asked her friend.

Tessa groaned. "I said for him to create a grand gesture. Not show up at your party to embarrass her."

"Too late," Chiara murmured. "Come on, let's move closer. I want to hear."

Emma and Arthur were alone in the corner, chatting and sipping drinks. Mike marched up to them and stopped in front of Emma. The woman gasped. "Michael? What are you doing?"

The flowers were a burst of bizarre colors and types all blended together to resemble half a forest. Malia winced, but at least it was definitely a grand gesture. The blooms hid half his body and most of his face, but she caught his profile, which was set in hard determination.

"Emma, I made a terrible mistake. All this time, I thought you were too good for me. You're an educated, well-respected, kind woman who spent her life dedicated to teaching kids. I'm not well read, I never graduated college, and I own a diner. I thought you were making fun of me."

Emma's eyes widened. Malia gave Arthur some credit—the man stepped back from the spotlight and let Mike have his time. "Why would you think such a horrible thing? Have I ever said or done anything to make you think that?"

"No, it was my own shit—stuff. I want to apologize and ask you to . . . ask you to . . ."

The woman's voice softened. "Ask me to what, Michael?"

Mike gulped. "Ask you to come back to the diner for your pancakes."

Malia closed her eyes. She waited for Emma to lose her temper and send him away. After all this, he still couldn't get up the nerve to ask her out on a damn date. But the woman surprised her. Malia caught an expression of humor flicker across her face, a softening of her gaze as she looked at Mike. "Okay, Michael. I'll come back to the diner."

He blinked. "You will?"

"Yes. Are those for me?"

He thrust them at her, and she caught them to her chest. "Yep. I'll see you Monday. I'm sorry to interrupt." He nodded his head at Arthur and came over to the three of them. Sweat glistened on his brow, but he looked at them hopefully. "How'd I do?" he asked.

They all began to laugh and gave him a group hug. Tessa sighed. "You did good, Mike. Let's just see what happens next, okay?"

And at that moment, Malia believed Mike would win back Emma. Because lately, she believed anything was possible.

~

They lay in the shadows, naked bodies entwined. The moonlight trickled through the window and cast patterns on Palmer's skin. She trailed her hand over the scattered beams, enjoying the soft glow. "Our first official party was perfect," Malia said.

He pressed a kiss to her shoulder. "Agreed. Did you see our sisters together? It looked like they were planning something big."

She laughed. "I saw, and it was scary. By the way, my parents want us to come over this Sunday for dinner, and they're already talking about Thanksgiving."

"Yep, mine too. It's not even Halloween. Is it a gene thing that you have to begin planning everything months in advance?"

"Hope not. Chiara said she and Ryder are always talking about what's for dinner, and it's now their new foreplay conversation."

His chest rumbled. "Is that what's going to happen to us?"

"No, because we're the wild ones. We don't have to worry about our families' intentions or wedding planning or baby making. I kind of like it. I feel free of all those pressures I used to live with. I'm a changed woman."

"We're the navigators of our own course, on our terms."

"Exactly!"

"I just hope you don't like being free too much."

She shifted around to look at him, puzzled by his statement. Then she saw the diamond ring shimmering before her in all its glory.

Her heart stopped. Malia stared at the exquisite piece of jewelry, a perfect emerald-cut stone with tiny diamonds around the band. It caught the moon's reflection and exploded prisms of light.

Her body began to shake as he turned to face her, lifting the ring. His eyes were filled with all the things she'd dreamed of in a partner. Love. Humor. Joy. And home.

"Malia Evergreen, you once told me you believe in beginnings and avoid endings. I'm asking you to be my beginning every day of my life. I love you, my queen. Will you marry me?"

She was struck mute. She stared at his beloved face and the ring and tried desperately to say that one word. The word she'd dreamed of saying her whole life.

"It's happening again, huh?" he asked, his voice ripe with humor. He pressed a kiss to her lips. "How long do you think it'll take before you can speak and make it official?"

Malia tried; she really did. She opened her mouth and squeaked, but nothing emerged.

"We're going to institute new rules for this one, baby. All you need to do is nod, and I'll get this ring on your finger and make you come at least three more times. Then we'll live happily ever after."

Wild joy burst inside her, and she threw her arms around his shoulders.

Then she nodded.

And Palmer made good on his promise.

AUTHOR'S NOTE

This is my fiftieth published book.

There's no way to express my humble gratitude for being able to fulfill and live a lifelong dream from when I was seven years old. I can only thank all my readers for accompanying me on this journey and the endless support along the way.

To celebrate, I tried to do something special with *So It Goes*. You'll find hidden "golden" nuggets throughout this book from five of my previous series and titles—special character drop-ins or mentions to surprise and hopefully delight my loyal readers. Here they are if you'd like to check them out:

The Sunshine Sisters series—Gabe Garcia from *Temptation on Ocean Drive*

The Stay series—Owen Salt and Chloe Lake from *Begin Again*

The Billionaire Builders series—Al from *Any Time, Any Place*

The Searching For . . . series—Kate Seymour and Robert from *Searching for Someday*

The Marriage to a Billionaire series—Alexa and Nick from *The Marriage Bargain*

Enjoy! I can't wait to get started on the next fifty books.

ACKNOWLEDGMENTS

This is a special book to me, and I have a lot of people to thank.

Hugs and gratitude go to the amazing Maria Gomez and the Montlake team for supporting my work through the years. From edits to cover design to proofreading, I'm grateful for your stellar work. To Kristi Yanta for always working so hard to get my books to the highest level. To Kevan Lyon, my talented agent, and my team behind the scenes: Nina Grinstead, Mary, Christine, Kelley, and Kim from Valentine PR. Thanks to my amazing assistant, Mandy Lawler, who keeps things running as I write.

Thanks to my son, Jake, for inspiring me with his love for Kurt Vonnegut.

Finally, thanks to readers, bloggers, podcasts, book clubs, and social media moguls for supporting my books along the way.

This industry rocks.

ABOUT THE AUTHOR

Photo © 2012 Matt Simpkins

Jennifer Probst is the *New York Times* and *USA Today* bestselling author of eight series, including The Sunshine Sisters, Stay, The Billionaire Builders, Searching For . . . , Marriage to a Billionaire, The Steele Brothers, Sex on the Beach, and Twist of Fate. Like some of her characters, Probst, along with her husband and two sons, calls New York's Hudson Valley home. When she isn't traveling to meet readers, she enjoys reading, watching "shameful reality television," and visiting a local animal shelter. For more information, visit www.jenniferprobst.com.